# HELLO,
# STRANGER

# HELLO, STRANGER

### VIRGINIA SWIFT

HarperCollins*Publishers*

HarperCollins books may be purchased for educational, business, or sales promotional use. For information, please write: Special Markets Department, HarperCollins Publishers, 10 East 53rd Street, New York, NY 10022.

FIRST EDITION

Designed by Nancy Singer Olaguera/ISPN Publishing Services

Printed on acid-free paper

Library of Congress Cataloging-in-Publication Data
Swift, Virginia.
     Hello, stranger / Virginia Swift.—1st ed.
        p.   cm.
     ISBN-10: 0-06-054333-7
     ISBN-13: 978-0-06-054333-4
     1. Alder, Sally (Fictitious character)—Fiction. 2. Women
college teachers—Fiction. 3. Women historians—Fiction.
     4. Laramie (Wyo.)—Fiction. I. Title.
PS3569.W516H44   2006
813'.54—dc22                                          2005046174

06 07 08 09 10 ❖/RRD 10 9 8 7 6 5 4 3 2 1

*To Katie and Hal and Kath and Audie—*
*Let 'er buck*

# Acknowledgments

AS THE GRATEFUL DEAD used to say, it's been a long strange trip. But thanks to wonderful friends and family, when the going got weird, the world kept going. Sam and Annie Swift were wise and loving and provided always useful, occasionally alarming information of various kinds. Trey Cole offered timely expert advice on firearms, and Miguel Gandert explained the revolution in photography. Dr. Jim Scharff and Dr. Mike Crossey answered my medical questions. Kudos to the folks who keep it all going: Yolanda Martinez, Helen Ferguson, Barbara Wafer, Dana Ellison, Cindy Tyson, and especially the saucy and convivial Scott Meredith at UNM; John Gray, Steve Aron, and Carolyn Brucken at the Autry.

As always, I rely entirely on Elaine Koster, my patient and supportive agent; Carolyn Marino, my patient and illuminating editor, and Jennifer Civiletto, Tim Brazier, Pat Stanley, and John Zeck at HarperCollins. Thanks, too, to the amazing people who have brought my books to the public: Kay Marcotte, Bonnie and Joe at Black Orchid, Barbara Peters, Chris Acevedo, Cindy Nye, Lauri Ver Shure, the great crew at Bookworks, and the very understanding Kat McGilvray.

Peter Swift and Hal Corbett have been my best readers and

gentlest, most meticulous critics. The Scharff, Levkoff, Swift, Broh, and Bort families weathered the storms with grace, cheer, and love, and little Benny Scharff provided inspiration and faithful companionship.

There's nothing like girlfriends. Melissa Bokovoy, Jane Slaughter, Beth Bailey, Katie Curtiss, Harriet Moss, Laura Timothy, Wendy Conway Schmidt, Mim Aretsky, Nancy Jackson, Kathy Jensen, Marni Sandweiss, and María Montóya have been there for me, for years, through all of it. I do mean all.

Hal Corbett and Katie Curtiss, and Kathy Jensen and Audie Blevins have made me very joyously and comfortably at home in Wyoming for years. Steve Aron, Amy Green, and Daniel and Jack Aron have welcomed me in Santa Monica on my new southwest commute.

Chris Wilson has made me see things in new ways, to my amazement and delight. Okay, Chris. What's next?

# HELLO, STRANGER

# CHAPTER 1

# THE RULE OF THUMB

THE RULE OF THUMB was one of those grotesqueries of English common law. For centuries, it had stood rock-solid, entitling—no, make that *obliging*—a man to "correct" the misdeeds of his wife and children with physical force, but holding that the instrument of household justice be no bigger around than a man's thumb. Some kind of limit, that. A switch cut from a tree, hickory or willow; a leather whip, braided rough; a well-knotted piece of rope; objects close to hand, within the reach of a modest man. A prince might have more means at his disposal: the blade of a fencing foil, say, or a length of iron chain. Such things would certainly remind a woman of her duty to submit to her husband's authority. As God and nature and the Bible and everybody had decreed.

The hell you say, thought Professor Sally Alder.

Whenever Sally taught the course titled Women's Rights in America, she opened the class on domestic violence with a few minutes on the Rule of Thumb. Talking about the rule made her a little sick to her stomach every time she gave the lecture, but it was something that had to be done. The students needed to know, or at the very least, to be reminded, that history could be a horror show. That a woman's right to be secure from bodily abuse should never be taken for granted. Even in the twenty-first century, there was plenty of reason to assume that not everybody had gotten the message.

Some students stared vacantly back at her, or surreptitiously checked their cell phones. More scribbled busily in their notebooks, knowing that this Rule of Thumb was likely to show up on a test. She might just as well have been telling them the names of the states, or the atomic weight of zinc. But at least the scribblers would have some memory of this lecture, unlike the girl who'd taken out an emery board and spent most of the class happily filing her nails.

Sally brooded all the way back to her office, huddled into her coat against the wind. Did she really imagine that bearing history's lousy news was actually doing any good? They had given a new meaning to blasé today, she thought as she entered Hoyt Hall and climbed the stairs to the fourth floor, headed for her office hours.

She already had a customer. Sally had put a chair in the hall outside her office, a molded plastic thing with a fold-down desk, so that students waiting their turn to see her wouldn't have to hunker down on the floor. Just now, a girl slumped uncomfortably in the chair, a knit cap pulled down over her head. She'd put a backpack on the desk and lay on top of it, her head on her arms, motionless, the picture of dejection.

What in the world had happened to Charlie Preston?

This was the first time Sally had seen the girl in nearly a month. Charlie was registered in Sally's class, but she hadn't been around before spring break, hadn't returned in the week after.

Plenty of students bagged lots of classes. They dropped out, or failed, or contented themselves with Cs and Ds. But Charlie hadn't struck Sally as your typical half-assed student. A third of the time she didn't show, true, and she'd missed a number of assignments. She never said a word in class. But she listened. And it seemed as if she got it. And Sally's real measure for intelligence in a student: She laughed at the professor's jokes.

When Charlie did turn in the work, she showed real spark and insight. She'd come to Sally's office hours more than once, simply to talk about women's history. Sally'd been delighted, encouraged her interest. Charlie was only a freshman, but Sally was already imagining writing recommendations to get her into graduate school.

"Charlie?" she said, touching the girl on the shoulder. "Are you okay?"

A moment passed.

The girl raised her head, and it was excruciatingly obvious that she was not close to okay. The cap covered her ears, but revealed a face that was a mass of bruises, darkening, it seemed, before Sally's eyes. Her lower lip was cut and swelling fast, and one eye was nearly closed. It occurred to Sally that the spike Charlie wore through the eyebrow, the ring through the lip, would be trouble soon, if she didn't get them off.

It wasn't the first time Sally had seen a woman who'd been beaten up. Back in her own student days, she'd run the University of Wyoming Women's Center, which had taken calls for the local shelter. More than one woman had called up crying, asking what to do, where to go. And more than one woman had shown up at the center, grim or shaking or shamefaced, mumbling something about having walked into a door.

This was the worst she'd ever seen.

"Come in with me," she told the girl, bending over to rub her back briefly before unlocking the office door. "I'll call an ambulance and go with you to the hospital. And we'll call the police."

Charlie hefted her backpack, an effort that cost her, and followed Sally in. But then what Sally had just said seemed to sink in. A look of terror swept over Charlie's face. "No!" she exclaimed, grabbing Sally's arm, grimacing at the pain that opening her mouth had caused. "I can't. Can't go to the hospital. No cops." Tears sprang into her eyes, leaked down the sides of her cheeks.

"Charlie," said Sally, as gently as possible. "Sit down a second."

The girl collapsed into the broken-down easy chair in front of Sally's desk, the backpack slipping to the floor with a clunk. These kids. Sally bet there wasn't a backpack at the University of Wyoming that weighed less than forty pounds. They'd all be in back braces by the time they were thirty.

Sally took off her coat and hung it in the closet, moving deliberately to calm herself down. "You're badly hurt," she said, turning back to Charlie. "You need medical attention. I know you're scared, but let me help you. Let the police help. Sheriff Langham's a really, really good friend of mine, a truly incredible person. Trust me, he'll take care of you."

"Yeah, right," said Charlie Preston. "Just like they always take care of me. Nobody ever believes me. Every time I manage to get away, they always send me back to him and the bitch. He's such a great liar, I even believed him this time. He's all, 'All I want to do is help you,' and I fucking believed him. I must be the stupidest person in the world."

Sally moved her briefcase and purse to the floor next to the desk, sat down in her chair. "You've got to see a doctor, honey. I'd drive you myself, but my car's at home. I could call a friend, if you don't want an ambulance." She thought a minute. "You wait tables at the Wrangler, don't you? I'm sure Delice wouldn't mind giving us a ride."

Delice Langham, owner of the Wrangler Bar and Grill, was one of Sally's best friends, and known for being a demanding but compassionate boss. Sally knew that on more than one occasion, Delice had slipped a waitress money to get away from a loser boyfriend, had called the cops when angry men showed up looking for "their" women, had been known to take them on herself, with a bag of quarters, or even the Colt .45 she kept below the counter. Sally was also aware that Delice had fronted the down payment for one of the bungalows used by the Laramie Safe House. Delice was probably at work now, but she would leap into her Explorer and speed over in five minutes flat if Sally called.

But Delice was also the sister of the Albany County sheriff, Dickie Langham. Charlie shook her head. "I got a car," she said. "I can drive myself. I'll go to a doctor, I swear. But not the hospital. They ask too many questions. And I'm serious, there's no need to get the police involved."

Sally looked at the girl very steadily. "Listen to me, Charlie. Somebody hurt you, a whole lot. Nobody's entitled to do that. They need to answer for it."

Charlie bristled, tried to sit up very straight, wincing. "I got it. I can take care of myself. I know a doctor I can go see. She's helped me out before."

Sally asked the obvious question. "Then why didn't you go straight to her?"

"She's not in town. She's somewhere else—I don't want to say where."

"You're in no shape to drive a long distance."

"It's no big deal, Dr. Alder," said the girl. She looked down, shook her shoulders, looked up again, screwing up her courage. "I'm sorry I missed class again. I didn't want any of the kids to see me. I knew you had office hours after, so I waited here. I almost waited outside the classroom, but I thought I might miss you. I couldn't go to the Wrangler. I didn't know who else to ask."

"For what?" Sally said.

"Money. I need money, Dr. Alder. I need to see a doctor, all right. And I need to get out of here for a while, figure out what to do next."

"Your parents . . ." Sally said, pointlessly.

Charlie just glared.

"Okay. What about the Safe House?"

"They know where it is," said Charlie. "It's not safe for me."

"There's more than one," Sally pointed out.

"It doesn't matter. They'd find me." Charlie slumped in the chair.

"Your friends . . ." she tried.

"My dad scares the shit out of them, and my stepmother makes them think they're all going to hell." She sat up straighter, and Sally had to admire the effort. "Please, Dr. Alder. Help me out this time. I swear I'll pay back every cent."

"It's not the money, Charlie. Do you promise to call and let me know where you are as soon as you've seen the doctor? To keep in touch with me? You can't just run away. And you don't have to."

"I can handle myself!" the girl insisted. "I just need some cash."

Sally took a deep breath. "How much?"

Charlie took a breath of her own, but the air caught in her lungs, hitched out in a small grunt. Broken ribs too?

"How much do you have?" Charlie asked.

"Just a second," said Sally. She reached down for her purse, took out her wallet, extracted bills. She'd just been to the ATM. She had more than two hundred dollars. It wouldn't be the first time she'd given money to a woman in trouble, no questions asked. She handed over the cash.

Charlie stuffed the money in her pants pocket and closed her eyes when the tears came again, blinked them away. "Thanks," she said, not looking at Sally. "I really mean it, Dr. Alder. This is the best thing you could do to help me."

Sally sincerely doubted that. She reached for the phone. "One more time. Please let me call the police and the ambulance. It's really the smart thing to do."

"If it were the smart thing to do," said Charlie Preston, "I wouldn't be in the shape I'm in. I gotta go now. I'll be in touch, I swear to God. You don't know what this means to me. Just promise you won't call the cops. Please."

"I can't make that promise. This is the best I can do," said Sally.

"Just a couple of days? Please?"

"This is a terrible idea," Sally said.

"Look. I gotta get going." The girl got up. She was wearing a snug T-shirt, low-slung jeans, Doc Martens shoes. The knit cap. No coat. Sally heard the wind howling through the budding branches of April trees, banging loose doors and rattling the window casings, the kind of wind you had to lean hard into, just to stay upright. "Where's your coat?" she asked.

"I'm fine," said Charlie. "It's warm out."

Right. And Sally was Maurice Chevalier. "You can't go driving off to who the hell knows where without a coat. Take mine."

"Really. I'm good. I got it," said Charlie.

"Goddamn it, Charlie. I must be crazy to let you out of here at all. At least take my coat, and stop acting like a moron," Sally told her, getting up to go to the closet.

"Won't you be cold walking outside?" the girl asked, taking the soft black wool coat with the warm liner.

"I'm good," said Sally. "I got it."

A few more tears. Sally opened a drawer, pulled out a box of tissues, put it on the desk.

Charlie got up, put on the coat, took a wad of tissues and jammed them in a pocket. She leaned over, pain in every movement, and picked up her backpack. "Thank you," she said. "You don't—really, I can't—anyway, thanks. See you."

And she was gone.

Sally picked up the phone. She'd agreed not to call Sheriff Dickie Langham. She hadn't made any promises about the sheriff's sister.

Delice answered on the third ring. "Oh, it's you," she said when she heard Sally's voice. "I'm waiting for a call from my meat guy. It's blowing like hell up in the passes, and the truck with my order had a problem somewhere between here and Denver. Hamburger all over the highway."

"Can you come to my office?" Sally asked. "There's something I need to talk to you about, and it requires some privacy."

"I can't really get away," Delice told her, "but it sounds like an emergency. Can you come down here?"

"No car," said Sally. "I'd walk down, but I don't have a coat."

Delice was silent a moment. "I'll pick you up," she said. "This is something bad, right?"

"Yeah," Sally answered. "I'm going downstairs now. I'll be watching for you out in front of the building."

Ten minutes later Sally was sitting in Delice's tiny office, hands around a cup of the Wrangler's terrible coffee, listening as Delice ripped a new orifice in a meat supplier who'd had the bad luck to lose a truck to the balmy breezes of a Rocky Mountain spring.

"I don't care how many orders this sets you back!" Delice hollered into the phone. "You're going to get my goddamn stuff up here by dinnertime, or you're going to start looking into the butcher protection program." She slammed down the phone, jangling a dozen silver bracelets, took a swig from her own coffee mug, and looked at Sally. "Okay. What's up?" she asked.

"Charlie Preston," said Sally.

"She's supposed to be working four to midnight," Delice said. "She's missed some shifts, but she usually calls ahead. What about her?"

"She won't be coming in," said Sally.

Delice pursed her lips, thought a bit before she spoke. "She's got some problems."

Sally leaned her elbows on Delice's desk. "The latest problem is that somebody beat the hell out of her. She came to my office, looking like a train wreck. She wouldn't let me take her to the hospital or call the police. She claimed she knew a doctor who could fix her up, but she needed money."

"So what'd you do?" asked Delice, eyes somber.

"She seemed like she was at the end of her rope. I gave her all the cash I had."

"Gave her your coat too, huh?" Delice said. "The really cool one you got last fall on sale at Bloomingdale's. The coat I want to kill you for."

"It's just a coat," said Sally.

Delice nodded. "I'd probably have done the same. And I'm not just saying that to be reassuring. Sometimes there isn't much choice."

"I couldn't keep her in my office," Sally said.

"Uh-huh. If they're gonna run, they'll run. I can tell you two things. One is that you'll never see that money again." Delice drank a little more coffee.

"It wasn't a loan," said Sally.

"The other thing is that there's a better-than-even chance you'll never see Charlie again," Delice told her.

"I know. That's what worries me. She was really messed up, Dee."

"Yeah. I can imagine," Delice replied. "But at least she admitted she needed a doctor, and had some idea of who she could go see. How much do you know about her?"

Sally shook her head. "Very little. She's bright, but frustrating. She misses lots of classes. She works for you."

"She's also been a tough case since she was a little kid. She ran away from home when she was, like, nine years old, probably not for the first time. Her father and stepmother reported her missing, and a trooper picked her up hitchhiking on I-80, just west of Green River, in the middle of a snowstorm. She was half frozen to death, but from what I heard, she wasn't exactly oozing gratitude for the ride. She clammed up and wouldn't talk, and they took her straight home. After that, she just fell into trouble, a couple of shoplifting incidents, and a real problem with running away."

"How do you know so much about her?" Sally asked.

"Last year the parents gave up and agreed to temporary foster care. She was living with Mike and Julie Stark when she came in here asking for a job. She had that look in her eye—wounded but brave. I like that. I hired her on the spot. Mike and Julie filled me in on the background later."

"Mike and Julie Stark? Maude's nephew and his wife?" Sally asked.

"Yeah. Nice people. They've got a fourteen-year-old daughter, always wanted more kids but couldn't have them, so they take in foster children now and then," Delice explained.

"So did Charlie keep running away because she was being abused at home?" Sally asked.

"She didn't talk about it with me," said Delice, "and the Starks didn't go into detail. But it's what I suspect. For their part, the parents claim they've tried everything, but she's an incorrigible juvenile delinquent who runs with a rough crowd, a pathological liar and thief."

Sally thought a minute. "From what she said, it sounded like she was living with her parents again."

"For about the last month, yeah. I don't know what happened, but I guess, somehow, they managed to talk her into coming home. I know they bought her a car—maybe that had something to do with it. Bradley Preston has bucks."

"Bradley Preston?" Sally frowned. "The name rings a bell, but I can't place him."

Delice made a face. "He's a heap big bwana corporate lawyer and a pompous jerk. You'd never know I had to kick his ass out of my bar twenty-some years ago."

"Wait a minute. There was a guy who used to hustle pool and hassle waitresses. Bad Brad. Used to work as a roughneck on drill rigs, right? You're not saying he's Charlie's father?" Sally said.

"Same guy, but different M.O. Quit the Oilpatch, went to law school, married and divorced his secretary when she ran off and left him with a three-year-old kid. Faster than you can say 'rebound,' he married an upright Christian woman and got born again. He represents insurance companies who want to deny claims to little old ladies and Cub Scouts."

"He was a rude bastard, back in the day. I recall him getting a huge snootful of Yukon Jack, reaching across the bar, and ripping the T-shirt off Lizzie Mason when she was in the middle of making a tequila sunrise," said Sally.

"And that," said Delice, "was the last time he set foot in my place. Stupid son of a bitch."

Nobody messed with Delice Langham.

"What about the stepmother? If the father is a batterer, where does this good professing woman fit in?" Sally asked. She was Jewish herself, but the situation struck her as, well, unchristian.

"Who knows? Beatrice is probably too busy minding other people's business to notice," Delice said with a sneer.

"So she's that kind of Christian," said Sally. "Maybe she just doesn't want anything to do with the leftovers of Brad's first marriage."

"Or maybe it's just easier for her to see nothing. You know how it goes. Family members look the other way so it doesn't come down on them." Delice picked up a pen and drew circles on her desk blotter.

"Or maybe she's convinced herself that the kid deserves what she gets," Sally said.

Delice put down the pen, sighed heavily, looked up. "It happens," she said.

"I'm feeling better about giving Charlie the money," said Sally.

"And the coat," said Delice. The wind was really kicking up by now, pounding the dingy little window of Delice's office with dust and gravel from the Wrangler parking lot. "She'll be glad she's got that coat. It's getting really evil out."

# CHAPTER 2

# THE AMERICAN EXPERIENCE

A WEEK WENT BY, then two, and as Delice had predicted, Sally heard nothing from Charlie Preston. The girl's predicament was on her mind, though, lurking under the surface of consciousness. Sally dreamed that she was driving down the highway, gripping the wheel hard and going faster, far faster, than she should. It was pitch-dark and the road was slippery, and she was scared. Then she looked over at the passenger seat, and there was a large, hideous man with a furious face and a huge fist drawn back. When she opened her mouth to scream, no sound came out. She almost felt the blow as she awoke, gasping for air.

"Mmph," said Hawk, when she startled him out of a sound sleep by practically leaping on his back. He stirred enough to reach out an arm and pull her close, and immediately fell back asleep. It was comfort enough. Having Hawk Green share your house and your life and your bed was, altogether, a vastly comforting thing.

And as much as she worried about Charlie, life went on. Sally was so overextended, she had started making lists of her to-do lists. Urgent interruptions continually interfered with pressing matters. She thought about taking a time-management seminar, decided what she really needed was a stress-management workshop, then decided she had neither the time nor the patience for either and resigned herself to being content with accomplishing forty percent of what she'd hoped to get done in any given day.

And found herself brooding about Charlie even when there were a hundred other things buzzing in her brain.

"You should go to my yoga class," said Edna McCaffrey, accepting a glass of cabernet from a server. Sally was hosting a reception following a preview screening of a new *American Experience* documentary on Margaret Dunwoodie, the Wyoming poet. Sally, as Dunwoodie's biographer and head of the Dunwoodie Center for Women's History, had been a consultant on the documentary, and had arranged to do the screening and reception as a fund-raiser for the Dunwoodie Center. It was a bit of a scam. Everybody who'd attended had paid fifty bucks for the honor of watching a film they could see on television two weeks later, and chatting over wine and cheese with people they were likely to run into at the supermarket.

Still, this was one of those times when it didn't hurt that everybody in town knew everybody else, and half of them were related. Meg Dunwoodie was a world-famous poet, and had been one of their own. The Performing Arts Center auditorium held five hundred, and every seat had been filled.

"Your yoga class?" Sally asked Edna as she took a sip of the adequate sauvignon blanc they were pouring. "Since when have you gone in for instant karma?"

"Since I went to the doctor and found out that my blood pressure's a trifle higher than it ought to be," said Edna. "This business of being a dean isn't all glamour and glory."

"You wear it well," Sally told Edna, and meant it. They'd been friends for years, and it had been Edna who, as dean of arts and sciences, had hired Sally for her current job. Edna remembered and rewarded productivity, creativity, and loyalty, and never forgot laziness, smugness, or opportunism.

You really didn't want to get on Edna's list.

She was nearly six feet tall, given to wearing dramatic colors and short skirts that displayed her showgirl legs. Tonight Edna had on a form-fitting red silk cocktail dress, short-sleeved with a sweetheart neckline, and black patent leather spike heels. She could literally look down on most of the people in the place.

"Thanks for the compliment," said Edna, "but I've been feeling like shit. So I started this yoga thing right after Christmas, two or three times a week, and it's changed my life, I swear to God."

"You probably shouldn't be swearing to God if yoga's changing your life," said Sally. "Think I'll stick to running. By the time I've done forty minutes of dragging my ass around town, I've sweated out all the demons."

"You can't sweat out *all* the demons," Edna replied. "Sometimes you just have to stretch out and let them go."

"By George!" said Sally. "There is a divinely serene aura around you tonight, Edna."

Edna laughed. "And if letting the demons go doesn't work, of course, there's always the possibility of kicking the shit out of them."

Now Sally laughed.

"I'm loving this event," Edna said, surveying the crowd like Big Bird on the set of *Sesame Street*. "You've raised twenty-five grand, made everybody here feel like an insider, and pulled it off with class. See that gang of thieves over there by the buffet?" she asked, gesturing with her wineglass. "They could be good for a couple hundred thousand down the road."

Sally looked in the direction Edna pointed, having to crane her neck to see. "Yeah, I've seen some of them at Democratic fundraisers. How come trial lawyers always stick together?"

"How come piranhas swim in schools?" asked Edna. "Go over there and see if you can enchant them into opening up their wallets."

Sally made her way over to the corner where the lawyers were discussing the coming elections. "If they run him for Congress," said a substantial blond woman in a poison-green power suit, "the widows and orphans better watch out. Make way for the malefactors of great wealth!" The blond slugged down some wine, speared a cocktail meatball from a chafing dish.

"Hey, easy now. I'm partial to malefactors of great wealth when they're paying my retainer," replied a sweet-faced young man in a blue blazer with—of all things!—a crest on the pocket. "Rich folks are people too, you know."

"Nobody denies that, Flip," interjected a lanky, slightly older (forty-something? fiftyish?) man in a tweed sport coat and gray sweater. "But they can probably get along okay even without the extra advantage they'd derive from having a tool like Bad Brad in Washington."

And then he noticed Sally. "Oh hey, Professor Alder. Great job on the documentary!" He turned and put down a paper napkin to shake her hand and introduce the group. "I'm Dave Haggerty," he finished. "I've got a little office downtown."

A little office. Uh-huh. Haggerty, Hebard, and Bright was the state's foremost civil rights and criminal defense firm, and Dave Haggerty was senior partner, chief mastermind, and by all accounts, courtroom hypnotist. She could understand the appeal. The man had a voice like Godiva chocolate.

Most right-thinking people in Wyoming considered Dave Haggerty a rabble-rouser at best, possibly a commie. She'd seen him around, but never been formally introduced. "You're too modest, Mr. Haggerty. I know all about your work, and I'm a great admirer. I wanted to tell you in person how grateful I am for the support you've given the center."

Haggerty smiled. "It's Dave. I had Miss Dunwoodie for freshman comp. A truly merciless woman. I still can't bring myself to use an adjective," he said.

"Except when you're talking to a jury, Dave," said the blond in the green suit. "I've even heard you resort to adverbs."

"Actually, Dave," Sally observed, "I believe you just used the adjective 'merciless' to modify the noun 'woman.'"

"Merciless of you to point that out," said Haggerty.

Sally laughed.

"We're just speculating about the election. Looks like the Republicans are going to run Bradley Preston for our lone congressional seat. Don't know if you're familiar with him. It's a pretty alarming prospect." Haggerty sipped a little wine.

Bradley Preston? That got Sally's attention.

"It's just a stepping-stone," the blond explained. "The Republicans have Bad Brad in mind for greater things. The bastards have been dying to get a right-winger on the Tenth Circuit bench, and it looks like they're lining it up for Brad. They might as well revoke the Bill of Rights right now."

"Maybe not the whole Bill of Rights," said a small woman in a black dress. "I'm thinking he'd leave the Second and Tenth Amendments."

"So that the states would have all the power, which they'd never use, of course, except to enforce public prayer and assure every American of his or her God-given right to carry an assault rifle into an elementary school," the blond said.

"Preston hasn't even announced for the House yet," said the guy with the crest. "And even if he wins, it's hardly the end of civil rights as we know it."

The other three lawyers just looked at him.

"Okay, you're right. It is," he conceded.

Sally liked their politics, but she wanted more information about the man they were dissecting.

"So this Bradley Preston," she said. "He's the darling of the GOP machine?"

"Professor Alder," said Haggerty, looking directly at her, "this guy's just one of the many standing in line to soldier forth for the cause of righteousness and tax cuts for the obscenely wealthy. He just happens to be slightly smarter and a whole lot more ruthless than the average."

"Call me Sally," she said, noting that Dave Haggerty's eyes were an interesting golden color. Amber? Topaz? Tiger eyes.

"And Preston's got a secret weapon," said the blond. "The B-Bomb."

"His wife," the woman in the black dress explained. "One of those people who makes you wish women hadn't gotten the vote."

"I never wish that," said Sally. "But why would I?"

"Bea's head of the Traditional Family Fund. They're new, but they're incredibly well organized and well funded, so they will be. Every time there's a bill in the legislature that allocates a little money for day care for single mothers, or family violence shelters, Beatrice Preston sends out one email and mobilizes a hundred fanatics to bury legislative staff in messages and letters and phone calls, and hold prayer vigils outside their offices—they even send little kids to pray outside the houses of everyone from the representatives to their lowliest aides. Pretty intimidating," the blond said.

"Not to mention creepy and fascist," the black dress added.

"Oh yeah. I've heard of them." Sally tried to imagine life as Charlie Preston, with a stepmother like that. "What about the Preston family?" Sally asked. "They must at least have one or two skeletons in the closet. A gay nephew, a brother who writes bad checks."

"Who doesn't? Bea's got an ingenious approach—she puts the family troubles right out front and uses them for all they're worth. Brad has a daughter from a first marriage. The kid's always in trouble. Bea suffers and prays a lot, very publicly," said the blond.

"It's disgusting," Haggerty said quietly. "And effective."

"Which is why you've got to run against him, Dave," the guy with the crest told Haggerty. "We can't have Bad Brad in Congress, and the B-Bomb running things behind the scenes."

"Look, I'm hardly Brad's biggest fan, and I'd even consider the run. Except for three things. One, I wouldn't have a chance in hell of getting elected. Two, the party knows that, and would never run me. Three, I don't want to be a politician." Haggerty drank some more Perrier.

The blond gave him a half smile. "We'll see about that, Dave," she said, and turned to Sally. "Now, Sally, tell us more about the

Dunwoodie Center. Flip here just won a big case, and I'm sure he'd like to make a generous contribution."

"Hey, I'm cash-poor," said the younger man.

"Oh, I forgot," the blond said. "Your latest client was the poor slob they so unjustly accused of cocaine trafficking. He paid you in giant plasma TVs and weekends at a time-share in Cabo."

Just then, Haggerty got a call on his cell phone. At the same time, Sally noticed Maude Stark, chair of the Dunwoodie Foundation, trying to get her attention. "You'll have to excuse me," she said to the lawyers. "It's been great meeting all of you."

"Let's keep in touch," said Dave Haggerty, putting his hand over his phone, looking at Sally's wedding ring–less left hand, and then smiling into her eyes.

Hoo boy.

Sally shook off the vibe as she approached Maude, who happened to be chatting with, among others, Hawk. Dave Haggerty was a fox, Sally decided, but Josiah Hawkins Green had been lighting her up a long time. Hawk's wardrobe ran to jeans and T-shirts and flannel, but he cleaned up very nicely. Tonight he wore a black turtleneck, a black cashmere sport coat, black jeans. His thick black hair, streaked with silver, was caught in the usual ponytail, halfway down his back. It was a careless, dangerous look, underplayed but not to be underestimated.

Maude was a formidable presence in her own right, nearly as tall as Hawk and just as lean. She wore a trim pantsuit with an Eisenhower jacket, steely hair pulled back, her eyes as pale and clear as a prairie lake at sunrise. Sally hoped she looked half as good as Maude did at half-past sixty. "So did you talk those legal eagles out of big bucks?" Maude asked.

"Working on it," Sally said. "David Haggerty's actually already made a contribution, but I'd never met him until tonight."

"He's probably good for more," said Maude, nodding approvingly. "I'm just introducing Hawk to my nephew and niece, Mike and Julie Stark. They're so busy saving the world, I hardly ever get to see them myself."

"That's you, Maude," said Julie, a comfortable-looking brunette with a round face. "We're just humble high school teachers."

"And you're not introducing Mike and me," said Hawk. "I've played against him in the city basketball league. If he's interested in saving the world, tell him to start with my ribs. I've been introduced to his razor-sharp elbows on any number of occasions."

"Welcome to the city league," said Mike, grinning. The man was unmistakably related to Maude—same build, same eyes, same air of confidence. "This is great, Dr. Alder. I mostly remember Meg Dunwoodie as the scary old lady that my auntie Maude used to keep house for. She really came to life in the film."

"What do you teach?" Sally asked Mike.

"Photography," he said, "and Julie teaches math."

"They don't get enough of obnoxious teenagers at school," said Maude, "so just to keep things interesting, they take in everybody else's problem kids."

"That's incredibly brave of you," said Sally. "Teenagers scare the hell out of me."

"Us too," said Julie. "Especially since our own daughter turned fourteen. It seems like just yesterday I was buying her underpants with the days of the week printed on the butt. Now she's going down to the mall in Fort Collins with her friends and smuggling Victoria's Secret bags into her bedroom."

"She thinks she's wily," said Mike, "but she forgets who takes out the trash."

"Agatha's a great kid," said Maude. "You've probably seen her out jogging around town. She's out there in the early morning like you, but she's about sixty times faster. And she runs with a little dog."

"Thanks, Maude," said Sally. "You always raise my self-esteem."

"Just the verbal version of Mike's elbows," said Hawk.

"So you balance out the elbows by taking in troubled teenagers?" Sally prompted, trying to work things around to Charlie Preston.

"Every now and then," said Julie. "Usually they show up in

Mike's photo classes just about the time they're flunking every-thing else. We've gotten so we can tell when they're getting ready to run away or the parents are about to kick them out. Sometimes we have to go through the courts, but usually it's more informal."

"And it's not always a great thing. They get into certain pat-terns, and a lot of them can't get out. I can't tell you how many times we've been lied to, ripped off, or gamed," said Mike. "When there are drugs involved, it's almost an impossible situation."

Sally decided to go for it. "Actually, I've got a student—her name's Charlie Preston. I heard she'd spent some time with you. She hasn't been to class in a couple of weeks, and I wondered if you might have heard from her."

Mike frowned. Julie looked worried. "No. We haven't. She moved back home about six weeks ago. We haven't talked to her since," said Mike.

"That Preston kid's a handful," said Maude. "I doubt those parents can cope with her."

"How do you know so much about her?" Sally asked.

"She lived with these kids," said Maude, adding, "and I've done some work for the Safe House. No need to elaborate."

Not that she could. As Sally well knew, for Maude even to imply that the girl had sought the services of the Safe House bor-dered on violating confidentiality.

"So Charlie hasn't been coming to class," said Julie. "Bad sign. I wonder if Aggie's been in touch with her?"

"They got to be pretty good friends, almost like a big and little sister," Mike explained. "They bonded over Aggie's puppy. Char-lie really loves dogs. So does Aggie."

"Charlie Preston," said Maude, "needs a hell of a lot more than a dog to cure what ails her."

"Would you mind asking your daughter if she's heard from Charlie?" Sally said, choosing her words carefully. "She's a really bright girl. I'd hate to have to fail her if something's wrong."

"Oh, make no mistake about that," said Maude. "When it comes to Charlie Preston, something is very definitely wrong."

# CHAPTER 3

# RUNNING WEATHER

THE NEXT MORNING DAWNED clear and remarkably calm, a day made for running. As Sally took her usual circuit around Washington Park, she passed and was passed by pretty much everybody she'd ever seen running around Laramie in the morning, including a leggy girl in short shorts, a light fleece warm-up jacket, and a knit cap, running the legs off a little dog who was scampering hard to keep up. Sally realized she'd seen her often. The girl ran with a long, easy stride, all smooth speed and muscle efficiency. A joy to watch, until she turned a corner and she and the dog disappeared. If the girl was indeed Aggie Stark, Sally reflected, panting, the mere idea of trying to casually catch up with her while out jogging was enough to threaten a coronary.

It didn't do her heart any good either when she turned onto Eighth Street and saw Sheriff Dickie Langham's Albany County truck parked in front of her house. Dickie had been known to drop in for a visit now and again. He and Sally had been friends for a hell of a long time, and he played poker with Hawk every other Wednesday night. But this was Friday morning, and the sun had been up barely an hour. Not the time for a social call.

Dickie was sitting at the kitchen table, tapping an unlit Marlboro on the tabletop. He was a big man, well over six feet tall and more than half that around the middle. He cleared a lot of space. Hawk navigated around him, working up breakfast and making a pot of coffee.

Sally went for cheerful, giving them each a smacking kiss and plopping down into a chair. "How divine to come home to my men in the kitchen and the smell of coffee brewing," she said, and gestured at the cigarette. "Don't even think about lighting that."

Dickie gave the cigarette a mournful look and put it down on the table. He glanced up at Sally. "You have a student named Charlotte Preston?" he asked.

So much for cheerful. Sally pressed her lips together, then nodded. "Yeah. She's in my women's history class. Smart kid, but not given to regular attendance. I haven't seen her in a while. What's going on?"

"We had a call early this morning from her father, a lawyer named Bradley Preston."

"I've heard of him," Sally said. "A pretty influential guy, I'm told."

"Whatever," Dickie said. "He's reported her missing."

It had been a good two weeks since Charlie had shown up in Sally's office. Why would the parents just now file a missing person report? Despite her own promise to the girl that she wouldn't call the cops, she'd been tempted to do so every day since the girl had disappeared. But at least she hadn't said anything about what she would do if the sheriff himself came to her. "I haven't seen her in a little more than two weeks," Sally told Dickie, accepting a cup of coffee from Hawk and taking a quick swallow. "She came to my office. Somebody had beaten her up, pretty bad. She asked me for money and I gave her some. Then she left."

Dickie's eyes narrowed. He picked up the cigarette and began tapping it again. "Why, may I ask, didn't you call me?"

"She begged me not to," Sally said. "She said she was on the way to a doctor she knew would help her."

"Somebody in town?" he asked.

"Charlie said not. She didn't give me a name," Sally answered. "She was terrified. Evidently there have been problems at home for a long time, and Charlie doesn't seem to have much faith that bringing in the authorities will help her out."

"So what'd you do, Mustang?" asked Dickie. "Make the informed decision that you, personally, know better than law enforcement, social workers, judges and juries and doctors and shrinks when it comes to assault on a young girl? That all that was necessary to save this poor misbegotten victim was for you to throw a fistful of dollars at her and tell her to have a nice life?"

Sally's temper spiked, but she could understand his being pissed. Dickie, after all, had more than one point. "No. I did everything I could to convince her that she needed to get to a hospital and let me call you. She absolutely refused. If I'd picked up the phone, she'd have been out of there before I could dial nine-one-one. I could have wrestled her to the ground, I guess, but I didn't see it as a good idea.

"She was a mess, Dick. The poor kid didn't even have a coat. I did what I could. She said she had a car."

Dickie sighed heavily. "Yeah. Bradley Preston reported that missing too. A British racing green Mazda Miata. A gift from him to her."

Hawk looked at Sally. "You think the father beat her up? What kind of father batters a child and gives her a Miata?"

"Weirder things have happened," said Sally.

"All the time," Dickie assented. "Like a kid who blames her parents for everything, including stuff they haven't done. Not"—he said, as Sally sputtered to explode—"that I'm saying that's what happened. But it's at least possible. Did Charlotte say that her dad had hit her?"

"Oh, for Christ's sake, Sheriff!" Sally said. "I think I can trust my own eyes to see when somebody's had the shit beat out of them. Do you want me to paint you a picture? Bruised, swollen face, eye half shut, gasping and flinching like maybe some cracked ribs. Then again, maybe no broken bones. She insisted she could drive. Obviously, I'm not that kind of doctor, but of course, neither are you." She glared at Dickie.

"Settle down, amiga," said Dickie.

She took a deep breath. "Okay. All right. I just know what she looked like, and what she said. She was one broken, frightened kid, and she made a point of telling me that her friends were afraid of her father."

"There could be any number of reasons why," said Dickie. "The girl's got a juvie record—shoplifting, vandalism, minor-in-possession, one marijuana charge that didn't stick. The father's a no-nonsense, law-and-order kind of guy."

"From what I've heard," Sally said, "it wasn't always that way."

Dickie's eyebrows twitched. "It's said that there was a time," he said, "when Bad Brad was one of those people who liked to show up for last call at Dr. Mudflaps's tavern."

As Sally was well aware, Dickie was referring to customers who had showed up at the bar at closing time, because the bartender, in addition to making a mean tequila and grapefruit, was known to do a brisk business in blow. The entrepreneurial bartender in question had been, in fact, Dickie Langham, back before he'd gone underground, gone into rehab, gone straight, and gone in for catching criminals instead of being one.

"Charlie's dad must be some kind of serious hypocrite to blame her for straying from the path of righteousness," Sally pointed out.

The eyebrows wiggled again. "Who among us would have our kids do what we did? We're fucking lucky to be alive, and I'm guessing this Charlie Preston does a very good job of pushing her own luck. She hangs out with some pretty dubious types. Her boyfriend, for example. He's nineteen, and he's been in and out of jail since he was ten. He's out now, with two auto thefts and some forgery charges pending. I went to see him, but his roommates told me he wasn't home. I'm guessing he might not be home for a while," said Dickie. "But we'll keep checking."

"Anybody else who might have some idea where she's gone?" Sally asked.

Tap, tap, tap went the cigarette. "She waitressed for my sister. Who told me that she doesn't keep tabs on her employees, because she's their boss, not their mom. Which is, of course, a complete crock of shit. I mean, if Delice was worried about the girl, you'd think she would have seen the wisdom of letting me know what was going on, but she claimed she just assumed Charlie'd gone AWOL and hired another waitress. No big deal. Very un-Delice-like. I wonder why?" He twirled the cigarette between his thumb and third finger and shot a glare at Sally.

She was saved from having to dream up an answer when Dickie's cell phone rang. He unhooked it from his belt, stood up as he answered. "Yeah. Yeah. Let's cordon off a four-block radius all around. Crap. Okay. We'll just have to detour 'em off Ivinson and Grand. Yeah, I know. I'll be there right away."

"What's going on?" asked Hawk.

Dickie took his gray Stetson off the table and put it on. "There's a new ob-gyn in town who has, very discreetly, let it be known that he's willing to perform therapeutic abortions. I mean discreetly—no advertising, no listings on the web, no intent to provoke the right-to-lifers. Just a guy who's got the idea that there's a problem when women can't exercise their constitutional rights in the state of Wyoming because doctors are being intimidated.

"I guess the word's gotten out. Some group's holding a 'prayer vigil' on the front walk of his office this morning, and there's a crowd building up. I gotta get down there."

Sally frowned. "I'm not surprised that the doctor's trying to keep a low profile, but I'd have thought I might have heard about him. Where's his office? I think I want to go down there."

Hawk reached over and put his hand on her arm. "I'll come too," he said.

"I wouldn't advise it." Dickie said. "Ignore these guys and

hope they preach themselves out, and go away. I wouldn't mind doing the same, but I don't have the option."

"You know that's not the way it works," Sally told Dickie. "It's not just prayer vigils. Bomb threats. Bullets through the window. Anthrax, for God's sake."

Hawk finished her thought. "Which is why no doctor has been willing to do abortions anywhere in Wyoming for the last four years," he said. "Some Equality State." He got up and walked into the mudroom to get his denim jacket. Sally went to the counter, rummaged in her purse, grabbed her cell phone, driver's license, and a ten-dollar bill to stuff in the pocket of her fleece pullover.

"If you're going to drive," Dickie said, "you'll have to park a few blocks away. We're setting up barricades. Just to be on the safe side," he added, too casually.

The office was on a side street between Ivinson and Grand, only ten blocks from their house. They decided to walk.

The building that housed the doctor's office wasn't much, a one-story tan brick cube with a still-brown crabgrass lawn and a straggly cottonwood tree out front. Somebody had planted a ring of pansies around the base of the tree, a month earlier than they should have. A waist-high chain-link fence formed a border between the sidewalk and the grass.

A dirt parking lot adjacent to the building held only two cars, parked in the spaces farthest from the building, leaving room for patients' cars closer in. The front door bore a placard with the doctor's name, followed by the letters M.D., OB-GYN. Nothing else.

The struggling pansies were in imminent danger of being trampled to dust. Several dozen people milled on the grass or paced the sidewalk, some holding signs with messages like "Stop the Death Doctor" and "Abortion Is Murder." Others prayed silently or aloud, some very loud. Clouds were rolling in fast from the mountains, and the wind was kicking up, boding to kick hard. The protesters had to raise their voices to be heard at all.

More people came, streaming toward the building. Some were

obviously supporters of the group holding the demonstration. Others sported buttons that said "Pro-Choice" or "It's Between a Woman and Her Doctor." Sally saw lots of people she knew, including Dave Haggerty, recognizing him from the Dunwoodie opening. Looked like the pro-choice people hadn't had time to make signs of their own. Pretty much everyone wore a grim expression, including Sally and Hawk.

One woman caught Sally's eye. She was quite simply stunning, blond hair perfectly styled for a television-anchor-grade wind-blown look that was undisturbed by the rising gale. She wore a beautifully tailored pantsuit and shoes Sally instantly envied. She stood at the edge of the crowd, holding hands with two well-groomed young women, heads bowed, looks of terrible sadness on their faces. Her immense blue eyes seemed to brim with tears that didn't quite fall.

Within minutes, the yard was packed with protesters, the crowd jostling and muttering in ominous anticipation. At that moment, Sally heard a familiar voice behind her.

"Excuse us. Excuse us," said Maude Stark, softly but clearly. Sally turned to see Maude making her way toward the gate to the front walk, her arm encircling a girl in a hooded sweatshirt. From what Sally could see of the face, the girl was absolutely petrified.

"I can't do this," Sally heard the girl say. "I'm too scared."

"I know, I know," said Maude. "It's entirely up to you, dear. If you'd rather come back another day, we can do that."

"No. It won't get any better, and I want to get it over with. We might as well go ahead," said the girl.

"We'll just get you inside," Maude said soothingly. "It'll be okay. I promise."

Sally and Hawk exchanged a look and made their way to Maude's side. "You're an escort?" Hawk asked Maude.

Maude nodded curtly. "I'm on a list. Got the call this morning."

"Can we help?" Sally asked.

"You're not trained," said Maude. "You'd better keep your distance."

"We'll follow your lead, Maude. Tell us what to do," Hawk said softly, moving to the girl's other side. Sally took a place between them and behind the girl.

Maude made a decision. She kept her arm around the girl as she turned to face Sally and Hawk. "All right. Just stay close to my friend here. Keep yourself between her and the people who've come out to exercise their free speech rights. Some of them are going to say hurtful things, and we'll all just ignore that and keep moving."

Sally put a hand on the girl's shoulder, for comfort and protection.

"What if they start pushing us around?" Hawk asked. Some of the protesters were pretty big. Sally noticed a clean-cut blond guy who looked like he could hold down the center of a defensive line.

Maude's eyes iced. "Move fast toward the door. If somebody gives you a shove, or throws a punch, don't respond. It's the cops' job to keep the peace."

Under the hood, the girl's eyes grew huge.

Sally craned her neck, caught sight of Dickie talking fast into his cell phone, and felt a small measure of reassurance. "We'll keep moving," she said, rubbing the back of the girl's sweatshirt, leaving her hand on her back. "Remember," she said, "you're just here to keep a doctor's appointment."

The chain-link gate was ajar. They walked through. Angry faces surrounded them, drawing closer.

"Baby killer!" screamed a boy in a high school letter jacket. He jostled Hawk hard. Hawk gritted his teeth and kept walking forward.

A girl with a Mohawk, black lipstick, and multiple face piercings sidled up to Sally's side. She leaned over and whispered to the girl in the sweatshirt, "Are you prepared for eternity in hell?"

"You'll excuse us," Maude said quietly, keeping moving even as, Sally noticed, she stepped on Mohawk Girl's foot.

At that moment, Sally chanced to glance over at the beautiful blond. Time slowed. The woman began to chant the Lord's Prayer, softly. The crowd took up the chant. At "Deliver us from evil," she gave an all-but-imperceptible nod. The protesters continued chanting but closed ranks, blocking the walkway.

The wind rose with a moan that turned into a howl, hurling sharp grains of dirt in eyes, flinging small pebbles, roaring its power. Maude, Hawk, and Sally huddled closer around the hooded girl as they pressed forward.

"*Murderer!*" shrieked the crowd, shoving up against them, hemming them in.

The girl began to sob wildly.

"Grip my forearm," Maude ordered Sally, putting her other arm in front of the girl and instructing Hawk to do the same. Within moments, the three of them had locked arms around the patient. "Now put your head down," she told the girl, "and when I say 'Do it!' we move forward as fast as we can go. Three deep breaths," she instructed.

One. Two. Three.

"Do it!"

But they never did. An ear-shattering explosion ripped the air, lashing the crowd into pandemonium.

People screamed and cried and ran. Sally smelled gunpowder, hot glass, scorched metal. In a daze, she watched Maude pull the girl in the sweatshirt to her feet, saw them rushing back out the gate, into the street, away from the building. Everyone who could was heading in the same direction.

Sally had just enough time to register a car in the parking lot, windows and windshield blown out, wipers and window frames grotesquely twisted and blackened, before Hawk yanked her by the hand and they started running.

It was a regular stampede. The crowd heaved down the street, blindly seeking escape. Half went south toward Grand, half north to Ivinson. Sally and Hawk were headed north.

"Come on!" Hawk hollered. "Let's get the fuck away!"

Halfway down the block, he veered left and pulled her into an alley. Lungs pounding, breath ragged, she ran as hard as she could, Hawk half dragging her along. The screeching wind pounded them with hard gusts of dirt and pebbles, coating her mouth, searing her eyes.

Amazingly, no one followed them. They crossed streets, but by silent agreement stayed in the alley. Within three blocks, she began to feel as if they'd gained some distance on the panic-stricken crowd, the madness of a morning gone hideously wrong.

That was when they nearly fell over the body, sprawled in the gravel in the middle of the alley.

# CHAPTER 4

## DEMONS

SOMEONE WAS SCREAMING. Not surprising, of course. The horror of the demonstration, the shock of the blast, and now a body in an alleyway. Who wouldn't scream?

What surprised Sally was that the person screaming was, evidently, she.

"Sally! Don't. Don't look. We'll get the police. Come over here, honey, just come with me. Come on, Sally. Come on, sweetie. Oh fuck. Stop it!" said Hawk.

Somebody was shaking her, and hugging her tight, and shaking her some more.

Her ears were still ringing from the blast at the doctor's office. God, there was so much blood.

Demons were loose in the town of Laramie.

They needed the police, right away.

Like the police had nothing else going on at the moment.

"I saw you put your phone in your pocket," said Hawk. "Come on, girl. Get it out."

With hands that shook until she felt her elbows rattle, she dug into her pocket and found her cell phone. Managed to punch in 911. Got a busy signal.

"K-keep trying," said Hawk, rubbing her back, his own teeth chattering.

Sally kept hitting redial until the operator answered. All available officers, she said, were currently on emergency call.

"I know," Sally said. "I was at the demonstration. But we're standing here in an alley, looking at a person who appears to be, erk, dead."

That got the operator's attention. She told Sally to wait there for an officer.

Sally felt the cold gale, heard the scream of police sirens, the honking of fire engine klaxons. Every detail of the scene sharpened, in surreal focus: the weathered plank fences that lined the alley, the bare branches of cottonwoods peeking above the fence tops, flapping in the keening wind, the garbage cans, chained down to board boxes to keep them from blowing away, the clattering sound of dust and gravel flung against hard surfaces.

And the body on the ground. Now she looked at him. Blue pinstripe suit, black wingtip shoes. Not, Sally thought with an unbelievably inappropriate giggle, a Laramie look. He lay in a twisted heap, facedown, head covered with blood. She could only glance at his head for a moment. Someone had bashed his skull to pieces.

A brown Toyota 4Runner pulled into the alley, and Detective Scotty Atkins, chief investigator of the Albany County Sheriff's Department, got out.

Ever a man of few words, Scotty merely nodded at them and went to check the body. Sally and Hawk stood waiting. Finally he turned to them.

"You didn't touch anything?" he asked.

"No," Sally said. "Of course not."

Scotty pursed his lips. "You recognize this man?"

They both shook their heads.

"Well," he said, "I do."

They waited. Finally Hawk asked, "Are you going to tell us who he is?"

Scotty took a deep breath, expelled air out his nose. "His name is Bradley Preston. He's an attorney."

"Sweet Jesus," said Sally.

"Your student's father," Hawk said, moving to hold her up when her knees buckled.

"Take it easy," said Scotty. "I'll get the sheriff. He's pretty tied up, but he'll want to take a look. Don't go anywhere."

"Why don't we sit down," said Hawk, walking Sally over to a pile of cinder blocks stacked against a leaning fence. The blocks had evidently been there for some time. Weeds had grown up around them, crackling against Sally's legs as she found her way to take a seat.

She didn't know how long they sat side by side on the cinder blocks. Scotty Atkins's voice, calling in the sheriff and crime scene team, registered dimly above the moan and rattle of the wind. Sally leaned back against the fence and looked off to one side, the better to use the fence to support a head grown suddenly too weighty to bear.

And then she saw it. There, in a tangled patch of dried weeds, amid back-alley litter that hadn't quite made it to the garbage cans. A faded and flattened cardboard beer carton, soda cans and broken bottles, a disposable diaper improperly disposed of. And a long, thin metal tube, bent at one end, fitted with a socket fixture of some kind.

No bigger around than her thumb, except for the socket. Crusted with drying blood and some kind of gelatinous substance Sally didn't want to name.

"Do you see that?" she asked Hawk.

With great effort, he turned to look. His eyes narrowed, then opened wide. "Oh God."

"What do you call that?" she asked, fatigue and shock washing away on a wave of bright awareness. "A tire iron?"

"Lug wrench," said Hawk, leaning forward for a better look. "Some kind of fancy one. See how it's jointed there? It telescopes. Compacts down to fit in the tool compartment of even a little car."

"Like a Mazda Miata?" Sally asked, feeling sick all over again.

"Yeah," said Hawk. "Maybe. But it wouldn't be standard equipment. You'd go out and buy yourself something like that if you wanted a little extra leverage."

"For example, let's say you were a girl," said Sally, "and you wanted to be able to change tires yourself, without having to ask some guy for help."

"For example," Hawk agreed.

"Detective!" Sally called. "Come here. You need to see this."

Atkins, talking on his cell phone, held up one finger.

"No," Sally insisted, "really! Really, Scotty, right now!"

He said something more into the phone, clicked off, walked their way.

"Look at that," she told the detective, pointing into the weeds.

Atkins looked. His mouth hardened. He glared at Sally, closed his eyes tightly, shook his head hard, and opened his eyes. "Let me think a minute about the facts I know as of this moment," he began. "Bradley Preston"—he nodded in the direction of the body—"is dead, by all appearances, victim of a very recent assault."

"An assault with a blunt instrument, it looks like," said Sally, pointing at the object in the weeds.

"You're getting ahead of me. The guys will be here soon enough to make that determination."

"But much as you hate to admit it," Sally put in, "that's what probably happened."

Scotty continued as if she hadn't spoken. "This same Bradley Preston's daughter has disappeared. Gone, who knows where, and it seems she herself had been assaulted at the time she took off. Meanwhile, this very morning, the man's wife is involved in a demonstration at an abortion clinic, and for the first time in the history of the state of Wyoming, there's a car bombing."

"Beatrice Preston? Is she blond, pretty in a sort of permanently blow-dried, network anchorwoman way? Prays a lot and acts like she's not trying to attract attention, when she is?"

Scotty winced, scrubbing his palm across his forehead. "May I ask what you know about Mrs. Preston, Sally?" he asked.

"We went down to the demonstration," said Hawk. "Just getting our fair share of abuse."

At that moment, Sheriff Langham peeled into the alley, the tires of his Blazer spitting gravel. An Albany County patrol car was right behind.

"What's going on over there?" Atkins asked Dickie.

"FBI's on the scene," he told Scotty. "Guess they headed over from Cheyenne the minute they heard about the demonstration at the clinic. ATF will be here within the hour. We've got a half-dozen people heading for the hospital with cuts and bruises, but nobody seriously hurt. It's a fucking miracle." Dickie glanced over at the body in the alley. "What the hell's happened here?" he asked of no one in particular.

"We were down there at the doctor's office," said Sally. "When that car blew, we just started running this way. That's how we found him," she finished, tipping her head in the direction of the body.

Dickie walked over to the deputies pulling crime scene kits out of their vehicle. Atkins followed him, Sally and Hawk trailing behind. "I know things are a little crazy right now," he told the deputies, "but take your time here. Do this right. Pretty soon every investigator within a four-hundred-mile radius will be stomping all over that doctor's office, treating the incident like the federal case it is. In other words, not the county's case. Our job over there is to render assistance as requested. But over here," he continued, "looks like we've got a murder on our hands."

# CHAPTER 5

# SICK

UNDER NORMAL CIRCUMSTANCES, SALLY'S first move upon wakening was to wash her face and brush her teeth. Her second was to head straight to the kitchen counter, fill the coffee grinder with Peet's French Roast beans, and perform the ritual that transformed her from a lump of protoplasm into a thinking human being.

After what she'd seen and been through, she wasn't sure she wanted the feelings that came along with thinking. Then again, she told herself as she lay in bed, loath to face the day, give a creature a big enough brain, and consciousness came with the territory. Get a grip on the feelings by focusing the thinking.

She didn't wait for coffee. She hauled herself up, grabbed a notepad out of a kitchen drawer, pulled a pencil out of a jar on the counter, and sat down at the table to try to draw, from memory, the object she'd seen in the weeds in the alley the day before. She wasn't the world's best artist, but fortunately her subject was simple. It took three sketches to get the bend in the bar right, to get to the point where the socket seemed to her the right size. Eventually she was satisfied.

Turned out she was a step behind Hawk, who'd taken the more rational if perhaps less artistic tack. He'd been on the computer, searching the web for auto parts. He'd found scores of websites that offered lug wrenches of various kinds, half a dozen more that specialized in gear for Mazda Miatas. He'd printed out pictures of several possibilities, but only one matched both Hawk's excellent memory and Sally's imperfect drawing: the Nut-Buster extendable lug wrench.

"That thing isn't only for Miatas, right?" Sally asked. Despite her automotive nickname, you could put in an eyedropper everything Mustang Sally Alder knew about cars.

"No. It's a pretty generic tool. But we do know that it works for Miatas, since I found this one on a Miata site. Most people would just use whatever lug wrench happened to come with their car. You'd buy something like this, maybe, if the original was gone, or as I told you yesterday, if you wanted a little extra leverage," Hawk explained.

"That doesn't mean it's a girl tool," said Sally. "It could be, sure. But think about it, Hawk. Who actually wants to work harder than they have to? I can imagine some big giant former football hero whose knees have gone to sludge and bone chips, deciding that the Nut-Buster would save him the trouble of having to get down on, and back off of, the ground. Or some trucker who has to change tires a lot wanting an extendable jobbie that would cut down wear and tear on an arthritic elbow joint. Things that save anybody's labor aren't just for girls. That's one of those myths that are meant to reinforce men's images of themselves as manly and make women think they're too weak to do stuff like be president of the United States."

"Presidents probably don't change a lot of tires," Hawk replied dryly. "But I catch your drift. You know, all this serious thinking about gender roles won't ultimately mean shit if they find Charlie Preston's prints all over that Nut-Buster."

"Or possibly her boyfriend's prints. And given the fact that both kids have records, it wouldn't take the cops any time at all to make a match. I really wish I could talk to Charlie before that happens. They'll catch up with her eventually. The sooner she's back here, telling her side of the story, the better."

"If, in fact, she didn't do it," Hawk said.

Sally bit her lip, thought a minute. "Even if she did, which I can't believe at this point. I think," said Sally, "I'll give a call to the Stark household. See if young Agatha's around."

Julie Stark answered. Aggie, she said, was at a track meet at the Laramie High stadium. She was running the 800-meter lap in a medley relay, running the mile, and doing a little pole vaulting.

"Pole vaulting?" Sally asked. "Aren't you terrified she'll impale herself?"

"Yes, I am," said Julie. "But when I mention it, Aggie just says 'Mother!' in that disgusted way they do, and tells me not to get all girlie on her."

"I'd like to talk to her about Charlie," Sally said. "Have you heard what happened to Bradley Preston?"

"It was in the *Boomerang* this morning. Horrible. What's this town coming to? You've heard, of course, about the blast at the doctor's office. Maude's calling it a bombing, but the newspaper said the police are calling it a prank—some kids hauled a derelict car into the parking lot and set off a bunch of firecrackers inside."

"I was there," said Sally. "I can't believe firecrackers would do that much damage. But I guess the police are still sorting it all out. Meanwhile, I'm hoping Aggie might be able to tell me something that could help Charlie."

"Hmm," said Julie, considering the pros and cons. "I guess that's okay."

"Today would be good," said Sally, pressing, but, she hoped, not too hard.

"I think she's planning to go out with friends to get something to eat after the meet. Your best bet is probably to go down to the stadium and try to catch her between events. She'll be there most of the day. The athletes are always up and down from the stands, getting water and snacks, and talking to people. Look for Mike. He took the dog down to cheer her on. Or if you don't see him, look for a gaggle of kids wearing brown and gold sweats. She'll be one of them."

"Thanks," said Sally. "Think I'll do that." She hung up the phone and turned to Hawk. "Feel like going to a high school track meet?"

"You know, Mustang," said Hawk, moving behind her and wrapping his arms around her, nuzzling her neck. "Yesterday was a bad, bad day. I could use a little comfort and care. I was just thinking to myself that it might be fun to try to talk you back into bed for an hour or so."

The nuzzling was having the effect of liquefying her limbs, from the knees up and back down again. "I really ought to talk to Aggie Stark," she said, undermining her position with a sigh that edged into a moan when he put his hands into action.

"I used to run track in high school," Hawk told her. "I'm partial to the distance events."

"I've always admired that about you," Sally said, reflecting on the prospects.

"If you want to know the truth, a track meet is mostly a matter of standing around. Another hour," he said, emphasizing the point with roving fingers, "won't hurt."

"No," said Sally, turning around to put her arms around him, raising her face for a kiss. "I think, in fact, it'll probably feel really good."

"I'm compelled to warn you," said Hawk, lips against her mouth. "If we dawdle around here, you might miss the pole vaulting."

She made a semirude remark about doing some pole vaulting of her own.

By the time they got to the stadium, the sun was high in the sky. The field was full of fit teenagers in various combinations of brightly colored sweats and shorts and tank tops, stretching, high-stepping, striding, jogging, milling, and flirting with one another. Over a loudspeaker a voice so distorted as to be, to Sally's ear, unintelligible announced the results of previous events and called athletes to line up for the next race. Out on the oval track, runners sauntered to staggered starting lines, shaking out their legs.

Up in the stands, clusters of uniformed team members mingled with parents and friends, forming islands of color all up and down the concrete steps, the metal benches. Sally spotted the group in brown and gold. The kids were chattering gaily, slugging water and Gatorade out of bottles, chomping on PowerBars and sandwiches and raw vegetables and an enormous assortment of junk food. One group of leggy girls clustered around Mike Stark, babbling baby talk to a miniature schnauzer they were passing hand to hand.

Could anything appear further removed from the brutal and bitter world of battered children?

"Hey, Sophie!" said a girl busily banding up masses of chin-length black hair into two stubby pigtails. "Don't give him Goldfish! Last time we got Beanie home from a meet, you guys had been stuffing him full of junk and he yakked all over my mom's Oriental carpet. Come here, Beanie boy," she cooed, finishing confining her hair to reach out for her dog.

Beanie the schnauzer looked up at the sound of his name, an expression of utter innocence on his face. Sally wondered how any animal that looked that much like a photo negative of Groucho Marx could also appear the soul of guilelessness. All black, with white eyebrows, white whiskers, and fluffy white shins, he was, she had to admit, adorable. Very useful, Sally thought, if you were the kind of dog who thought being stuffed with Goldfish and Fritos and Cheez-Its was heaven enough to put up with a bit of barfing later on, if indeed you had a big enough brain to make the connection. Beanie looked intelligent enough, but he probably had a brain the size of a walnut.

Sally'd had a black Lab. They loved people as much as schnauzers, but they had a little more dignity, she thought. A spear of longing for that dog, struck down by a speeder on Hilgard Avenue in L.A., stabbed through her. She shook it off.

Mike Stark caught sight of them. "Hey, Sally, Hawk. Are you guys big track fans?" he asked.

"Actually," Sally told him, "we were hoping to get a chance to talk with your daughter."

The girl with the pigtails raised enormous brown eyes. The dog whimpered in her lap, wagged his stumpy tail, licked her hand. "I'm Aggie," she said. "And you're Sally Alder."

"Wow!" said a freckle-faced girl with mile-long legs and a mouthful of braces. "You're the one who got her hat shot off at the Wrangler Bar!"

Sally took a moment. It wasn't the sort of thing one put on one's résumé, but as claims to fame went, it wasn't half bad. "Yep," said Sally, "guess so."

"She's also the professor who lived in Miss Dunwoodie's house and writes all those books, Jenny," Aggie told her friend. "It's not like people go around getting their hats shot off every day or anything."

"You know about my books?" Sally asked.

"Duh!" said Aggie. "Like, my aunt Maude worked for Miss Dunwoodie for about a thousand years. And she's your boss now, right? If you don't write books, don't they fire you or something?"

"Not hardly," Aggie's freckled friend retorted. "Once you're a professor, you have to be a serial killer or something to get fired."

"Julie just called me on my cell, saying you all were coming down here," Mike interjected. "Ag, why don't you give me the dog, and go over there and talk to Sally and Hawk for a few minutes. Your next event isn't for half an hour anyhow."

Sally gave him a grateful smile. "We won't be long," she said, as they walked up the steps and found a vacant bench.

Sally got right to the point. "Aggie, I just wanted to let you know that I'm really worried about Charlie Preston. She's my student," Sally explained. "She came to see me right before she left town. I gave her some money and a black wool coat."

Aggie nodded, saying nothing.

"Any chance you already knew that?" Hawk prompted.

Aggie cocked one eyebrow, then nodded again.

"Feel free to use your words," Hawk said.

Aggie laughed. "Sorry. I don't like to talk to adults about Charlie. I mean, my mom and dad are cool and all, but Charlie has enough problems without me ratting her out to some grown-up who comes on all well-meaning, but who'll just get her busted and sent back to her dad . . . oh."

Aggie looked down at the ground, shook herself. "I guess she won't be getting sent back to him anymore."

"Aggie," Sally said, putting a hand on the girl's arm. "Charlie could be in danger. At the very least, she's in a lot of trouble. Somebody beat her up before she left."

Aggie looked up now, her face fierce. "For a change! Do you know how many times they did it to her? She told me it used to be a weekly thing. She didn't say much more than that. But I figured some of it out. Her shoulders were all scarred from where they'd used a belt on her, buckle end out."

Sally closed her eyes, took a slow breath.

"If somebody did that to me, I'd get as far away as possible, and cover my tracks," Hawk said quietly.

"If they did it to me, I'd bust a cap in 'em," said sweet little Aggie.

Sally swallowed an inappropriate laugh, composed herself for a serious question. "Aggie, do you think somebody did?"

"You mean," she asked, "do I think that Charlie killed her dad? No! Well . . . I don't know . . . it's pretty hard to believe. I mean, with everything he did to her and all, you'd think she'd want to. But mostly she just seemed sad and scared all the time. Like she thought everything bad that happened to her was her own fault."

"It's like that a lot with people who've been hurt the way Charlie's been hurt," Sally told the girl. "Get beaten on and belittled enough, you start to believe you deserve what you get."

Aggie pressed her lips together, scratched at a scab on her knee.

"But you didn't think she deserved it, did you, Aggie? You're her friend," Hawk said.

Aggie nodded again, eyes intent on her knee. Then she looked up. "Nobody deserves it. That's what Billy kept telling her."

"Billy?" Hawk said.

"Billy Reno," Aggie told them. "He's Charlie's boyfriend. He's got this really sick tattoo of a dragon that winds from his wrist up across his shoulders and around his neck."

"That does sound sick," Sally said.

"'Sick,'" Hawk told her, "means 'cool.' Try to keep up, Sal."

Sally leaned in. "Aggie," she said, "I don't want to keep you. I know you've got to get ready for your race. But is there the slightest chance you know where Charlie is?"

Aggie's face went blank. "No," she said.

"But you've heard from her?" Hawk pushed.

"Maybe. But that doesn't mean I know where she is. That's her business."

This was one tough fourteen-year-old; there was a lot of Maude in her. And there was no point pushing so hard that she'd clam up permanently. Better to hope for more, another day. "Okay. Fair enough. How about this? Do you have any idea where we might find Billy Reno?"

Aggie considered. "The police probably know already, since he's on probation. I guess it wouldn't hurt to tell you. My aunt Maude is the sickest person I know, for somebody who's like a hundred years old, and she thinks you're okay."

"Glad to hear it," said Sally. "I think Maude's the best, myself."

"Okay," said Aggie. "I gotta go." She stood, shaking out her long legs. "You can probably find Billy at this apartment he shares with some roommates. It's up on North Fourth." She gave the address, started to head down the steps, and turned. "Actually, you might be able to leave a message for Charlie with Billy. I think she might be in touch with him."

"Can I maybe leave a message for her with you, in case I don't connect with Billy?" Sally asked, following Aggie as she strode down the steep stadium steps, already putting on her game face.

Aggie turned. Frowned. Shook her shoulders. The pigtails bobbed.

"Come on, Aggie!" yelled one of the long-legged girls, now jogging in place on the grass inside the oval, down on the field. "We need to warm up!"

"What's the message?" Aggie asked, getting her own legs going.

"Tell her I'll do anything I can to help. Here." Sally dug in her pocket, produced a business card. "That's got my work phone and email on it. I wrote my home and cell phone numbers and my home address down too. Anywhere, any time. Charlie knows they're looking for her. And I'm not just talking about the cops. It's possible that she could be in danger from whoever killed her father."

"And if she's driving that Miata, she'll be pretty easy to spot. It's not like they're everywhere in Wyoming," said Hawk.

"Tell her she needs to come back. I can't protect her, but I'll do everything in my power to help her out. If she stays out of sight, nobody can do a damn thing for her."

"Nobody you know," Aggie said, thrusting the card in the rear pocket of her shorts, impatient to get going.

"You think anybody's protecting her now?" Hawk asked.

"Do you think," said Aggie, "anybody ever has?" and took off at a dead run down the hard concrete steps.

# CHAPTER 6

# CODE VIOLATIONS

ON MONDAY SALLY SAT contemplating the menu at El Conquistador, waiting for Edna McCaffrey to arrive for their monthly lunch date. Why she was bothering with the menu, she didn't know. She always ordered the same thing. Edna always ordered the same thing. They had beer if their afternoons didn't include any classes, or appointments with people smarter than they were. Sally had a class to teach, and planned to go looking for Billy Reno after that. She was nursing an iced tea.

"Sorry I'm late," said Edna, dashing to the table. She was wearing a lime-green silk suit that Sally was pretty sure had come from Armani . . . in Milan. "The provost is on a tear about fundraising. All us deans are supposed to show balance sheets at the end of the year, with at least twenty million in outside funding in the plus column. It's one thing if Halliburton is bankrolling your petroleum engineering students to practice their skills for drilling the Alaska National Wildlife Refuge. It's another thing to try to figure out who wants to be the millionaire to give some English professor a big bunch of money to write about how *The Virginian* is just another version of *Tristan and Isolde*."

The waitress arrived with chips and salsa. Sally and Edna ordered the usual.

"So," said Sally, loading up a chip with salsa hot enough to take the skin off the roof of her mouth. "I presume you're about to get on my case about fund-raising."

Edna grinned. "Obviously, you've developed an understanding of how universities work."

"How all institutions work," said Sally. "The big boss gets a bug up his ass, and pretty soon, they're passing the Preparation H down the line."

Edna raised one eyebrow. "You do have a way with a metaphor, Professor."

"I merely state the obvious," said Sally, "and then bend over to take my medicine."

Edna dipped a chip. "I am eating," she said.

"Okay. No more metaphors. Who do you want me to—I almost said 'grease'—approach?" Sally asked.

Edna looked down, drew a little circle with her fingertip on the paper placemat festooned with Wyoming cattle brands. "I'm thinking about corporate gifts to the Dunwoodie Center."

Sally gave her a one-sided grin. "I don't think we're exactly in line for contributions from the oil, coal, and gas guys. And we're not a military base, so that rules out the government. Who else has big bucks in Wyoming?"

"It's not about Wyoming, or not exclusively," said Edna. "Look, Sally. You started with Meg Dunwoodie's bequest, and you've gotten some Hollywood money. You need to enlarge the circle, as they say in the development biz. Think 'liberal money.' What Wyoming lefties have the national prominence, and the connections, to bring in bigger money from outside the state?"

Sally thought a minute. "Golly," she said, "I ought to be able to come up with both their names."

"You're so amusing today," said Edna.

"I live to entertain," Sally replied.

Their plates arrived. "I'm talking about Dave Haggerty. He's already given you a nice contribution. He's not afraid to support the sisterhood. He might be willing to up his own commitment, especially with what happened at that doctor's office last week. Get him to be your point man, and maybe he can hook you up with people who might be good for a whole hell of a lot more," Edna said, tucking into her flautas.

"He's wired to people with that much money?" Sally asked, loading her steaming chicken taco with salsa and biting in.

"He's the grid," said Edna. "First of all, he's on the boards of half the progressive organizations in the U.S. Second, the guy's got some big bucks himself. Three years ago, he won a *huge* settlement in a product liability case, which meant that he gets brought in on all kinds of similar suits—on both sides. Sometimes the plaintiffs want his expertise, and sometimes the manufacturers hire him to cover their asses."

"You mean, he's on retainer with tobacco companies and the like?" Sally asked.

"I don't know. There was a piece about him in *Mother Jones*—the interviewer asked him what he thought the major problem with big business was, and he answered, 'Big greed.' And since he does so much pro bono work, it'd be out of character, to say the least, for him to sell out to the biggest greedheads. But the people in the university development office, who keep track of charitable giving, tell me he's started handing out money like somebody who's got something to prove. He's not making that money representing the broken and busted. Draw your own conclusions," Edna answered.

Sally sneered. "And I liked him when I met him," she said. "Does he also go hunting with Supreme Court justices?"

"No. But I hear he plays chess with Paul Allen from time to time."

"Microsoft Paul Allen?" Sally gaped.

Edna grinned.

"So, maybe I should set up a meeting with him," said Sally. "Sort of lay out my vision for the center, ask his advice."

"If it were me," said Edna, "I'd buy him dinner at the Yippie I O first, just to get acquainted. It wouldn't be a big chore. From what I've seen, he's a pretty fascinating guy."

From what Sally'd seen, Dave Haggerty had tiger eyes and an interesting mouth. "I don't know about that."

"Oh for Christ's sake, Sally. You think he's never been out for a business dinner? Or are you worried Hawk will object?"

"Hawk understands the demands of business," Sally said. "I'm sure he's done his share of working dinners with attractive women."

"If I'm not mistaken," Edna said, "Professor Green's job requires him to spend days at a time camped in remote locations with graduate students, some of whom are females. Some of whom are triathletes who enjoy exhibiting their muscle tone. And you don't seem to have any objection to those professional responsibilities."

"Professor Green," said Sally, "is a free man in a free country. I don't inquire about muscle tone."

Edna smirked. "So why would he have a problem with a business dinner? Or is it you who has the problem? Just do it. You're getting way ahead of yourself."

She was right, Sally reflected. Better slow that Mustang down. "All right," she said, "I'll give Haggerty a call."

"It's not as if I'm asking you to suck up to somebody really odious," Edna said. "Although I certainly reserve the right to do that. In fact, maybe I should give you a long list of loathsome people to court. Might keep you out of trouble," she finished.

Okay. All right. Right away. Sally told herself she'd just take a stab at finding Billy Reno, then she'd get down to business and make the call to Dave Haggerty.

Maybe it was the size of the town; maybe it was just that, as Lorelei Lee, the gentleman's favorite blond, had observed, fate kept on happening. When Sally pulled up in front of the dilapidated two-story duplex at the address she'd gotten from Aggie Stark, a small crowd was gathered on the sidewalk. A sheriff's deputy was stapling a notice to one of the front doors. Three young men in baggy pants and limp T-shirts stood smoking cigarettes and watching morosely as another deputy tossed a motley assortment of gear on top of a heap of similar stuff in the front yard. But the crowd on the sidewalk was focused on Dickie Langham, sucking on a Marlboro of his own, leaning against his truck, getting an earful from none other than Dave Haggerty, casually dressed in jeans and a fleece jacket.

"Come on, Sheriff," Sally heard Haggerty say as she worked her way into the midst of the onlookers. "My clients paid their rent on time. And what about their right to be safe in their own home? Broken light fixtures, appliances with shorts, bare wires hangin' out all over the place—it's no wonder they had a fire in here! I thought you people were public safety officers."

" 'Course we are, Dave," Dickie told him in a soothing voice. "The building inspector's been here a time or two and cited the management company for code violations. According to the paperwork I've got, the place has been brought up to code. It's not clear who's responsible for those broken light fixtures, I'll grant you, but I might mention that your clients," he said, gesturing toward the young men, "appear to have done some damage to the place themselves. There's trash everywhere, spray-painted graffiti on the walls; hell, somebody ripped the bathroom door right off the hinges! It don't exactly look like these lads have spent their time in this place memorizing Bible verses and polishing their Eagle Scout badges."

"They're entitled to the protection of the law," Haggerty retorted. "This morning at seven A.M., the apartment manager came into their apartment without knocking, waving a forty-four, yelling, 'If you punks don't get the hell off this property in fifteen minutes, I'll blow every damn one of you to Kingdom Come!' No prior notice of eviction, not to mention the threat of bodily harm. What do you plan to do about that?"

Dickie contemplated his cigarette, flicked the ash. "Maybe tell him to watch his language?"

"Come on, Sheriff. The guy manages half the slum properties in town. The owners rent to kids who don't know jack shit about their renters' rights, and half the time they end up getting evicted, taken to court, and charged for enough repairs and renovations to build the Trump Tower. We get a case like this every day at the university law clinic. It's a slumlord's racket, and you know it!"

"I also know," said Dickie, "that these fine, upstanding young citizens have been partying and trashing their place, off and on for the last two weeks. We've had at least three complaints about noise, and on one occasion had to come in and shut things down. My officers busted three kids for drugs and wrote twenty-five minor-in-possession citations that night. Your boys here might be of age, but some of their guests were still suckin' on pacifiers. I wouldn't be surprised if some of those cases have showed up at your university law clinic. 'Scuse me a minute."

Dickie had caught sight of Sally. He tilted his head, took a last drag on his cigarette, and flicked the butt away as he walked toward her, took her hand, pulled her aside, Haggerty at his heels. "What brings you out today, Mustang?" he asked, only a hint of irritation slipping into his voice.

Haggerty turned to look at her, more than a glimmer of annoyance still on his own face, but quickly covered the emotion. "Sally Alder," he said. "What a surprise."

"I had no idea what was happening here," Sally told them, hoping to explain away her awkward presence. "I didn't come just to gawk at the spectacle. I'm hoping to have a chance to speak to Billy Reno."

Both men looked at her. "And why would that be?" Dickie said. "You need a cheap TV or a Jeep Cherokee?"

"Watch it, Sheriff," said Haggerty. "Mr. Reno's paid his debt to society for his juvenile indiscretions."

"Indiscretions!" Dickie laughed. "Last time I encountered little Billy being indiscreet, he wasn't a juvie anymore, and he was in the midst of hot-wiring a Lexus that happened to be parked right out in front of the county courthouse. In the middle of a blizzard! There's your indiscretion, and then there's your bein' a sociopath. But then, of course you probably recall that episode yourself, Dave, seeing as how you went straight out and hired away the PD who got the little shit off by convincing the Lexus's owner that Mr. Reno had merely been a good Samaritan, thinking he was helping out with a dead battery."

"Since the owner had been at a bar where Billy happened to be, and had slammed down six or seven vodka gimlets by the time he got back to his car, his recollection of the incident was a little hazy. The public defender merely presented the owner with a plausible explanation, which he chose to accept, rather than having his own DWI record become an issue," Haggerty pointed out blandly. "Come on. You have to admit it, Dick. That was a pretty sweet little piece of lawyering. No reason to revictimize the Lexus guy, or contribute to jail overcrowding and police overwork, when you can make everybody happy by getting a case dismissed. By the way," he said, shifting gears suddenly and turning to Sally, "how *do* you know Billy Reno?"

When in doubt, the truth. "He's Charlie Preston's boyfriend. I thought he might know something about how she's doing, maybe take her a message."

"Why don't you give me the message?" Dickie said. "I happen to be looking for Charlie Preston myself, you know."

"And you're hoping Billy Reno can lead you to Charlie," Sally said.

"Better me than you, being as how I'm doing my job, which involves assaults and missing persons and homicide, for example, and last time I checked, you worked for the university. What kind of message are you trying to send this girl, Sally?" asked Dickie.

She was a little embarrassed. "I just wanted to tell her to come home, and to talk to you."

"Thanks a heap," said Dickie. "We peace officers need all the moral support we can get."

"Give me a break, Dickie. I'm really worried that whoever killed her father might be dangerous to Charlie. Maybe she found out that Brad was in some kind of trouble. Maybe she even got beaten up in the first place for seeing or hearing something she wasn't supposed to know about. She was in a hell of a hurry to get out of town, right? Maybe it wasn't just her father she was worried might be coming after her."

"Or maybe it was," said Dickie. "And she had something to do with what happened to him. I'm sorry if it hurts your feelings to think that one of your students could be involved in murder, but it's a possibility I have to consider."

"Which is precisely why this girl is so scared of you, or any cop. The system hasn't been any help to her. She must know that you all see her as a suspect in her father's murder."

Getting no reaction from Dickie, Sally appealed to Haggerty for support. "I thought, since I'm her teacher and she came to me for help before she disappeared this last time, I might be able to be, oh, I don't know, a kind of go-between."

"A bridge over troubled waters?" Haggerty asked, aiming the tiger eyes at her.

Sally looked into those eyes and fought not to mentally finish the line of the song, having to do with laying herself down. "Something like that."

"Charlie Preston's a troubled kid," Haggerty said, gaze steady on Sally's. "She's lucky to have a professor who cares about her. I admire you for that."

This was a man who seemed to know a thing or two about admiring. Sally's heart was beating a little faster than it should. "I'm really not trying to interfere," she told Dickie.

"Oh yes. I could tell," said Dickie. "And I'm really not going to have to tell you that you really don't want to interfere, for reasons that ought to be really obvious to a person of your really large intelligence."

"Sarcasm. Really unbecoming," said Sally, and then pointed at the punks on the lawn. "Which one's Billy Reno?"

"Well now, that's an interesting question," said Dickie. "Because none of them is. Matter of fact, Mr. Reno's not at home. You wouldn't happen to have some idea where the young man might be?"

Sally shook her head. "I haven't got a clue—I've never laid eyes on him. Any chance he just went out for a pack of cigarettes?" she asked.

"Oh, there's always a chance," said Dickie, glancing down at his watch. "But I've been here an hour or so, and he hasn't made an appearance. Odds are, he's cleared out entirely. Our Billy has reason to skedaddle when the law comes calling, of course, but moreover, there's no reason for him to hang around here. His name, naturally, isn't on the lease. Even slumlords don't like renting to incorrigible criminals."

"So Billy Reno wasn't actually living here?" Sally asked.

"Oh no. This is the address listed with his parole officer," Dickie told her. "But you know how it is with these kind of places, Sal. People come and go. Sometimes the rent gets split five ways, sometimes ten, and sometimes, as we see here, it doesn't get paid at all. Then everybody's got to find someplace new to tear apart."

Sally looked at the boys on the lawn, noting the shaved heads, the tattoos, the wife-beater tank tops. One was lighting a cigarette off the butt of the previous one he'd been smoking, squinting against the smoke. Another, wearing a large, gem-studded cross around his neck, was slumped against a rusting car in the driveway, hand over one ear, cell phone at the other. A third bent to pick up something off the lawn: a handmade afghan, crocheted in pinks and purples and blacks. That afghan was something only a mother or grandmother could have made, and the kid was treating it like it was the Shroud of Turin. He stood, shook out the afghan, folded it neatly, and set it carefully on a La-Z-Boy lounge chair with half the stuffing coming out of it. There was a tattoo of Bob Marley's sad-hopeful face on his arm, and something so poignant about the sight of him that Sally felt tears spring into her eyes. "Who knows who did the tearing apart, who's responsible, and who just happened to be in the wrong place at the wrong time," she observed.

"I can think of one person who falls into both of the last two groups," said Dave, "as you'll probably be interested to know, Sally. Charlie Preston. It appears," he said, looking at the notice of eviction now firmly stapled to the front door, "that her name was on the lease."

"Charlie signed the lease? Why? These guys look to me like they've got a few years on her, and she didn't even live here, from what I've heard."

"These boys also have worse credit records and rap sheets than she does, not to mention parents whose pockets aren't close to being as deep as the Prestons'. I also think she was spending a fair bit of time here with Billy," said Haggerty.

"Which is why I'm going to excuse myself, much as I enjoy your company, and chat with the roommates over there." Dickie jerked his head toward the boys on the lawn. "And just in case you should happen to succeed in making contact with Miss Preston before I do, I'll tell you one other thing. I haven't entirely given up hope that Billy Boy might show up here at some point. He knows that, at the very least, Charlie's liable to have to go to court over what happened at this place. He's completely crazy, true enough, but in his twisted, amoral, borderline way, Billy's one of the most loyal people on this green earth. He's very protective of the younger punks and losers and lost girls who follow him around and look up to him, God help him. Kid thinks he's fuckin' Robin Hood."

Sally and Dave watched Dickie walk toward the boys on the lawn. As he approached, each of them stopped what he was doing. Some slouched, some stood with their legs spread, arms folded or flexed at their sides. Their eyes grew flat, their faces expressionless.

"Those guys," said Sally, "are a little bit scary."

"They're also a little bit scared," said Haggerty. "More and more, I see kids these days who seem to be running out of options.

What is it about our world that makes people with their whole lives ahead of them stop believing in possibility?"

Haggerty's lips were pressed together, his sandy brows slanting downward. They both watched as the sheriff engaged the boy who'd folded the afghan with such reverence, now affecting utter boredom with the experience of dealing with the law. "As it happens," said Haggerty, "I've represented Billy Reno in the past. And will again, if it comes to that. Charlie Preston may need a little help in that department too."

"You're a good guy, Dave," said Sally.

"Thanks," he said reaching in the back pocket of his jeans, pulling out his wallet, handing her a business card, and catching her with the tiger eyes. "Let's keep in touch."

"Uh, maybe we could get together for lunch or dinner," Sally managed. "I mean, ever since the *American Experience* event, I've been meaning to call you. About the work I've been doing in the center. Talk about some projects," she finished, wondering if she sounded as lame to him as she did to herself.

Haggerty smiled. "Projects. Yeah. Definitely. Maybe some fund-raising too?"

"How'd you guess?" Sally smiled back.

"I'm clairvoyant. Plus your dean sent me a note saying it was nice to see me at the reception. So I've been expecting a pitch."

"I'm not that good at the pitch," said Sally, "but I do think we care about a lot of the same things, and I'd like to pick your brain."

Now the tiger eyes softened. "Looks like one thing we both care about is messed-up kids. We could start with that, and see what else develops." He glanced once more at her bare-fingered left hand. "Why don't we make it dinner next week at the Yippie I O? I'll email you to firm things up."

"I'm involved with somebody," Sally said. "We live together."

"Right. I believe I heard something about that." Another glance at her hand. "The world," said Haggerty, "is a complicated place."

# CHAPTER 7

# THE SANCTUARY OF THE INNER WITNESS

"HEY, HAWK. WHAT ARE you doing this afternoon?" asked Sally, putting down the newspaper. "Want to go to a memorial service?"

Hawk eyed her suspiciously. "For whom?" he asked.

"Bradley Preston," she said. "There's a service for him this afternoon at three, at a church out on the east side. I kind of feel like I want to go."

"Why?" he asked. "He wasn't a friend, or even an acquaintance."

"Maybe Charlie'll show up," Sally said.

"Not friggin' likely," said Hawk. "And if she does, you won't get near her. The family will close ranks, first of all, and second, the minute that service is over, Dickie and Scotty will be hauling her in. In case you'd missed it, she's a suspect in a murder case."

"No, I hadn't missed it, though I definitely object to it," Sally said.

"Why?" Hawk asked. "From everything you've told me, she had reason to want to hurt her father. Maybe she didn't have it in her to strike back, but she could have gotten somebody else to do it. And how well do you really know that girl, anyhow? How do you know she doesn't get herself wired up on meth every night and go bust windows, or doors, or somebody's head? Hell, maybe she was the one who tore up the apartment on North Fourth. You don't have any idea."

"Okay. I don't know her very well. But I've worked with victims of domestic violence. When they're that beaten down, they don't have the strength to fight back. It takes incredible guts just to run away. And you're right, she'd be crazy to come back for the memorial," Sally acknowledged. "But the *Boomerang* says that Beatrice Preston will be delivering the main eulogy. There was a picture of her in the paper. She was the one at the doctor's office, leading the hymn singing. I think she gave the signal for the protesters to rush the patient," Sally told Hawk.

She handed over the newspaper.

"Yeah, that's her," said Hawk, putting the paper down on the table. "The caption says this photo was taken in 2001. Her hairstyle hasn't changed one hair since then."

"Neither has yours," Sally pointed out, "since 1975."

"If it ain't broke . . ." Hawk began.

"Come with me," she said.

The Sanctuary of the Inner Witness was a large, flat building that looked more like a warehouse discount store than a church. It was surrounded by a sea of parking lots, filling up fast with pickup trucks and SUVs disgorging men in cowboy hats and women in conservative dresses, children with combed hair and clean, pressed clothes, older people leaning on canes and walkers.

The place was packed. Sally and Hawk, dressed in their most nondescript dark business suits, joined the standing-room crowd at the back of the chapel.

Laramie wasn't as small as Sally was used to thinking. There must be hundreds of people in town who went to church at least once a week, whose values were in many respects 180 degrees away from hers and Hawk's. She'd probably seen some of them at the supermarket or the bank, but she had absolutely no recollection of anyone she saw in this crowd.

Then she caught sight of two people she knew. Off to the right, sitting unobtrusively in the second-to-last row, Dave Haggerty leaned his elbows on the pew in front of him, resting his chin on his folded hands. He didn't see her.

But Scotty Atkins did. By the time she found him, standing far back in a corner, she knew he'd seen her for a while. He nodded very slightly when their eyes met. He didn't smile.

All these people in a church so new and makeshift, it didn't even have fixed pews. The congregation sat on folding metal chairs, noisy on the concrete floor. The dais was raised a good six feet above the seating area, so they had a clear view of the proceedings. At one side of the platform, a trio consisting of guitar, bass, and synthesizer worked through a lugubrious arrangement of "What a Friend We Have in Jesus." Most people in the church were still fidgeting, chatting, getting settled.

Then the minister walked down the center aisle, shaking hands as he went. He was young and handsome and greeted with warmth by his parishioners. Ascending the steps, he took his place in the pulpit. Brad Preston, he said, had been a pillar of the community, an upholder of traditional family values, a heck of a first baseman for the church softball team. He'd shouldered his earthly burdens, and was now released from those bonds. Pretty familiar, tame stuff, to Sally's mind. She'd been expecting hellfire, or a little damnation at least. She caught herself wondering, as Beatrice Preston ascended the steps, received a hug from the minister, and took her place in the pulpit, whether what she'd heard about Evangelicalism was vastly overstated.

Beatrice wore an exquisitely tailored black crepe suit, with a cream-colored blouse secured at the neck with an oval brooch—a cameo, visibly handsome even from Sally's distant vantage point.

Bea's blond hair was in its trademark perfect sweep, her face a matching cameo of composure and compassion. She dipped her head for a moment, closed her eyes, raised her chin, opened her eyes, and began to speak.

"Bradley Preston was my husband," she intoned, her voice as sweet and clear and ringing as a church bell. "But he was also your son." She nodded toward a weeping white-haired woman in the front row. "Your brother." She extended a hand toward the grim-faced man and woman flanking the mother. "Your neighbor, your colleague, your friend. Brad dedicated his life to timeless values. His death should be a call to us to build a world where the godly are not scorned, where the wicked see the path to righteousness."

In the front and middle of the church, people were crying. Even back where Sally and Hawk stood, she could feel people reaching for handkerchiefs, see them wiping their eyes. Beatrice Preston had a lovely speaking voice, and she used it with confidence and skill.

And now Bea lowered the pitch of that voice, confiding in the crowd. "My husband," she said, "was brutally murdered. In the days and nights since, I have wondered how such a good man could come to such a horrific fate. How could the just and merciful God be so senselessly cruel? I came close, brothers and sisters, to doubting God's wisdom and His will."

Audible gasps. Hawk leaned over and whispered, "Guess she isn't known for her skeptical nature."

"Unlike you," Sally whispered back, putting a hand on his arm to prevent a reply.

"Yes, I came within the merest feather's breadth of doubting the will of our Lord," Beatrice's voice, breathy for a moment, began to rise. "But the Lord holds us in His hand." Sally got a mental image of a little family and a little house in a big hand, some insurance commercial. A friend of hers had once observed that the true history of the West was about real estate. Maybe the true religion too?

"Or He can, if it is His will, simply open His fingers, and let us fall," Bea said. "Like a feather, suspended on the air, we can drift, down and down, at our peril. Or the weight of our sins may be upon us, and we fall, like a rock, like a boulder, plummeting down and down to be swallowed up in the fires below, oh yes, swallowed up!"

And now they felt it. The whoosh of the air. The heat of the fire.

"The Lord tested me, as He tests us all. And faith came to me, like a sweet breeze, lifting me back up and up, saved me from the danger, from the very flames of hell. Faith found me, and LIFTED ME UP!"

"Praise the Lord!" someone shouted.

"Praise the Lord!" came echoing shouts.

And now Beatrice's face began to glow, and she lowered her eyes and half whispered, "Oh, praise the Lord, yes, praise Him. And in the moment when faith saved me, I remembered something I had known a long, long time."

The crowd waited.

"The Lord," she said, "made Bradley Preston for a purpose. He took Brad from us too soon, to show us the way. But we will carry on his work, oh yes, we will!"

"We will!" came the shouts. "We will!"

Will, thought Sally. Brad Preston must have left a will. Maybe there was something in it that had caused somebody to kill him. At the very least, the will ought to give her a sense of how he'd felt about Charlie. She wondered if Dave Haggerty, her new friend, could find some way to get her a copy of that will.

"This is getting genuinely strange," Hawk whispered to Sally.

They were just about to find out precisely how strange.

"And for those still lost, we say, come, come into the fortress of God's love."

Fortress?

"For ye wander as survivors on the terrible killing field, and if ye seek not the shelter of His love, oh, what a fiery fate awaits! Come, come and be saved, lest ye burn forever!" she cried.

"Amen!" cried a woman in the third row.

Bea returned to her stage whisper. "Do not think I speak only to strangers to the house of God. For do we not have those in our own house, in our own families, who may yet be lost forever to the flames? Is there one among us who would not save someone we love, a child, perhaps, hopelessly perplexed, in danger of falling forever?"

"Uh-oh," murmured Hawk. "I think I know what's coming."

"Shhh," said Sally. "I don't want to miss this."

"As God loved His only Son, so Bradley Preston loved his only daughter, Charlotte," said Bea. "A love that surpasses all time. Brad showed her that love, spoke to her in words and deeds of love. But the forces of evil shut her eyes and stopped her ears. She spurned him. She cast him away."

Someone choked out a sob.

"Instead of divine love," Beatrice told the congregation, "Charlotte's ears were tuned to the filthy whispers of the beasts of darkness. 'Leave your home,' they said. 'Don't honor your father and your mother,' they said. 'Seek your own gratification, your own grandeur.' The secularists and the feminists tempted her away from the true path, brainwashed her in their philosophy and psychology and women's studies courses, seduced her with their evolutionist science, which denies God's Creation. And there are so many children, lost in the killing fields. Your children, and mine. Right here, in our own town. Right now, even as we worship here, in the house of the Lord. They bore from underground, plant their vile seeds, spew their poison."

"Mixed metaphor," Sally mumbled.

"And they are not content merely to enslave the minds of our children; oh no, far from it, I am sorry to say." Bea looked genuinely sad now, shaking her head. "They want their bodies. The want their very souls!"

"As a women's studies professor, do you want your students' souls?" Hawk asked Sally.

"Nope," she answered. "And I definitely don't want their bodies. Their minds, well, I think I get paid to want their minds, right? Now shut up and let me listen," she told him.

Bea had taken a long pause, a drink of water, a very deep

breath. "On the day my husband was murdered, many of us were but a few blocks away, standing up for righteousness. You will recall, as I do, the explosion, the panic, the terror. It felt like the beginning of a holy war, right here in Laramie."

"Oy veh," said Sally.

"You know, and I know, the story the authorities are telling, the 'official' story," Bea said, the faintest mocking tone creeping in. "A nasty prank. Firecrackers in a junk car. Probably some high-spirited teenagers, trying to stir things up. But we were there. We heard it with our own ears. Saw everything with our own eyes. And surely there is a more plausible story."

"You'd think," said Sally.

"But I bet it isn't the one she's going to tell," Hawk replied quietly.

"Has it not occurred to you," Bea asked, "that the bombing at the abortion factory might be the work of feminists and others? They will stop at nothing to kill the unborn—would they hesitate at blowing up a car?"

Murmurs in the crowd.

"I don't frigging believe this," Sally said. "The woman's crazy."

"Something is terribly, terribly wrong here in Laramie," Bea Preston intoned, shaking her head. "Something is terribly wrong in my heart, in the bosom of my family, in my beloved community. I say to my daughter: Charlotte, come home. Your father was taken from us for a reason. Take my hand. And I say to all of you here, join together. Take the hand of your neighbor."

Sally felt the woman to her right take her hand. She took Hawk's hand. He glanced at her, but hesitated as the man on his left reached for his hand.

"Will you join together? Will you defeat the enemy that stalks the righteous, right here at home? Say yes!"

"Yes!" thundered the crowd.

"Say yes!" Bea cried, lifting her hands.

"Yes! Yes!" The chorus rose and rose.

Never had the word "yes" filled Sally with such dread.

# CHAPTER 8

# FRIED

SALLY HADN'T BEEN HOME more than an hour before the phone rang.

"I hear Bea Preston's launched a crusade to clean the devil worshippers out of the university," Delice Langham told Sally.

"How'd you hear already?" Sally asked.

"A bunch of 'em came in all fired up after the memorial service for Brad Preston," Delice told her. "They were denouncing you all over their chicken-fried steaks."

"Me?" Sally asked.

"Well, feminists. And evolutionists. And I forget what all else. Evidently old Bea was on fire," Delice said.

"I was there," said Sally. "It was everything you imagine and more."

"I don't like this." Delice fumed. "This town's full of people who manage not to hate each other, mostly by ignoring each other. This kind of stupidity brings out the nutcases and puts all the bad shit on the surface. People get all righteous and start subjecting each other to tests nobody can pass."

"And what, precisely, do you suggest I do about it?" Sally said.

"Hell if I know. This could get out of hand pretty quickly, especially if Bea keeps beating the drum. She looks sweet and delicate, but when she gets her teeth in something, she's like a fucking Gila monster. You'd have to cut her head off before her jaws would let go. And she's got a lot of influence with the Holy Roller crowd. There's got to be some way to get her to back off."

"I seriously doubt that I'm the one to do that," said Sally. "You know her, right?"

"Not really. I mean, I've known her most of my life and all. She went to Laramie High. But she's younger than me, and we didn't exactly hang out. I was beads and bongs, and she was Campus Crusade. Once Brad hooked up with her, we didn't see much of him around the watering holes. Oops—my dishwasher's about to quit again. Gotta go."

The phone rang almost immediately. "Just got off the phone with a guy who was a little incoherent," said Edna McCaffrey, "but as I pieced it together, he's under the impression that women's studies is the academic equivalent of the KGB. And that was the third call today."

"This is ridiculous," said Sally. "It'll blow over."

"I devoutly hope so," Edna agreed. "In the meantime, I'd advise you to keep your mouth shut and be nice to people."

"I'm always nice to people," said Sally.

"Hah!" Edna replied, and hung up.

*Ring, ring!*

"Heard about the memorial service," said Maude Stark. "Guess we're in for it."

Sally took a deep breath and actually prayed for patience. "Look, you guys want me to be a women's historian, that's what I'm going to do," she said. "I just ask myself what Susan B. Anthony would have done."

"My guess? She'd have launched a counterattack. Susan B. never stepped back and never looked back," Maude said.

Sally sighed. Sometimes, Susan B. (and Maude, for that matter) made her tired. "For the moment, I want to concentrate on being a good college professor." And of course, finding and assisting one promising student, recently gone missing. "So I think I'd better quit talking and get after the mountain of work that's piling up. I'll leave the counterattacking to you."

As she hung up, Sally reflected that maybe that wasn't such a good idea. Maude was a good Wyomingite. Her idea of a counterattack might involve live ammunition. She comforted herself with the thought that Maude was too smart to get into a shooting war when she'd be outgunned ten to one. No point fretting about it now.

And she'd worry about Charlie Preston later too. She had plenty to do. Papers to grade. Programs to plan. People to schmooze. Books to write.

She didn't feel like doing any of those things, so she took the slacker's way out. She decided to check her email.

She made herself a cup of coffee, set her laptop on the kitchen table, sat down, and dialed up her Internet connection. The weasel in the machine screeched, and she was wired to the world.

If she was looking to avoid work and controversy, checking email might not be the best course of action. Since the last time she'd checked, less than twenty-four hours earlier, fifty messages had piled up in her already overstuffed inbox. A dozen of them were junk—daily blab from airlines and travel sites, offers of great deals on wine, flowers, books, and home furnishings. Just the nuisance cost of the convenience of online shopping. She knew she could have blocked them, but she'd never bothered. She deleted the messages without reading.

Half a dozen were from addresses she didn't recognize, with subject headings like "Bring God Back to the Classroom." Looked like the crusaders had gotten her email address. No surprise. It was available through the university website. She hit the delete button again and again.

As she scrolled down what remained, one return address caught her eye: *Dhag@legalequal.org.* She located the business card Dave Haggerty had given her at the eviction: yep. That was his address.

The subject line read, "Re: Projects." Haggerty was a lawyer. He understood discretion. He wouldn't headline a message, "Your Search for Charlie Preston." Or "Our Dinner Date," for that matter.

She clicked on the message. "Nice to see you," it read. "Please open the attached for information about your projects."

She clicked on the little paperclip symbol, to open the attachment.

The attachment screen appeared, with a very brief message, written in red letters. "Stop looking. Next time it won't be just a machine. You've been fried."

Suddenly her laptop began spewing out incomprehensible code. Then the screen went black. She tried to reboot, but nothing happened.

"Shit," she grumbled. Stared at the screen and said, "What?" And then, "Crap!" And then, "Hawk!"

Fried. The attachment had been infected. She'd been victimized by a virus.

"What happened?" Hawk asked, walking in and sitting down.

"Fucking virus. Shit shit shit."

They had a pattern. When things went wrong, the crazier one got, the calmer the other. "Take a deep breath, Sal," said Hawk, the voice of cool for this crisis. "We can take your laptop to a computer geek, and they'll probably be able to fix it in a day or two. The more you can remember exactly what happened, the easier time the geek will have."

She sucked in air, blew it out. "Okay. Okay. I'm an idiot. I should have known. I opened a contaminated attachment. There was a message, then the machine started spitting gobbledygook, then it shut down."

"What did the message say? You should write it down," he told her.

"Let me get this right." She pulled a pencil and pad out of her laptop case and wrote as she spoke. "It said, 'Stop looking. Next time it won't be just a machine. You've been fried.'"

Hawk frowned. "Stop looking? Looking for what? What was the return address on the message?"

She showed him Haggerty's card still sitting on the table, beside the now forlornly silent laptop. "That's the address. I got the card from Dave Haggerty when I went out to see Billy Reno, and caught that eviction instead. Turns out Haggerty's representing the renters. Since Charlie's name is on the lease, he needs to find her. And I'm trying to hustle him for money for the center, so we're trying to schedule a dinner."

"So the 'stop looking' part could be about Charlie Preston." Hawk gave her a measuring look. "When you told me about the eviction and about Charlie having signed the lease, you didn't mention Dave Haggerty. Or dinner. How come?"

"I don't know. Slipped my mind, I guess." Of course it had. No deliberate evasion there.

"So . . . have you been emailing with Haggerty, then?" Hawk asked, voice in neutral.

"No!" said Sally.

"I'm not accusing you of having cybersex with him, darlin'. Just want to know if you're in his address book, or vice versa. That's how worm viruses work. They get into somebody's Internet address book and send themselves to everybody," he said reasonably.

"Oh. Sorry. But really, no. This is the first message I've gotten from him, and I've never sent him anything. I just got the card yesterday."

"Hunh. This is weird." Hawk picked up the open laptop, held it high, looked at the bottom, like a guy checking under the hood. "You know what I think?" he asked.

"You think," she said, "that I should call the police."

"You should call the police," he replied. "And we should also called the computer support desk at the U. and let them know you've got a worm. They're going to need to send out a warning and get everybody to update their virus protection."

An hour later, an Albany County patrol car pulled up in front of the house. A very young, crisply uniformed deputy got out, opened the back door, pulled out a large, rectangular toolbox and a laptop case. She introduced herself as Sally opened the door. "I'm new to the force," she told Sally. "IT specialist."

Information technology specialist. Crime fighting in Laramie. It wasn't just for cowpokes anymore.

The IT specialist set up her own laptop at the kitchen table, along with some kind of machine that made Sally think of fifties sci-fi flicks, plugging cables into boxes and ports and holes, testing this, trying that. Sally's laptop remained obstinately dead. "Hmph," said the high-tech deputy at one point. "This is a tough little mother of a virus. Think I'd better take your laptop to my shop. I need to put it up on the bench and see what's what."

"How long will it take?" Sally asked, trying hard not to whine. A uniformed deputy was not, after all, some spotty-faced twenty-year-old with a computer science degree and enough credit card debt to float an aircraft carrier, the usual kind of person who came to the rescue when Sally's techno-structure crapped out.

"Can't say. Maybe a couple days, maybe a couple weeks. We've got a lot on our plate," said the deputy.

"Look, it's probably just a garden variety pain-in-the-ass virus. Maybe I should just take the machine to somebody who can get to it quickly. I've got a lot of work to do." Sally gave in and whined.

"Not an option," said Scotty Atkins, striding into the kitchen. "Figured you wouldn't mind if I came in without knocking, since you called us," he told Sally. "And don't bother objecting. If there's any possibility that what happened to your machine has anything to do with what's happened with Charlie Preston or her father or her trashy boyfriend, we want to take a look at it."

"Will you fix it?" she asked.

"We can give it a try. But as you can probably guess, Dr. Alder, we're not in the computer repair business. We're a lot more interested in identifying a virus-writing pattern that might lead us, eventually and with a lot of luck, to the hacker."

"You could start with the threat that appeared before the thing started chucking out flames and fire, Scotty," Sally told him. She was feeling pretty crabby. There were files on that computer that existed nowhere else, and she hated the thought of losing them. Not to mention certain emails that might prove embarrassing, if not exactly actionable.

"Always the drama queen, aren't we," said Atkins.

She showed him the message she'd written down. "The flames and fire might be a slight exaggeration," she said.

"The return address belongs to David Haggerty, the defense lawyer," Hawk told Scotty.

Scotty squinted at her. "That doesn't mean anything where viruses are concerned. Generally, the return address is a blind, an address-book link, though sometimes it helps with tracing. But having said that, how well do you know Mr. Haggerty, Professor?"

Sally put on a disgusted look, spoke with disdain. "You guys make me feel like I've been caught necking with him at the park! Come on. I barely know the guy. He'd have no reason to mess with my computer, or anybody's."

"How the hell do you know that?" Hawk said, revving up as she ratcheted down. "You say you've barely met the guy—for all you know, he might spend his spare time hacking into Justice Department files and dropping charges on political prisoners. For that matter, he could be an axe murderer for the ACLU."

"Oh yeah," said Sally. "I hear that's pretty common."

"Hmph!" said the techie deputy from the kitchen table. "This is weird."

"What's that?" Scotty asked.

"I sent a message to the university tech support, letting them know about the virus. And I just got a message back saying that their diagnostic indicates that the thing isn't acting like a worm."

"What do you mean?" Sally said.

"It doesn't appear to be replicating itself at random," said the deputy. "The problem is localized."

"What's the pattern?" Scotty inquired.

"They didn't send that information."

Hawk said, "Excuse me a minute. I think I'd like to check my email." He headed toward his desk in the corner of the living room.

"Thanks," said Scotty. "Let's get packed up and get out of here," he told the deputy, motioning to Sally as he walked toward the front hall.

"Look," Scotty continued. "I know you're worried about your student . . ."

"Yes, as it happens, I am. And about finding her father, dead. And about this new crusade her stepmother is launching against godless commie college professors. And maybe five or six other things. Do you really think I have the option of laying low at this point, Scotty? Apart from that virus message, my inbox was full of stuff from people who want me fired unless I hold revivals in my classroom. Do you really think I can just lie back and nibble on bonbons?"

Scotty's face didn't change, but he was giving what she said some thought. "Okay," he said at last. "I'm not going to tell you how to do your job. But don't do mine. We'll find Charlie Preston. We've got some leads."

"What leads?" Sally asked.

"I can't tell you that. And if I could, I wouldn't, because the next thing I knew, you'd be barging in and getting in my way."

That hurt. She didn't think of herself as getting in the way. In fact, she rather thought she'd been a help a time or two. "I don't think that's fair," she told him.

Scotty ignored the remark, pressed on. "We will also find out who killed Brad Preston. And if it should turn out that the girl is involved in the father's murder, you're going to have to figure out a way to deal with that."

Was that a glimmer of compassion on his hard face? Impossible. "I can deal with it. I just can't believe it," she insisted.

"Doesn't matter whether you do or not," he said. Nope. Not compassion.

"Hey, look at this," Hawk called from the living room. They went to look at his screen, along with the deputy. "A bunch of messages from addresses I don't recognize. Some God Squad stuff in the title lines, and this one headed 'Family Photos,' with a series of attachments."

"Did you get that message?" Scotty asked Sally.

She thought a moment. "No. I'd remember. But it could have been sent after my computer crashed."

"Don't open it," said the IT deputy. "Forward it to this address, with all the attachments, and then delete the whole thing. I'll check it out. Dr. Alder, you'd better give me your password, so I can access your account and see if more funny stuff has showed up." She put a business card on Hawk's desk.

"Family photos?" said Sally. "Wonder what that's about."

"Maybe just the hook to get you to open another bad attachment. We'll find out," said Scotty.

"If they really are photos," Hawk told him, "and either of us are in them, that'd be pretty weird. We'll hear from you, right?"

Scotty pressed his lips together. "If they're photos of you or your families," he said, "you can bet you'll hear from us."

# CHAPTER 9

# CROSSES TO BEAR

BY THE TIME SCOTTY and the IT deputy left, it was cocktail hour. Maybe half past cocktail hour. She requested a Jim Beam. Hawk complied.

She took her first sip. "Bea Preston," she said. "I need to go talk to Bea."

"I'm sure she'll welcome you with open arms," Hawk told her.

"She'll have to see me," said Sally, "because I'm going to tell everyone I know that I'm going to see her. To make peace. We may be far apart on many issues, but we're both women who want the best for her daughter and for the community. I'm sure we can find some common ground."

The Preston residence was listed in the Laramie phone book. Sally took a deep breath and dialed the number. She'd probably get voice mail, but she could at least leave a message and start the ball rolling.

Bea Preston answered on the first ring. "Professor Alder?" she said, when Sally identified herself. "Oh yes, of course I know who you are. Charlotte's teacher." Bea's beautiful voice was as cool and creamy and all-American as banana pudding. Not welcoming, but at least she didn't hang up on Sally.

"Yes, Mrs. Preston. I'm very concerned about Charlotte. I wanted to talk to you about that. But I also want to offer my condolences. I know how hard a time this must be for you," Sally said, taking a surreptitious sip of her Jim Beam. Kentucky courage.

A pause. "Yes. It's very hard. The sheriff told me you'd been the one to . . . find Brad. It must have been a terrible shock for you. I'm sorry."

"Thank you," said Sally, hearing a hint of compassion creep into Bea Preston's voice, and going with the connection. "I'm certain the police are doing everything they can. And I wanted you to know that I attended the memorial service yesterday. I don't want to impose, at this very difficult time, and I know you're distraught, but I think there are things we should discuss. Matters of mutual concern. Mrs. Preston, we differ on many things, but we at least have a desire for Charlotte's well-being in common."

Another pause. Sally began to think the idea of calling had been insane. Then Bea spoke. "Professor Alder, many people would be appalled that I'm even speaking to you. If you were at the service, you understand my feelings about your work, your ideas, and the influence of people like you on impressionable young people like my daughter. I can't imagine why you'd think I'd want to talk with you."

Yep. Insane. "I understand, Mrs. Preston. I'm sorry you feel that way. I won't bother you again," Sally said, preparing to hang up, finish her bourbon, and chalk the whole thing up to a crazy impulse. And what would be gained by letting it be known she'd made the call?

"Just a moment, Professor," said Bea. "You must admit yourself, this is a very strange conversation."

Sally found herself almost smiling. "Yes. Pretty strange."

"The Lord works in mysterious ways. I think we should meet, and talk. Why don't you come to my house tomorrow afternoon at five?" She gave an address on Tenth Street, south and west of the university, in a neighborhood Sally recognized as high-end. Big old houses, some historic Victorians, beautifully kept. It wasn't Laramie's richest—that honor was reserved for the sprawling brick and glass tract houses with four-car garages, springing up like weeds in the new developments on the edges of town. Still, it took some bucks to live where the Prestons did, and some taste to choose a historic house instead of a McMansion.

So it was a date. Beatrice Preston had been nicer than Sally had expected. A hell of a lot nicer, when you considered that less than twenty-four hours previously, Bea had been pretty much damning Sally and all her ilk to hell, five ways.

But there were some possible explanations. Even while she publicly celebrated Brad's life, Bea could not have been oblivious to what he'd been doing to his own flesh and blood. Maybe he'd abused Bea too. Now that he was gone, no longer a threat, maybe she was looking for a push to come out of shame and denial, and confront what had really been happening behind closed doors. All that rage and righteousness might really be a fierce disguise for guilt and regret. Maybe Bea was reaching out.

Or maybe she figured she could get something out of Sally that she could use later. Sally had no illusion that she was dealing with a lightweight.

Sally dressed carefully for her meeting with Beatrice Preston. Nothing too foofy or pandering, nothing that would identify her as a fanged feminista. No pink angora, but no black tunics or big ethnic jewelry either. On an April day like this, the wind could cut you to pieces, so she chose gray wool slacks and a soft orange sweater. Professional, but cheerful.

The house was three stories tall, brick painted gray with maroon, cream, and black wood trim, with a turret at one end and a deep front porch furnished with wicker chairs and a couch. The high windows gleamed. The front door was painted the same maroon that appeared on the trim.

Bea Preston answered the door wearing gray wool slacks and

a melon-colored sweater only slightly paler than Sally's orange. They looked at each other and laughed.

Sally spread her hands. "Common ground," she said, still smiling.

"Maybe we should call each other in the morning and do a wardrobe check," said Bea.

It took a deft touch to keep Victorian furnishings under control. Enough generally shaded over into too much, into over-doilied, antimacassared parody. Whoever had done the Preston house had managed the trick. There was a crystal chandelier, fringed tassels on the tie-backs for the drapes, the obligatory piecrust table. But not too much. Sally felt as if she'd stepped back in time, into the nineteenth century, into a slower, more gracious time.

Bea led her to a settee upholstered in deep-rose watered silk, poured tea from a silver pot into gold-rimmed, pink-and-white Limoges cups. A matching plate held thin lemon cookies. The teapot, silver creamer, sugar bowl, and spoons were all the same pattern, something heavy and ornate, a lot like the Chantilly pattern Sally had inherited from her grandmother. Pink linen napkins. Even a small cranberry glass vase, with a delicate little array of pink and white flowers. Bea was a detail woman. And though she probably hated Sally's guts on principle, she was showing a lot of class.

Sally tasted the tea: Earl Grey. A safe, nice choice. "Mrs. Preston," she said, "Let's start out by agreeing that we both want what's best for your stepdaughter." A safe, nice statement, right?

Bea stirred milk into her own tea. "I'm sure we do," she responded, aiming her enormous blue eyes at Sally. "But I doubt you have any real understanding of the depth of Charlotte's problems. How much do you know about mental illness?"

Sally gave it a moment. "I'm no expert. From time to time I've had to deal with students who've had problems of one kind or another. I've done what I can to understand what they're up against."

"I would be surprised," said Bea, "if you have any idea of the seriousness of Charlotte's disorder. She first began exhibiting signs of behavioral problems when she was only six years old."

"Behavioral problems?" Sally asked, setting down her teacup.

Bea nodded. "She'd be completely withdrawn, or fly into uncontrollable rages. She did destructive things: tearing up the garden, setting little fires. That was also when she first began hurting herself."

"How?" Sally asked.

"Scissors. Matches. We had to lock up anything we thought she could use. But she was endlessly creative. Once she threw herself down the stairs. We tried doctors. They put her on medication. It would help for a while, then not."

Proceeding carefully, Sally said, "What do you think caused her to act that way?"

Bea shook her head. "Some might say the cause was spiritual. The doctors, of course, had their ideas. They suggested that there might be a genetic predisposition toward psychiatric problems. Since there was no history of such things on Brad's side, we assumed that the affliction must have come from her mother's family."

A convenient explanation, thought Sally. Another plausible cause would have been the beginning of a pattern of abuse. Would it be possible, Sally wondered, to get a look at Charlie's medical records? "That must have been hard on you, as her stepmother," she said.

"The woman who gave birth to Charlotte saw fit to abandon her. I married her father when she was five. I've always called myself her mother, Professor. And yes, it was hard on both Brad and me. We prayed for guidance. We told ourselves that everything that is, exists as part of the Lord's plan. God had sent Charlotte's suffering to strengthen our faith. She was our cross to bear."

Wow. With parents like that, a kid would be carrying a heavy load herself, Sally thought.

"We did the best we could," Bea continued. "But then, when she was nine, she started running away from home. She got as far as West Laramie, that time. She was incoherent, and she fought us all the way home. We were forced to put her in a psychiatric clinic. We simply couldn't give her the care she needed."

Nine years old, and sent to a psych ward. Jesus. "What a terrible ordeal for such a little kid," said Sally.

"It absolutely tore her father apart. But he could never bring himself to do what the doctors told us we should."

"Which was?" Sally asked.

"Permanent institutionalization. Charlotte was a very sick child, who has grown into a desperately ill young woman. Brad kept hoping that medication and counseling, and firm parental guidance, would help her to stop the self-destruction, the violent outbursts, the pathological lying. Nothing helped.

"What you need to understand, Professor Alder, is that my daughter has no understanding of the concept of right and wrong, or even of how to live in the world. She sees conspiracies against her everywhere, and seems to trust only the worst kinds of people, people she knows will hurt her. Everyone else, she manipulates with lies and guilt, with the appearance of repentance and affection. Time after time, she'd wreak havoc on us, disappear, and reappear as the penitent prodigal. We would rejoice, reconcile, believe we were on the road to being a real family. And then she'd do something horrible and run away again."

"It must be hard to believe your own child would do such things," Sally said.

"You have no idea how devious she can be. She's not above finding a way to injure herself physically to make a point."

Could it be? Sally had seen Charlie's cuts and bruises—could the girl be crazy enough to have somehow done that to herself? The cops and the state had been involved in Charlie Preston's life a long time. Somewhere in her police files or case records, there had to be some answers.

Bea continued. "I know that you feminists believe that women have never had freedom of choice. As I'm sure you've gathered, I believe that God has ordained that men will protect and provide, and women be helpmeets to their husbands. There's a divine plan for us all, and our happiness and our salvation come from knowing what God has in mind for us. You may think you're helping young women seek independence and fulfillment, but are you asking them to deny and defy their nature? Are you simply sowing discontent and discord?"

"I believe I'm offering them the opportunity to use their brains, their hearts, and their talents to the utmost, Mrs. Preston. I don't think anyone has the right to withhold those possibilities from any human being. Yes, you and I do disagree, and I suspect that we'll go right on disagreeing on general principles. I hope you understand, however, that your daughter's well-being is important to me," Sally answered.

"Professor Alder," said Bea, controlling whatever emotions threatened to break loose, "you may find this hard to believe, but I pray for your soul. The Bible tells us to hate the sin, but love the sinner. All of us are capable of finding redemption in the Lord, no matter what our delusions and our transgressions. Seek God's love, and He will find you."

Sally said nothing. So Bea continued. "If nothing else, please understand one thing. Charlotte is the last person on earth who needs choice. The doctors told us: To function even minimally, she requires a strictly controlled environment, very definite discipline. The last thing on earth she needs is the kind of moral relativism, of boundless license, that people like you advocate. And with all that medical advice, still, I could never convince Brad to do the hard thing, the thing that was best for the child. He kept thinking he could buy her sanity with lavish gifts and endless acceptance. The more he gave her freedom, the worse it was. The drugs, the horrid boyfriends, the vile abuse she heaped on us, the lies she's told about us. That was the thanks we got." Bea's lovely eyes at last filled, and spilled tears. "And now Brad's paid the price."

"Mrs. Preston," said Sally, leaning toward the woman. "Are you suggesting that Charlie had something to do with what happened to her father?"

Bea reached into a pocket of her trousers, withdrew a hand-kerchief, wiped her eyes, composed herself before speaking. "Professor Alder, do you have any idea how many times that child threatened to kill us both?"

If Charlie had been treated half as badly as Aggie Stark had suggested, Sally could understand the threats. Angry words would have been the least of the conflict in the Preston household. But if Bea was telling the truth, and Charlie was half as crazy as she implied, such threats would have been scary, even without what had happened to Brad. Sally took a minute to think. "From what you've just told me, the person she's most likely to harm is herself."

"Possibly. Charlotte may well have gone into yet another phase of self-destruction. She has a history of drug abuse, and of involvement with criminals. She may well have persuaded that boyfriend of hers to do a deed she couldn't quite bring herself to do," said Bea.

Sally had to admit, Bea had a point. And if any of what she was saying was true, Bea had reason to be worried about what Charlie might do next. "One way or another, it's really important that she come back here. Do you have any inkling where she might have gone?" Sally asked.

"If I did, we wouldn't be sitting here now. I take it you've no idea, either."

"No, I don't," Sally admitted.

"I don't have much faith in the police," said Bea, "but at least they'll be looking for that Miata of hers. Brad held the title, of course. He didn't want to tell the police she was missing, but I finally convinced him, and he told them about the car. After he was killed, I reported it as stolen."

Now there was some motherly love. Then again, if Charlie had killed her father and threatened her stepmother, the bonds of familial affection were already pretty much shredded.

This visit had begun to feel like one of Sally's worst ideas ever. She picked up her purse, rose. "I guess we all do what we can. Please let me know if there's anything I can do to help out."

Bea stood up. "I doubt there is anything that you, or the police, for that matter, can do. In fact, I've hired someone to look for her. And in the meantime, all any of us can do is pray that she'll see her way clear to coming home, whatever she's done. Charlotte has never been able to take responsibility for her actions. Whatever the consequences, it's not only about justice for my husband. Charlotte's soul depends on it."

# CHAPTER 10

# FAMILY PHOTOS

"THAT'S THE BIGGEST LOAD of crap I've ever heard," said Hawk Green, the moment Sally finished filling him in on her visit with Beatrice Preston. They were sitting at a quiet corner table at the Yippie I O Café, drinking a fully realized pinot noir and grazing on salmon carpaccio and black bean hummus. "You saw the girl with your own eyes. She didn't get into that state walking herself into the wall."

"Obviously not. But for just one second, consider the possibility that Bea's telling the truth. Or if not the whole truth, then a story with a grain of truth. There's no doubt that Charlie's had big problems from an early age. It might not have been Brad who beat her up when I saw her, but kids who've been abused tend to grow up into people who expect, even try, to be abused. For all I know, Charlie's boyfriend was the one hitting her, and she thought that being hurt was pretty much what she deserved.

"As for Bea, she might want to blame Charlie's problems on heredity, but maybe she's just in denial about more obvious causes," Sally said, spreading hummus on a piece of homemade flatbread, and adding a strip of roasted pimiento.

"In other words," said Hawk, "you think Bea might be crazy enough to have blanked out the beating episodes. Because she let it happen, or because she was a victim too. Or even," he added, "because Bea herself was involved in the abuse."

"Any one of those things. Choose your nightmare. Whatever the real story is, it was clear to me that Bea believes what she told me. And she's got somebody looking for Charlie."

"Which has got to be bad news," Hawk said, disgust in his voice. "That woman's a horror, Sal. She's a fanatic, who at the very least has been trying to lock up her child in a psychiatric hospital since that kid was really little. She says Charlie's devious, but where do you think Charlie learned how to manipulate?" Hawk helped himself to a slice of the salmon. "Bea's a friggin' Svengali. You saw how her followers reacted to her at the doctor's office, not to mention the crowd at the church. If Bea Preston has her way, her people will be coming to our house with tar and feathers. You know all that, and even so, she managed to talk you into thinking that Charlie's the perp, not the victim."

"She did not!" Sally protested, setting her glass down hard enough to splash red wine on the white tablecloth.

"She made you doubt your own eyes and your instincts. Five more minutes and she'd have had you handing out Bible tracts on Ivinson Avenue. Or at least singing with the gospel choir."

It was a good thing that Bea hadn't tried that tack. Sally loved gospel music. "You're right. I let her control the conversation. I should have been grilling her about every time Daddy came home a little frustrated and took it out on little Charlie. I should have taken her on. I'm so fucking lame," Sally said.

"Forget about it. Consider it an achievement that you didn't get furious and piss her off so much that she'd never talk to you again. You have an in with her, and that might be useful. But next time, don't let her take charge."

Sally twisted the stem of her wineglass, narrowed her eyes.

"That might not be a bad thing. Being underestimated can be a big advantage. And I know now that she's looking for Charlie. I'm sure," said Sally, "that Dickie and Scotty will get there first, but what if they don't?"

Sally put down her wine, reached into her big black bag, pulled out her cell phone, and rummaged a little more, finding a pad of paper.

"Who are you calling?" Hawk asked.

"I want to talk to Aggie Stark," Sally said. The phone chimed. She'd had it turned off during her visit with Bea Preston, and when she turned it back on, the message symbol appeared instantly. "Oops—wait a minute. I've got a message."

Scotty Atkins. "I'm not getting any answer on your home phone, or at Hawk's or your office, so I thought I'd try your cell. We've been able to open up those email photo attachments from that message Hawk got," Atkins told her voice mail. "We'd like you to take a look at them, as soon as possible. Call me back." He left numbers for his extension at the sheriff's office, and his cell phone.

She reached Scotty at the office, told him they were on their way.

Hawk tossed money on the table, and they made for the door when a voice called out, "Hey, you two. Were you born in a barn or what? When it says RSVP, you're supposed to *respondez*."

Burt Langham. Gorgeously garbed, as usual, in pressed Levi's, a turquoise linen shirt, red lizard cowboy boots, and a silver bolo tie set with chunks of onyx and coral and turquoise, a work of art that had to have set him back a couple of grand at the Santa Fe Indian Market. Burt and his chef partner, "John Boy" Walton, had just come back from getting married in Massachusetts. They were throwing themselves a Wyoming wedding reception worthy of Barbra Streisand.

"Yipes. My bad manners, honey," said Sally. "But you just sent out the invitations to the reception last week."

"Hey, when you're dealing with the possibility that Congress or the Supreme Court is going to come in and try to void your marriage license, it's important to proceed with all deliberate speed," Burt replied. "It's must-see matrimony. All the local fiends from hell will be there." Obviously he'd heard about Bea Preston's eulogy, probably from Delice, his cousin and business partner. "You're coming, of course?"

Sally gave him a grin. "Are you kidding? If only to see what you and John Boy will be wearing," she said.

"I'm coming for the food," said Hawk.

"The menu's a secret," said Burt. "But I can tell you some of the ingredients."

"We'll have to worm it out of you another time," Sally told him. "We've gotta jet."

When they got to the sheriff's office, both Dickie and Scotty were waiting for them. They ushered them into a windowless interview room, a place that smelled of sweat and dust and bad coffee. They sat down on folding metal chairs that clattered against the dingy linoleum floor, pulling up to a Formica-topped table. Scotty took out a small digital recorder, set it on the table, and turned it on. Dickie opened a manila file folder, extracted a stack of eight-and-a-half-by-eleven-inch prints of photographs, and laid them out on the table. They both took notebooks from their back pockets and sat down.

Sally stared, appalled.

"They're all of us," Hawk said, uttering the obvious.

"Tell us where and when they were taken, as precisely as you can," Dickie said. No folksy wisdom, no attempt to soften the moment with humor, none of the usual hint of existential angst. All Sheriff Langham, all grim business.

She was a historian. She looked at the photos a moment more, then began to rearrange them in chronological order.

"Okay," she said. "These three were taken at the reception after the screening of the Dunwoodie documentary."

"Identify as many of the people as you can," said Scotty.

Sally blew out a breath. "This one, of course, is Edna McCaffrey and me. I can't really see the faces in the background. I'm not sure what time that would have been taken, since we talked several times over the course of the evening. This one," she said, pointing, "is of Hawk and me talking to Maude Stark and her nephew and niece, Mike and Julie. That was maybe halfway through the reception," she said. "Our glasses are full, so I guess that server in the corner has just given us all a refill." She indicated a girl in a white blouse and black pants, carrying a tray full of glasses.

"And this one's from the same night. Do I need to go into detail?" she asked.

It was a photo of Sally standing alone, back to a wall, a serious expression on her face.

"Try to remember when it might have been taken."

She searched memory. "I'd say that would have been late-ish in the evening, after we'd talked with Mike and Julie about Charlie Preston. It was a great evening for the Dunwoodie Center, but what they had to say worried the hell out of me. Kind of put a dent in my mood."

"That's right," said Hawk.

She looked at him.

"I remember the moment. I was talking to somebody and I glanced over and saw you standing there. The caterers had started clearing up, and it occurred to me to try to talk you into going home, but I knew I'd never get you out of there before everyone left. So I let it pass."

He had a kind of radar where she was concerned. The thought warmed her, enough to keep going.

"These," she said, indicating the next two pictures, "were taken at that demonstration outside the doctor's office. That's Hawk and me, standing around, obviously. You can see Bea Preston behind us, leading the singing. I don't recognize anybody else in this one. In this second one, we're helping Maude, who's escorting the patient into the building. I couldn't tell you who all those angry people are, shoving in on us, but I think that big blond guy was singing hymns with Bea Preston before he started pushing Hawk around. You've probably got some of them ID'd, since you've been investigating the explosion, right? Or should I say, the prank?" She couldn't keep the sarcasm out of her voice. "Hell of a lot of damage for firecrackers, Sheriff."

Dickie glanced up from writing in his notebook. "My kids get enough explosives every Fourth of July to blow Albany County off the face of the earth. Somebody hauled a derelict car into the parking lot and blew out the windows. A piece of malicious mischief, but not exactly an abortion clinic bombing."

"Right," said Hawk. "That's your story and you're sticking to it."

Dickie gave him a bland look. "We're still checking it out."

"I really don't like this one," Hawk put in. "That's the Laramie High stadium, at a track meet. The girl we're talking to is Aggie Stark."

They both looked at Scotty. "We're keeping an eye on her" was all he said.

"She's a nice kid," Dickie added. "Not much on talking, though."

Sally chose her words. "I'm glad you're looking out for her. But kids are funny about who they will and won't talk to."

"We've had that experience," Scotty said dryly. "Which is why we aren't forbidding you from talking to her. We want to know anything, and everything, she tells you."

"Fair enough," said Sally.

"Not to mention that we've pretty much given up on trying to get you to butt out completely," said Dickie. "So we guess we'll just use you in our cynical, fascist way."

"Let's finish up with the photos," Scotty said. He hated time-wasting banter. Possibly, he hated banter of all kinds. Sally had a decided fondness for banter, which made it all the more amazing that she sometimes felt little ripples in her innards when she heard Scotty Atkins's voice on the phone, or he walked up to talk to her, or looked right into her eyes.

"Do I need to go into detail about this one?" Sally said, pointing to a picture of herself and Dickie, standing in front of the apartment building where Billy Reno and his roommates were being evicted. "You probably can identify more of the people in this one than I can. Not a big deal, considering that the only people I know here are you and me. Oh—there's that blond guy from the demonstration. I guess that's worth mentioning."

Dickie nodded. "And this last one?" he asked.

"Pretty crappy quality," said Sally. "You can barely see Hawk and me through the crowd. But from the way we're standing up against that wall, the looks on our faces, that was the afternoon of the memorial service for Brad Preston."

"That's right," said Hawk. "That's us. That photograph was taken at the Sanctuary of the Inner Witness. And sent to me by email just a couple of hours later. This is very fucking creepy," he finished.

"These were obviously taken with a digital camera," Sally said. "Do you think it was one of those cell phone thingies?"

"Could be," Dickie said.

"Well, that certainly narrows it down," said Hawk. "Nowadays, everywhere you go there are sixty people talking on cell phones."

# CHAPTER 11

# THE CAVALCADE OF HUMANITY

SALLY GOT UP SATURDAY hoping she might just happen upon Aggie Stark on her morning run. What runner wouldn't be out on a day like this, one of those perfect mornings that almost had you thinking that spring in Laramie was like spring everywhere else— bright, warm, balmily breezy, alive, full of promise. Before long, the tulips and daffodils just poking their shoots up would burst into nodding bloom. On a day like today, you could almost forget that there was a fifty-fifty chance that the famed spring gales would rip the blossom off any flower foolish enough to show its head, if a hailstorm didn't hammer it flat first.

She spent forty minutes listening to Neil Young songs, pounding pavement, contemplating mortality and renewal, but didn't catch sight of Aggie. So once she'd returned, stretched, and made herself a cup of coffee, she got on the phone. Aggie herself answered.

"Didn't see you out running," Sally said.

"It was my morning to lift weights and do aqua-jogging in the pool," said Aggie. "The trainer won't let us run every day. He says it's too hard on our joints."

Hoo boy. If only somebody had given Sally that advice at fourteen, she might not be walking around on knees that crackled like fraternity bonfires on homecoming weekend. "Say," she began. "I just wanted to know if there's any chance you've heard from Charlie."

Aggie hesitated.

"I'm worried as heck about her, Aggie," Sally said. "She could be in really big trouble. She needs to know she's not all by herself."

Aggie made a decision. "Yeah. She called yesterday. She wouldn't tell me where she was, but she wanted to let me know she's okay," she said. "She said she missed Beanie."

"What else did she say?" Sally said.

Another pause. "Well, she said she had a place to stay, and that she's got a job. She's already gotten a paycheck. She told me she bought some great shoes."

Sally thought a minute. "Great shoes? She's probably not in Wyoming," she said.

"Duh," said Aggie.

"Aggie, did Charlie have friends in Colorado? Or anyplace else you can think of? She's probably crashing with somebody she knows."

Another pause. "Um, okay. She told me once that Billy Reno's got a lot of friends in Fort Collins. Once when we went shopping down there, she wanted to go see them, but my mom said we didn't have time. Charlie was kind of ticked off. She told me she wished she could just move to Fort Collins. She was sure she could get a job somewhere in the mall."

An opening. Sally probed. "Honey, is it possible that's where she is now?"

Sally heard Aggie swallow. "I don't know. Maybe. I guess. She said she'd been down there and hung out with people, and that it was pretty cool."

Sally wondered what "pretty cool" meant in Billy Reno's set. From what she'd heard, and from her own misspent youth, she could imagine: a bunch of wasted kids sitting around on thrift shop couches, listening to eardrum-shattering music, getting loaded one way or another. When you started the day stoned, and made every effort to stay that way, each repetition was a little more disappointing than the last. You spent a lot of time in a low-grade daze, with a low-grade headache and a very low level of motivation. Some people got stuck that way.

"So you're worried about her too," Sally told Aggie.

"No kidding," said Aggie.

"Maybe it would be good to go down to Fort Collins, and do a little shopping," said Sally. "Cruise the mall, maybe have lunch at that Mexican place. You interested?"

"Well, um, as a matter of fact, I'm going down there today with my aunt Maude," said Aggie.

Maude, going to the mall? This was a woman whose idea of fun was shoveling compost, not cruising the sale racks. "Maybe I could tag along," Sally said.

"Okay with me, but you'd better ask Aunt Maude," said Aggie. "We're supposed to leave in an hour."

Sally called Maude. "I hear you and Aggie are going shopping. I'm coming with you," she said.

"How'd you know?" Maude asked.

"I talked to Aggie," Sally said, without explaining further. "What's the deal, Maude? You hate shopping."

"Your kind of shopping, yes. Who in their right mind browses Victoria's Secret just for fun? I need to get a watch battery at Sears," said Maude. "That's my kind of shopping."

"What's going on, Maude? What do you know that I don't?" Sally asked.

It took Maude a minute. "Ordinarily, I'd rather save this conversation for the car. I don't really like to talk about this stuff on the phone," she said, "but I don't want to discuss this in front of Aggie."

"Okay," said Sally. "Fire away."

"As you're obviously aware, the options for young girls and women who get into trouble are pretty grim here in Wyoming," said Maude.

"What kind of trouble?" said Sally.

"The kind that's always referred to as 'getting into trouble,'" said Maude.

"Oh. Like that young lady who was trying to keep the appointment with her doctor, the one you were helping," said Sally.

"Yes. Poor kid. It's almost like the dark ages all over again," said Maude. She wasn't talking about the medieval era. As Sally knew, Maude had been pregnant and unmarried in Laramie in the 1960s. Meg Dunwoodie had helped her out of the jam, changing her life and earning her love and gratitude forever.

"Only worse, in some ways. Back in your day," said Sally, "there wouldn't have been demonstrations and explosions. There just wouldn't have been any choices."

"I'd never have thought we'd be back to underground railroads, but we are. Which is how I happened to be passing the time in a certain Fort Collins doctor's waiting room, a couple of days after that fiasco, and saw a large blond man walk up to the receptionist's desk and ask if anyone had seen his girlfriend. He said he hadn't seen her in a few days, and he was down from Laramie, trying to get word to her that her father had been killed."

"You happened to overhear this in a waiting room?" Sally said.

"I have excellent hearing," said Maude. "Unlike people who ruined their ears with loud rock 'n' roll."

"It helps if you don't care who knows what a busybody you are," said Sally.

"On the contrary," said Maude. "I had to hide behind a plastic ficus tree. I was worried the guy might recognize me—"

"Because," Sally concluded, "you remembered seeing him at

the demonstration. He was praying with Bea Preston and shoving Hawk around."

"How did you guess?" said Maude.

"Bea told me she had somebody looking for Charlie," Sally said.

"Since when are you and Bea Preston intimate confidantes?" Maude asked.

"I went to see her after the memorial service," Sally said. "We need to get down there, Maude. I hate to think this, but the right hand clearly knows what the left hand is doing around here. What if Bea's guy gets to Charlie before the police do? Bea makes no secret of the fact that she'd like to have the poor kid locked up. I wouldn't put it past her to take it into her own hands." She thought a minute more. "You know, I don't think we should take Aggie with us. What if we manage to find Charlie, and there's some kind of problem? I don't want to put her in that kind of situation."

"Obviously you don't know my great-niece very well," said Maude. "Aggie called me yesterday and asked me to take her shopping today. I think she must have heard from Charlie, and they've made a plan to meet. She's damn determined to ride to the rescue."

Sally thought. "Charlie would have told her not to go to the cops, and Aggie would feel like she had to agree. But why wouldn't she just ask her mother or father to take her? Why you?"

"My nephew and niece are loving, compassionate, wise, and honest people," said Maude. "They'd probably feel they had to call the sheriff. On top of which, they object to the notion of carrying concealed. Which, as it happens, I don't. As Aggie well knows," Maude finished. "And it seems she also knows about the underground railroad. Kids these days."

Oh good. Just a typical Saturday of schlepping around the mall, looking for a deeply damaged, possibly psychotic, perhaps homicidal girl-woman, with a hell-bent teenager and a pistol-packing sexagenarian. Potentially shadowed by an evangelical enforcer and God only knew who else, not to mention being one step ahead of or behind peace officers who would not look at all kindly on the interference of private citizens, however well intentioned (or well armed). Couldn't get much better than that.

Hawk was playing Saturday morning city league basketball. She'd better let him know where she was going. But how much detail? She left him a note: "Gone to the mall in Ft. C. with the girls, for some retail therapy. Call my cell if you need me."

Just another shopping spree with the gals.

"So tell me," said Sally to Maude as they hurtled south on Highway 287, Maude's Chevy Suburban having no trouble hauling the high road at eighty miles per hour, "how did you happen to be in the waiting room of a medical clinic that probably considers patient confidentiality on a par with nuclear secrets?"

Maude glanced over at her. "I've done some referrals, some counseling, and, well, some transportation. In cases where there's been recent violence, and where the patient is a minor, the clinic sometimes likes to keep the counselor of record in the loop."

"And you're that counselor for Charlie Preston," Sally said, drawing the obvious conclusion. "But Charlie's not a minor." Sally thought again. "So she's been there before?"

"Draw your own conclusions," said Maude, eyes on the road.

"But you didn't drive her down there this time. She had a car."

"I know about the clinic too," Aggie put in, leaning forward from the backseat. "Charlie told me she was going. She was really scared."

Sally reflected that at the age of fourteen, her biggest life concern had been whether her boyfriend's braces and hers would get locked if she let him kiss her. "Was that before somebody beat her up?" Sally asked.

"It was the day before she left," Aggie answered. "We talked on the phone, so I didn't see her. She didn't say anything about having been beaten, but she was freaking out." She looked out the window at a herd of antelope grazing by a snow fence.

"Abortion is a hard choice for anybody to make," said Sally.

"It's a lot harder if you've got a stepmother who tells you it's one more reason you'll burn in hell," Maude said.

Nobody said much of anything else in the hour it took them to make their way to the mall.The place was jammed. They finally found a parking spot about five million miles from the entrance, and once inside, had to weave their way among phalanxes of teenagers shouting at each other and gabbing on cell phones, oblivious mothers wrestling behemoth baby carriages and herding zigzagging toddlers, and supersize seniors moseying along at half the pace of the crowd. One part of Sally's brain told her that she should chill out and enjoy the spectacle. This was, after all, the cavalcade of American humanity, the modern-day equivalent of strolling the promenades of Paris in the days of Toulouse-Lautrec. Another part of her brain considered the virtues of neutron bombs.

There were sales everywhere; no wonder the mall was packed. They made slow progress, walking into every store to see if by any chance, the bored clerk talking on the phone, or the gum-cracking kid sullenly helping customers, might be Charlie Preston. Jewelry stores and shoe stores, shops selling potpourri and cell phones, beauty products and maternity wear, CDs, DVDs, pianos and eyeglasses. They walked the aisles of the bed and bath emporium, peering around every rack full of overstuffed, overprinted comforters, flimsy tables, and pillows hard and springy enough to bounce a quarter halfway to the moon. No Charlie.

They braved a trendy jeans-and-shirts store, dark, crowded, and deafeningly soundscaped with grating pop music. Aggie obviously knew and loved the place. Sally wondered whether the experts who developed marketing strategies for youth stores had cut their professional teeth in the military, prying Manuel Noriega from his palace by blasting Metallica at brain-splintering volume until the Panamanian dictator came out whimpering. Were the geniuses counting on the fact that parents would simply hand over their credit cards to kids piling up purchases, and then run screaming back into the mall, desperate for an Orange Julius?

No Charlie there either. They stopped for a lifesaving Orange Julius.

They tried Sears. Maude got her watch battery. Sally found a table full of cashmere sweaters at half price. No Charlie.

They hit the upscale department store. Aggie scored a pair of jeans marked down from two hundred to forty dollars. Sally wondered when jeans in the junior section of a department store had started costing more than a week's worth of groceries for a family of four.

Still no Charlie.

"That's about all I can take of the mall," Maude conceded. Maude was possibly the strongest person Sally had ever known, but consumerism had sapped her powers. "Let's go sit somewhere quiet and have a bite to eat."

Somewhere quiet? Fort Collins, like every town in the United States, had been taken over by franchise restaurants that specialized in gargantuan portions and acoustics designed to wake the dead. "Let's get something to eat, anyway," said Sally, as they headed out into the parking lot.

Two aisles away from Maude's Suburban, they saw flashing lights and heard raised voices, staticky radio transmissions. The Fort Collins police, it seemed, were making a bust. Sally caught sight of the backs of two officers, cuffing a young man in a backward baseball cap and a tank top revealing arms covered with ink.

"Oh my gosh!" Aggie exclaimed, thrusting her shopping bag at Sally, cutting away from them and heading between cars, toward the action. "That's Billy Reno!"

"How do you know?" Sally asked, hustling after Aggie.

"I recognize the dragon tattoo!" Aggie said, and shouted, "Billy!"

The suspect glanced over his shoulder. He had bewildered eyes and just about the sweetest smile Sally had ever seen. "Huh?" he said. "Oh. Hi, kid," he told Aggie.

"Eyes front!" barked one of the cops.

"What's going on here, Officer?" said Maude, a restraining

hand on Aggie's arm as she addressed the guy checking the hand-cuffs.

The officer ignored her.

Now a tow truck came down the aisle, lights spinning. The driver hopped out, and the other cop pointed at a Mazda Miata with County 5 Wyoming plates.

"That's Charlie's car!" said Aggie.

"See?" Billy Reno told the cops. "I told you! Charlie's my girl-friend. I'm just here to pick her up at work. I didn't steal no car, man!"

"Right, son. And I'm the king of England," said one of the officers, who did, actually, bear a slight resemblance to Prince Charles.

"I'm not shittin' you, Officer. This really, truly is my girl's car. I haven't done nothin' here."

The other cop, who looked more like Derek Jeter than the Windsor scion, sneered. "No, of course not. You're just a sweet young thing. The fact that you've got a sheet longer than that tat on your back is all an unfortunate misunderstanding, not to men-tion that the owner of this here sports car reported it stolen a week ago. Get the fuck in the car," he finished, shoving Billy's head down as he forced him into the back of the patrol car.

"Wait!" said Aggie. "He's telling the truth. This is my friend's car. She must be in the mall. Just wait a minute!"

The Prince Charles–ish officer let go of Billy Reno and walked toward them, picking up a clipboard from the roof of the patrol car as he approached. "Hold on there, young lady," he said, "is there some information you'd like to share with us?"

Aggie looked at the tow truck driver, attaching the big hitch to the Miata. Panic and puzzlement showed on her face. "That's—that's my friend's car. Her dad gave it to her. She works—I think she works, like, somewhere in the mall."

"Let's slow down a minute here," said Maude, addressing the officer. "My name is Maude Stark. This girl is my niece, Agatha. And the boy's girlfriend has disappeared from Laramie. Her name is Charlotte Preston."

The cop nodded. "Yes, ma'am." He took something off the clipboard, handed it to Aggie. "This wouldn't be the girl you're talking about, would it?"

Sally looked. It was a digital copy of a photo of Charlie. Probably her high school graduation photo. Perfect, airbrushed hair, phony smile, no facial jewelry. No bruises. The girl looked as if she'd been embalmed.

Aggie nodded. She looked like she might cry.

"We've received a missing person report on this Charlotte Preston. There are officers in the mall right now. We expect to have her very shortly."

# CHAPTER 12

# THE BRA

THE FORT COLLINS POLICE turned out to be more confident
than they had reason to be. Sally, Maude, and Aggie hung around
for the next two hours, while the cops took Billy away and
searched for Charlie Preston. To no avail. Sally wondered why.
Maybe the girl had actually been at the mall, working at her job,
when Sally and Maude and Aggie had first arrived. Maybe Charlie
had somehow caught sight of them and fled, without getting word
to Billy Reno. That would explain his coming to pick her up, and
Charlie being nowhere to be found.

Or possibly Charlie had seen them come into the place she
worked, and hidden in a back room until they left. And then gone
back to work for a while, or simply skedaddled.

Or maybe they'd just missed her, in all the mall madness.
Charlie worked her shift selling shampoo or candles or wireless
plans or chicken teriyaki, and when she got off, headed out into
the parking lot to meet Billy. She might have seen the cops and run
off then.

Or maybe Bea Preston's people had found her. Sally decided not to think about that, for the moment anyway.

Whatever the situation, it was Billy Reno's bad luck. The Fort Collins cops had ID'd the Miata, had made the driver's license Billy gave him as a fake, had connected the dots between the car, the missing girl, and the boy with the dragon tattoo. They'd tapped into Billy's rap sheet, put the cuffs on him, and hauled him off, complaining about how much paperwork it would take to get him extradited back to Wyoming.

Sally had no idea whether Billy Reno might have killed Brad Preston. She just didn't know enough about him, about the circumstances, about the crime. But she did feel damn sure he hadn't stolen the Miata. Aggie and Maude agreed with her on that point, and they kept one another spun up about it all the way back to Laramie.

"Billy's a really nice guy," Aggie kept saying. "I mean, he's a criminal and all, but that doesn't mean he's, like, evil or something. He just steals cars. And maybe some electronics and stuff."

"Aggie," said Sally. "I know that's what Charlie told you. But at the very least, he's got some serious problems." She wondered how to ask. "Is it possible that he's the one who's been beating on Charlie, and she's trying to cover for him? That's pretty common, among battered women."

"No! You should have seen her when she first started living with us, Sally. She was a mess. And she didn't even know Billy then. And she says he's really sweet. He gave her a diamond necklace."

"I bet he did," said Maude dryly.

"Don't be mean. Charlie says she loves him. So we've got to help him. He's been in so much trouble, if they put him in jail, they might never let him out."

"I don't think they can do that over a stolen car. But maybe we should see what we can do," said Maude.

"I think you should talk to Sheriff Langham," Aggie insisted.

"Billy's probably still in Colorado. They have to extradite him to Wyoming," said Maude.

"At the very least," said Sally as they pulled into town, "we can go down to the jail and see if Dickie's there. I think," she continued, "that we ought to take you home first, Aggie."

"Don't even think about objecting," said Maude, as Aggie opened her mouth to protest. "Consider what your mom and dad would do to me if we took you along."

That did it. She pouted a little, but she conceded the point. They dropped Aggie off, and Sally and Maude headed straight for the sheriff's office.

They walked into the reception area, separated by an upholstered half-wall partition from a bullpen where clerical workers took phone calls, stared at computer screens and clicked keyboards, relayed messages, and sorted piles of paper. At a desk in one corner, a woman clerk was talking quietly with Dave Haggerty and Scotty Atkins. The detective and the lawyer glanced up when Sally and Maude came in the door. Scotty's eyes narrowed microscopically, but he appeared otherwise indifferent to their presence. Haggerty bobbed his head in their direction and returned to the conversation.

"We might as well get out of here," said Maude. "The kid evidently called Haggerty to represent him. There's nothing else we can do. I've got animals to feed."

Sally didn't. And Scotty hadn't come out and asked them to leave, or even bothered to inquire what they might be doing there. She really ought to let the police know that Bea Preston had the blond guy out looking for Charlie. Plus Dave Haggerty had acknowledged them. So she felt like sticking around, at least for a while. Hawk would be wondering where she was. She'd better give him a call.

She pulled out her cell phone, realized she'd shut it off. When she turned it on, she found Hawk had left a message. An old friend of his from grad school had called to say he was in Cheyenne, doing a deal for a coal-bed methane developer. He'd offered to buy a couple of steaks at the Hitching Post, and that had sounded good to Hawk. He hoped Sally had been having a good therapeutic time at the mall and had spent lots of money. He'd have his cell phone if she needed anything, and he'd be back mid-evening.

No rush getting home then. Sally told Maude to go ahead and go, that she could walk home or get a ride with Dave Haggerty. Maude gave her a look, then told her to call with any news and took off.

And so she sat down in a grimy plastic chair in the waiting area, picked up a tattered copy of a three-year-old *Redbook* magazine, and nonchalantly strained her ears to filter out ambient noise, to catch anything she could of the conversation between Haggerty, the clerk, and Detective Atkins.

Years of practice picking out talky students in lecture halls had honed her auditory skills. And then, of course, she'd put herself through college and grad school playing country rock in honky-tonks. She'd spent hundreds of hours trying to tune a guitar in the midst of shrieking crowds, hollering musicians, shattering glass. Or it might be that she was just terminally nosy. She caught plenty.

They were holding Billy Reno in the Fort Collins jail on a count of grand theft auto. Nothing new for Billy, who was a congenital car thief, after all. They'd be transferring him to the custody of the Albany County sheriff's department by tomorrow.

But it seemed that they'd also nailed him for outstanding traffic warrants, giving false information to an officer, and a bunch of other things he'd piled up and run from since he'd last been in jail, not to mention a few that popped back up from years before. They'd added a count of malicious destruction of property: the trashed apartment.

Sally heard Haggerty ask Scotty about bail. Scotty answered, voice dropped down a notch, too low for her to hear. She wondered if she'd been too obviously eavesdropping. Of course, she was being pretty obvious just by sitting there. Still, she tried to act as if there was nothing strange about sitting in the sheriff's waiting area, reading an article about the miracle of cosmetic surgery. In fact, she read the piece about ten times. She was beginning to wonder what she might look like without eye bags.

"A hundred grand?" Haggerty exclaimed. "Come on, Detective. I really don't think any judge would go for that. It's a frigging car. And all that old stuff is just horseshit. If you'd been able to pin him down on that crap, you'd have done it by now."

Sally looked up from her magazine. Scotty glanced in her direction. The two men continued talking, in hushed tones. Did she hear Scotty mention the words "murder charge" and "Brad Preston," somewhere in the midst of an extended exchange? Then Scotty said in a normal voice, "The kid's a proven flight risk. Let it go, for now, and I'll work with you as this thing develops. It won't do him any good for you to yank my chain right now. I've got things to do."

Scotty turned and walked back through the bullpen, opened the door at the back, and disappeared. So much for getting the chance to tell him about Bea's effort to find Charlie.

Haggerty picked up his briefcase and told the clerk that he'd wait while she made copies of the paperwork. Then he walked around the divider that separated the work area from the waiting room, sat down next to Sally, and removed the magazine from her hands.

"Why are you here?" he asked her, voice cordial but inscrutable.

"I was at the mall in Fort Collins with Maude Stark and her niece Aggie," she said. "We were looking for Charlie—don't ask. At least right this minute," she added when he looked a question.

"We didn't see her, but we did see the bust. I just . . ." She shrugged. "I just thought I'd see what happened to Billy next. I don't think he stole that car, Dave. He was telling the truth about picking her up."

Haggerty nodded. "It's getting pretty complicated. What are you up to now?"

Sally looked around, as if there were someone standing over her shoulder who might tell her how to answer. "Um. Nothing much. No plans. In fact, I thought I'd try to talk to you, then walk home or hitch a ride. My, um, boyfriend can't pick me up. He's, er, in Cheyenne for dinner."

"Okay," said Haggerty. "So why don't we go to my place and fuck like wild animals?" he inquired in the same mild, friendly voice.

Sally's jaw dropped.

"Just kidding," he said. "An old attorney's trick of misdirection. What about waiting with me until I get the paperwork, and then we can go someplace and get a burger or something?"

They ended up at a brand-new restaurant down on Grand, facing the railroad tracks. The place called itself Le Brasserie de Laramie, which was enough of a hoot by itself. But when you got inside, you discovered that it wasn't Gay Paree on the High Prairie, but was instead a kind of fern bar (Laramie enters the eighties!). Sally hadn't been there before, and none of her friends was talking about it yet, since it had been open only about a week. There was a chance she'd end up running into somebody she knew. How often, after all, did somebody have the wild idea of opening a French restaurant in Laramie? Within two more weeks, all her friends would have been there, and if it was any good, they'd make it a regular stop. If it sucked, they'd soon be mocking it. She fast-forwarded to a time they might be referring to the place as The Bra.

But that was in the future. For now, a random encounter with a friend wasn't guaranteed at The Bra (she couldn't help herself) as it would be at the Yippie I O or the Wrangler or El Conquistador. Sally wasn't about to show up with Dave Haggerty at one of her usual hangouts. Particularly not after his astoundingly crude (not to say arresting) remark at the cop shop.

She reminded herself that this was, in a sense, a business meeting. There was a chance that Haggerty knew where Charlie was. He might even tell Sally. After all, they were both trying to help the kid. And besides, once they'd exhausted that subject, she might even lay the groundwork for hitting Haggerty up for some bucks for the Dunwoodie Center. Yeah, lots of business to do.

Like wild animals? Tigers, maybe? Ooh la la.

Haggerty ordered a scotch on the rocks. Sally thought that sounded good, but in the effort to protect her integrity, stuck with good old Jim Beam. She hadn't been born yesterday. You started out ordering "what he's having," and pretty soon you lost your head entirely.

So when the waiter brought their drinks, and Haggerty settled on the steak sandwich, she requested the salade niçoise, figuring that it had tuna, and that was brain food. It probably wasn't the greatest choice, given the season, the distance from the ocean, and the possibility that nearly every ingredient would, or possibly should, have come out of a can. She took a sip of Beam, standing her ground.

"You're representing Billy," she said. "How come?"

"I like to lose?" Haggerty inquired.

"I sincerely doubt it," said Sally. "How did you hook up with him, anyway? I can't imagine that you do a big business in car thieves. I'd have thought your practice would run more to victims of the system."

"It's a big system, so there's plenty of latitude for all kinds of victims," Haggerty said, contemplating his scotch. "And when you get to know the victims, nearly all of them are also perps. People aren't simple. When I first opened up my practice, there was this girl who worked part-time for me, filing and doing small stuff. She was something of a hard case, high school dropout, but really bright. Shitty taste in men.

"She got pregnant. I kept her on, even when she started having trouble showing up for work. She didn't take very good care of herself, to say the least."

"Billy's mother, I presume," Sally said.

Haggerty nodded. "She did what she could, on and off. But the boyfriends weren't a lot of help. And she had some real substance abuse issues. Put it this way. The best times of Billy Reno's childhood were when his mom took off and left him to shift for himself. That didn't exactly equip him to make wise life choices."

"So how were you involved with him?" Sally asked.

"Kind of an informal Big Brother thing. I tried to keep an eye out for him when I could. Gave her money when she asked. A time came when I figured out what she was buying with it, so I stopped. Billy ended up in foster care, and for a while I was his guardian ad litem. He was a handful, to say the least. By the time he was eighteen, he thought he was John fucking Dillinger."

"Violent?" asked Sally.

"Fights, starting in elementary school," said Haggerty. "Said he had to defend himself, and I bet he did. By high school . . . well, he wasn't in high school all that long, but you'd be surprised how many teenage boys have guns. They frigging love guns. Some girls too."

"Like Charlie Preston?" Sally said.

"I don't know," Haggerty answered. "Do you have any idea where she is?"

So much for Sally's hope that he knew. She shook her head. "I'm kind of hoping that Bea Preston doesn't know either."

"Charlie would probably be better off with the police," Haggerty agreed.

Sally asked the question. "Does Scotty think Billy killed Brad Preston?"

Haggerty bit his lip, took a swig of scotch, and said, "He's got some reason to think so."

"Do you?" she asked.

"I'm his attorney," said Haggerty. "I'll leave it at that."

"But from what you're telling me, if Billy Reno had wanted to kill Brad Preston, he'd have had access to a gun, and have known how to use it."

"True," said Haggerty. "But there's one little problem. As I understand it, you and your friend Green were the ones who found Preston. And you also found a lug wrench, which appeared to be the weapon used to beat Brad Preston to death."

Sally nodded.

"Well, it seems," Haggerty continued, "that the Miata the cops are holding down in Colorado, registered to Bradley Preston, contained a custom tool kit. All the tools were there, except the lug wrench. And it also seems"— and now Haggerty took a truly large gulp of scotch—"that the cops here lifted specimens of two different fingerprints off the wrench found with the body. One set belongs to Billy Reno. The other came from Charlie Preston."

Sally's shoulders sagged. "I guess I ought to be surprised, but I'm not. I'm probably out of my mind. I still want to believe that somebody's setting Charlie up."

"Why?" asked Haggerty.

"I can't see her killing him. Yeah, evidently Brad had been beating her up for some time, but she'd gotten away. Seems like she made it at least as far as Fort Collins. Why would she come back and yank him into an alley and kill him? I thought people usually chose between flight and fight."

"As I said," Haggerty told her, motioning to the waiter for refills, "when people have choices between one thing and another, they generally try to do both."

"So you'll be defending Billy on a murder charge?" she asked.

"Looks that way," said Haggerty, flicking his eyes at the waiter, who'd come to serve their food. They said nothing until their plates sat in front of them and the waiter had departed.

Her salad didn't look toxic, if you didn't mind pale lettuce, mealy tomatoes, Chicken of the Sea, and mushy olives. She didn't think she'd become a regular at The Bra. "What about Charlie?"

"Someone from my office will take the lead on her case. They'll undoubtedly charge her too, as an accessory at least." Haggerty picked up his steak sandwich, took a big bite. If you dealt with violent crime a lot, you probably needed to keep up your strength, no matter what the dinner-table chatter might be.

"So where do you start?" she asked.

"With the coroner's report. They gave me a copy. They put the time of death as some time that morning. Somebody came up behind Mr. Preston and hit him over the head, and kept on hitting, more than was absolutely necessary. Whoever did it wanted to be sure of the results. Sorry. I'm afraid I'm spoiling your dinner."

Sally stopped picking at the salad, set down her fork. "Don't worry about it. This whole thing pisses me off. The violence just breeds and breeds and breeds. What the hell was Brad Preston doing in that alley anyway? Don't you think the cops ought to be asking about that?"

"They are. So am I. And could it be"—and here he put down what remained of his sandwich, reached across the table, and stroked a finger down her face—"that you will too?"

She ignored the stroking, which felt at the moment more like one of his famous distractions than an enticement. "Look. Here's the way I see it. Preston was either looking for something, meeting somebody, or forced by someone to go into the alley. Now that they've got the fingerprints off the lug wrench, it seems clear that it wasn't some random assault by a thug looking for money."

"We don't get much of that around here anyhow," commented Haggerty.

"Yeah. Stay with me. Preston might have been alone when the attacker caught him. Or maybe he met whoever he was looking for, and there was an accomplice who did the beating. I can imagine somebody pulling a gun, say, marching him into the alley, and then the second person hit him."

"All plausible. So the question," said Haggerty, "is, what was he doing in that area?"

"Maybe he was on his way to the protest at the clinic," said Sally. "He'd surely have known it was coming."

"I doubt he'd have been going to the demonstration," said Haggerty. "Brad embraced the politics, but he steered clear of that kind of public display. He played it tough, businesslike, and detached."

Tough. Businesslike. Detached. And back behind the closed doors of his tasteful Victorian dream house, out of control. "I admit, the easiest explanation is that Charlie talked Billy into helping her kill him. Her father would have gone with her into the alley if she'd asked, or met her there. But why there and then?"

"Good questions," said Haggerty.

Sally pushed on. "You'd have to assume that whoever killed

him was either crazy with rage or standing to gain, in some way, from his death."

"Only two of those circumstances could apply to Charlie Preston," Haggerty pointed out.

"Granted. But play along, Dave. Who else had reason to be furious with him? And who was in a position to gain, financially or otherwise, from his death?"

Haggerty polished off the last of his sandwich. "On the financial front, his wife, obviously. As for anybody else, you'd have to get a look at the will, which I certainly intend to do. And then there's the fact that the Republicans were setting him up to run for Congress, a development that should have scared the shit out of everybody."

"Maybe. But who'd have been scared or pissed enough about that to actually want him dead?" Sally said.

"Maybe he had some old enemies," Haggerty replied.

Old enemies? Maybe Dave Haggerty himself? "How long have you known him? Can you think of anybody who really hated his guts?"

Haggerty polished off his scotch. "Twenty-five years, maybe? We went to law school together. He was brilliant, I'll give him that, but he was always a self-centered, self-righteous son of a bitch. He was a famous pain in the ass even before he started running to the right, and you didn't have to be on the other side of the political fence to know that. Not to mention that over the years, he's undoubtedly pissed off some of the people who lost to him in court. But that comes with the territory."

"Like who?" Sally asked. "What kinds of cases did he take? Anything especially notorious?"

"He made his bones representing insurance companies contesting claims," said Haggerty. "That's what his firm does. Whenever there's a toxic waste dump that needs liability protection, or a blind grandmother to be denied a couple of grand for some frivolous thing like a pacemaker, he's taken on the good fight. He's done at least one case that had to do with denying benefits to unmarried domestic partners. But I have a question for you. Why are you getting so involved?" he asked. "I know you care about Charlie Preston, but why? Most professors wouldn't go so far for a student."

Sally pushed her nearly full salad plate to the side and leaned forward. "She came to me for help. She'd been horribly beaten. I gave her money. I gave her my coat. The whole thing was a rude shock. It's been years since I actually had to deal with domestic violence face-to-face. I teach my students about it, but I hadn't personally dealt with a woman who'd been assaulted since I was in grad school, when I ran the women's center here. It's a vicious situation. The victims need medical doctors and cops and shrinks. Most of them never get to the point of getting out of the house, of even trying to get away.

"So when they come in the door, looking for help, they've already made a big step. But even then, most never press charges, and damn near all of them end up going back to their abusers. It makes you sick. When one of those women does manage to get away, and get justice, and start over, and you had some little part in helping, it's amazingly rewarding."

"Yeah," said Haggerty, smiling warmly. "You know, it really is."

"I've got friends who are still in the trenches, helping out personally." She thought about Maude, who never stood back. "But not me. I've been a smug little armchair feminist for a long time."

"There are lots of ways of being on the front lines," said Haggerty. "You don't have to be answering the Safe House hotline to be involved. You've done plenty for women."

"How the hell would you know?" said Sally. "I just met you. I'm proud of the things I've done with the Dunwoodie Center, but that's pretty ivory tower stuff, after all."

"You don't exactly hide in the tower, Dr. Alder," said Haggerty. "Seems to me that you take some risks. I like that in a woman. In fact, I've been watching you, seeing what you've done with the Dunwoodie, and liking what I saw, a long time. I like everything about you." He grinned. "You might say I have this little crush on you."

## CHAPTER 13

# NIGHTHAWKS AT THE BUS STATION

HAWK WASN'T BACK FROM Cheyenne yet when Dave Haggerty dropped Sally off at home. Haggerty leaned over for a hug, not an easy task since he drove a sweet little two-seater ragtop Beamer sports job, and the seats were leather buckets that hugged your bottom like a favorite pair of jeans. The steering wheel and his chest were closely acquainted.

But he was a hugger, this one. And he whispered in her ear as he wrapped his arms around her, "I don't think we should kiss tonight."

Sally put a restraining hand on his arm. "Right. I don't either, Dave. Thanks for the ride, and the dinner." He'd paid for dinner. She told herself that since she hadn't actually eaten her salad, she wasn't indebted. "I'll be in touch, or call me when you hear anything."

He did the tiger-eye thing. "I'll call. Sweet dreams."

Mmm-hmm. A battered girl, a murdered father, a boyfriend in jail, the girl gone missing, and some anonymous somebody taking creepy pictures of Sally and Hawk, and then sending them over the wire to pop up on Hawk's computer, in the intimacy of her own home. Just the recipe for lovely reveries.

What was Haggerty's game, anyway? True, there was electricity between them. Nothing you could do about that. Such chemistry originated somewhere way below the cerebral cortex, down in the lizard brain. But Dave Haggerty was a stranger to her. Obviously, he was aware of his sexual appeal. She was sure he wouldn't hesitate to use sex to his advantage. Was he messing with her? If so, why?

She was too damn tired to think about it. She managed to pull off her clothes and haul on her pajamas, and fall into bed. Her head hit the pillow like a rock.

She didn't know how much later she felt Hawk slip between the sheets and pull her close. Or how long they slept, nestled like spoons, comfort seeping into her from his warm, firm body.

The phone rang, jolting them both awake. The clock on the bedside table said it was almost two A.M.

"Dr. Alder," said the voice on the other end, sounding a little slurred. "This is Charlie Preston. Need to return your coat."

"Thank God," said Sally.

"I wasn't gonna steal it or anything. I mean, what do you think I am?" Charlie retorted, defensive.

"That's not what I meant," Sally said, trying to keep her voice calm. "Where are you, Charlie?"

"Ummmm . . ." she was trailing off, losing focus, passing out, maybe.

"Listen to me!" Sally said, forgetting about calm. "You've got to tell me where you are, okay? Don't be afraid. I've been trying to find you. I was down in Fort Collins, with Maude and Aggie Stark."

"Yeah. I know. Talked to Aggie," Charlie mumbled. "Aggie's nice girl. Lil' sis. So sweet."

"Are you in Laramie, Charlie?" Sally asked, hoping against hope.

"MMMMMmmmm. Laramie. Yeah. Took the bus. Hangin' by the station. Cold here. Sure you need your coat?"

"Stay right where you are. I'm going to come and get you. Don't move, Charlie. I'll be there in ten minutes at the most. Are you on your cell phone?"

"Cell. Yeah. Haven't cut me off yet." Charlie began to giggle.

"Stay on the line. Keep talking to me." Sally was out of bed by now, rummaging in her closet until she found a ratty fleece pullover, yanking it on, grabbing a pair of socks, searching for shoes. "I'm coming right there. Meanwhile, I'm going to put my boyfriend on the line. His name's Hawk. He's a good guy, Charlie. Talk to him." She handed the phone to Hawk, who managed to pull himself up on one elbow in the bed.

"Hawk? What kind of name is that for a boy?" Charlie asked, giggling some more.

"Charlie? What kind of name is that for a girl?" he answered.

By that time, Sally had dragged on the sweater, jumped into her shoes, and was headed out the door.

The gray and blue plastic sign glowed pale in the darkness. Gray-painted cinder-block wall, concrete sidewalk, curb, driveway, and a parking lot littered with soda cans and wrappers from vending machine food, discarded cigarette packs. The grime-streaked front window revealed the interior tableau: a few people slumped on chairs, haggard and dejected in the harsh fluorescent light, waiting for a bus that probably didn't come for hours. Nighthawks at the bus station.

Some small relief: she didn't have to go inside. Sally found Charlie sitting on the sidewalk around the corner from the entrance, legs splayed out and back against the wall, surrounded by cigarette butts and empty beer bottles. She was holding a cell phone halfway to her ear. Her eyes were closed, head drooping. Sally could hear Hawk still talking, tinny and faint. She took the phone. Charlie didn't seem to notice.

"I'm here," she told Hawk. "She's sitting outside the bus station, on the side by the parking lot."

"I'm coming down there," he said. "You probably need help."

"She's totally out of it," said Sally. "Come on down. I might have to carry her to the car."

Sally squatted, put a hand on Charlie's shoulder, gave a little shake. "Come on, Charlie.

Charlie startled, looked up, utterly dazed. "Oh. Umph. You're here."

"It's cold," Sally said. "How come you aren't inside keeping warm?"

"Too bright," said Charlie. "Hate those fucking lights."

"Okay. That's fine. I want to take you to my house, get you into bed. Can you get up and walk?"

"I dunno. Real tired." When Charlie tried to pull away from the wall, she toppled over. She curled up on the pavement. "Lemme sleep." She pulled Sally's now-filthy coat close around her. Sally got the feeling it wasn't the first time Charlie Preston had bedded down on a sidewalk.

She heard a truck pull into the parking lot. A moment later, Hawk knelt beside her. "Pathetic," he said.

"Yeah," she replied. "But at least she's here. At least Bea didn't find her."

"All right. Why don't you pull your car up to the curb here, and we'll load her in?"

Charlie was shorter and skinnier than Sally, but she was passed out cold. Dragging her up and maneuvering her into the Mustang was harder than they'd expected. It took them half an hour to get her out of the car, into the house, out of the coat, her shoes, her pants, and into their bed.

They'd debated loading her into the shower. Charlie reeked of cheap tobacco and bad beer. But they ended up deciding that she probably needed sleep more than she needed to be clean and awake.

So while Charlie slept the sleep of the dead drunk, they sat at their kitchen table, sipping herbal tea and discussing their next move.

"I'm going to call the sheriff's office. In just a little while," said Sally.

"Why wait?" Hawk asked. "You should call right now."

"Hold on a second. I haven't had a chance to tell you what happened today." She gave him the rundown on the day's events, including an apology for not giving him much detail on why she'd gone to the mall (he accepted) and a heavily edited summary of her encounter with Dave Haggerty (he frowned, but didn't say anything). "So the police are holding Billy Reno. Billy's and Charlie's fingerprints are all over that lug wrench we found. That's enough for them to charge him with murder. What do you think they'll do to her?"

Hawk pressed his lips together. "Probably the same. Or something close to it."

Sally took a breath, made herself imagine the sight of Brad Preston's shattered skull. The room tilted a little. "I can't do it. I can't see in my mind what the wounds in his head looked like. But wouldn't you think that the medical examiner will be able to tell whether the person who hit Preston was taller or shorter than he was? Wouldn't there be something about the angle of impact? Hell, they can probably tell whether the attacker was right- or left-handed."

"And then match the prints on the wrench. It's not rocket science. If two people accosted him, they could tell which one of them it was, or if both of them hit him, and whether he was standing up or on the ground." Sally looked crushed. "I'm sorry," said Hawk. "You really don't want it to be her."

"If it was," said Sally, "I want to know what drove her to do it."

Hawk put down his tea, reached over the table, and took her hand. "This isn't about you. You have to call the police. Call Dickie at home, if it makes you feel better. But you can't play cop here."

"She came to me before. She called me tonight," said Sally. "She trusts me. I just want to talk to her before they take her."

He gave her a long look. "She could be a murderer, Sally."

"You helped me undress her. All she had on her was a bus ticket, a ten-dollar bill, and half a pack of cigarettes. No weapons. No ID, even. She's a lost kid, Hawk. I agree, she might still have done something terrible. Maybe she was high on meth. Maybe her boyfriend decided they should shake down the old man, and she agreed, and things got out of hand. Or maybe, well, anything. But she's been in the system a long time. If ever there was a victim, it's her. She's used to thinking they're out to get her. She has reason to believe that they are.

"What harm would it really do if we let her sleep off her drunk and then gave her something to eat, and listened to her side of the story? Don't you think she deserves at least that much sympathy?" Sally asked.

"Why in hell do you think she'd tell you anything?" Hawk asked.

"I don't. Or at least I'm not counting on it. But it's worth a try," Sally insisted.

"So you're not going to call Dickie right now, are you?" he said.

"What difference does it make?" Sally replied. "If I call him now, they'll just come wake her up. She'll be miserable enough going with them in the morning, after she's had some sleep. We can give her that."

He didn't like it. "You know, if she didn't do it, every minute of delay might give whoever did more time to get away. And you also know that Dickie will be pissed at you, and he'll be right."

"He'll be pissed," said Sally. "But if he was sitting here, I bet he'd let her sleep."

Hawk looked at Sally, looked toward the bedroom, looked back at Sally. "Yeah. Okay. I could use a couple more hours in the rack myself."

They pulled out the so-called sleeper sofa in the living room. Hawk had gotten it at a garage sale when he'd first bought the house, and everyone who'd ever attempted to actually sleep on it had the same opinion: Are you kidding? They'd bought a new mattress for it, put an extra pad on top, but nothing disguised the fact that the thing was basically an assemblage of sagging springs and unforgiving metal bars. They finally gave up and put the mattress on the floor, but no sooner had they shut their eyes than birdsong and pearly light prodded them awake.

Birds and light and the muffled noises coming from the kitchen.

They found Charlie Preston sitting at the table, dirty and disheveled and fully dressed, writing them a note.

Sally looked over Charlie's shoulder, reading. "'Decided to split. Thanks for the bed.'" She sat down, facing the girl. "Where, exactly, were you planning to go?" she asked.

Charlie tried to glare at Sally, but she was utterly out of gas. She put her head down on the table.

Hawk sat down too. "You're out of options, Charlie. Your boyfriend is in jail. The police are going to charge him with murdering your father."

She lay motionless.

"I don't know what happened," Sally told her, "but you need to go in and tell them what you know."

Minutes passed. Charlie's shoulders shook a little, but she remained silently prostrate on the table. Sally and Hawk said nothing, waiting her out.

Finally, with huge effort, Charlie raised her head. Her eyes were a thousand years old. "It doesn't matter. They won't believe me anyway. They never do."

Sally took a chance, took Charlie's hand. "I have to ask you. Were you there? Did you see who . . ."

Charlie wrenched her hand away and leaped up with a shriek. "I didn't! I wasn't! I didn't fucking kill my old man! I wasn't even in Wyoming when he died. I don't know anything about it! I didn't hear about it until two days after it happened."

"Can you prove that?" Sally said. "Is there anybody who can back you up?"

Tears began to leak out of the corners of her eyes. She nodded. "I had, uh, s-some m-medical problems."

"I know," said Sally. "I saw you before you took off, remember?"

"Yeah. R-right. There's this doctor in Fort Collins. I don't want to tell you her name."

"If she's the person who's going to corroborate your story, you're going to have to let the police know who she is," Hawk said.

Charlie looked down. "I don't want her name getting out. They'll come after her. Do to her what they did to that guy up here. She volunteers at the shelter down there. She does all kinds of things."

"Like patching up people who've been battered, and dealing with unwanted pregnancies?" Sally asked.

Charlie nodded, took a big breath. "This wasn't the first time for me, Dr. Alder. I got pregnant when I was fifteen. Then again last year. This was my third, um, operation. The first one wasn't so hot. There'd been some problems, a lot of scarring. I thought I got through this one okay. I just went in for the day and had it done, then they let me out and told me to call if anything came up.

"For a few days, things were fine. I had a job and everything. But then, there were some complications. They had to do . . . some other procedures. I ended up in the hospital down there." Charlie shook her head. "Well, anyhow, I guess I can't get pregnant any more."

Dear God. At the age of eighteen, Sally Alder had been partying her way through her sophomore year at Berkeley. She'd been madly in love with a bass player from South Carolina, a sloe-eyed premed from Montreal, a chain-smoking radical preppie, and half her American Folklore class. Plenty of drama. Not much trauma.

At eighteen, Charlie Preston found out her father had been murdered, maybe the very day she'd learned that she'd never be able to have children of her own. Sally covered Charlie's hand with her own. "How did you find out about your father?" she asked gently.

"Billy came and got me when they let me out of the hospital. He was freakin'. The day after it happened, the cops came knocking on his door. He snuck out a back window and got the hell out of there. He came and told me as s-soon as he could. He didn't want me to be a-alone," she said, hiccupping down tears.

"I lost my mom when I was little," Hawk said. "It's the worst thing in the world."

"My dad . . . I mean, I can rememb-b-ber him bouncing me on his knee and singing to me when I was just a little, little kid. He'd sing and sing and bounce me until I was laughing and laughing. That was b-before . . . oh shit. Before. He'd get so mad at me. I d-don't . . . whatever." She was gasping for air. "Whatever! Then he'd try to make it all up. He'd be so sorry. He'd try to explain, and then—then I'd end up in . . . I can't . . . and then Bea . . . I just fucking had to get out of here. It was so fucking awful!"

"Aggie told me you had friends down in Colorado. Or at least Billy does," Sally said.

Charlie sniffled hard, breath coming fast. "They aren't the kind of friends, who h-hang around hospitals," she managed.

"So Billy knew what you'd been through." Hawk made it a statement, not a question.

"Billy," said Charlie, "knows every g-goddamn sorry thing about me." She sat up straighter, face tear-streaked but fierce. "And he loves me anyway. As soon as he gets his hands on some money this guy owes him, we're gonna get married and get the fuck outa Laramie! There's nothing for us here."

Sally leaned her forehead on her hand and closed her eyes, thinking. "Was Billy with you in Fort Collins?" she asked.

Charlie eyed her warily. "Some of the time," she said.

Hawk leaned in close. "Was he with you the day your father died?" he asked.

Charlie glared, despite the tears, her trembling mouth.

"How well do you know Billy Reno, Charlie?" asked Sally.

"Fuck you!" shouted Charlie. "I love him! Just because he's gotten in trouble doesn't mean he killed my daddy."

Not "my father." Not even "my dad." "My daddy."

"Sally's not saying he did," Hawk said. "But he loves you too, right? He knows who hurt you. Maybe he was trying to pay Brad back. Maybe things got out of hand. Does he lose his temper a lot?"

"Do you?" Charlie screamed. "Mr. Fancy-Ass college professor, do you ever get so mad you want to punch your fist through a wall? Doesn't everybody lose it sometimes?" She turned to Sally. "How about you? Does Ponytail Boy here ever get out of control and slap you around? Do you try to fight back? Or maybe he just sneaks off and gets his revenge other ways. Or maybe you do."

They stared, appalled. "We get mad, sometimes, sure," said Hawk. "But we don't hit each other. Ever. That's out of bounds."

Charlie sneered at them. "You say that now, but how do you know? Have you ever hit anybody else, Hawk? Anybody ever hit you?"

He had nothing to say.

"How do you know she won't piss you off so much that one day you'll just lose it? If there's one thing I've learned in my life, it's that you never really know anyone. You might think you do, but you don't. One minute they're all, 'I love you. I adore you. I'd do anything for you.' The next, they're smackin' you so hard you think your neck's gonna snap. And then suddenly someone's sticking a needle in your arm and hauling you off and you just can't, you just don't . . . you can't figure anything out, count on anything. My old man and his bitch wife were living proof of that." She began to laugh and sob hysterically. "But at least now he's dead."

# CHAPTER 14

# DO YOU WANT MY JOB?

SALLY HAD NEVER SEEN anything like it. One minute, Charlie Preston was hysterical. The next, she was motionless, incapable of speech, eyes dead. They tried to rouse her, rubbing her back, shouting at her, offering water. When Hawk put the glass to her mouth, Charlie didn't move. The water dribbled down her chin. Then Sally tried to take her hand, and Charlie grabbed her wrist, grasping convulsively before lapsing back into immobility.

She needed a doctor. She needed a lot more than that, but a doctor first. Sally called 911, then called Dickie Langham at home. "Charlie Preston's here," she told him. "An ambulance is coming. . . . No, no, it doesn't look as if she's physically hurt, but she's gone into some kind of catatonic state."

"I'll be right there," he said, hanging up without asking more questions.

Then she called Dave Haggerty. "We've got Charlie Preston," she told him. "But we're getting her to the hospital. I've called the sheriff."

"Thanks," said Haggerty. "She's gonna need a good attorney.

I'll call my associate, Melba Krich, and tell her to go down to Ivinson Memorial. Anything you want to tell me?" he asked.

Sally wasn't sure of the protocol. She knew that she needed to give Dickie the fresh version of Charlie's story. It was good to know that Charlie would have a lawyer on board when the police started asking her questions. When she was able to answer them. Whenever that might be.

But Dave Haggerty wouldn't be taking Charlie on as a client. He'd be representing Billy, who evidently *had* been in Laramie when Brad Preston was murdered. Charlie might want to believe that she and Billy were in this mess together, but who knew? Once the lawyers got into the act, it would be every man, woman, boy, and girl for himself or herself, and things would get exponentially weirder and messier. This, Sally decided, was a good time to say as little as possible. "Charlie wasn't there the day Brad was killed. She was down in Fort Collins. I don't want to go into detail now," she told him.

"Okay. All right. Thanks for calling," said Haggerty, sounding disappointed at Sally's reticence. But not all that surprised either.

Ivinson Memorial Hospital in the cold, pale dawn. Sally shivered, teeth chattering, as they walked toward the emergency entrance. In the course of her checkered career, she'd spent more than her share of time holding down a chair in the waiting area, drinking the toxic coffee from the cafeteria, trying to tamp down worry and pain and grief. The clicking of her heels on the linoleum floor stirred up all the fragments of fear and heartbreak she'd accumulated over the times she'd spent there. No wonder doctors and nurses wore soft-soled shoes. It wasn't just to save their backs and knees. The sound of their footsteps on that rackety floor would drive them crazy.

"I had to let her sleep, Dickie," Sally told the sheriff at the end of her story. They were sitting on a Naugahyde couch in the emergency room waiting area, miraculously unoccupied except for the three of them. That was probably good news for Charlie; they'd rushed her into the ER while Sally was still trying to figure out how to fill out the paperwork a receptionist had stuck in her hand the minute they'd arrived. "I know I should have called right away," she explained, "but the kid was drunk, maybe high, although she didn't really seem to be on any drug other than lots of beer."

"Enough beer," said Dickie, "can be powerful poison. Believe me, I know."

"Yeah. Jesus. I hope to hell I didn't make a terrible mistake," Sally said.

"You mean, 'We didn't make a mistake,'" said Hawk. "I didn't call either."

Dickie reached for his cigarettes, shaking his head. Realized he couldn't light up in the hospital, so he contented himself with taking a smoke out of the pack, tapping it in his palm, putting it back with a regretful sigh. "I don't know. I'm no doctor. I can't imagine sleeping did her any harm. From what you've said, she needed it pretty bad. We'll just have to see what happens."

Sally reached over and squeezed his hand. "She's got an alibi, God help her."

"But the boyfriend doesn't," Dickie replied. "He's got real problems."

"What do you mean?" asked Sally.

Just then, a doctor emerged from the ER, dangling a clipboard from his left hand. "From what we can tell," he said, "she's in a catatonic state. We want to get a lab workup, get an EEG, do some other tests. We've sedated her. Fortunately, we've got a pretty extensive medical history for her. I guess the good/bad news is that she's been here a lot before." He smiled very ruefully.

"Can you help her?" Sally asked.

"Yeah, we're pretty sure," said the doctor. "But we have to get permission to treat her further. Her paperwork's incomplete. We need to notify her next of kin."

Sally, Dickie, and Hawk looked at each other. "There are some complications," said Dickie. "It'd probably be her stepmother, Beatrice Preston. But they aren't exactly close."

The doctor closed his eyes and rubbed his forehead. "Anybody else?" he asked.

"There are foster parents," said Sally, thinking of Mike and Julie Stark. "How about them?"

The doctor scratched at the beginning of a beard. He looked exhausted. Sally could imagine why. He'd probably pulled an all-nighter; sometimes emergency doctors worked seventy-two-hour shifts. Brutal, not to mention scary. "This is not good," the doctor announced. "Especially given who the stepmother is. She's liable to reject medical treatment and get up a revival in the ER waiting room, not to mention the legal stuff. Okay. What do you say, Sheriff?"

"I doubt that Mrs. Preston would turn down treatment," Sally put in, "given what she told me about Charlie's medical history. But I don't think she'd be real sympathetic either."

The doctor breathed deep. "Okay. We probably have to call her anyway. In the meantime, would you happen to know if there's any chance that this girl might be pregnant?"

Sally, Hawk, and Dickie stared at the doctor. Sally said, "You examined her, right?"

"Yeah," said the doctor. "What are you getting at?"

"She had an abortion, followed by some kind of sterilization procedure, within the last three weeks," Dickie told him. "What is it you people do for a living?"

The doctor made a note on the clipboard. "Pelvic exams aren't standard procedure when we get somebody in here with a neurological emergency. We deal with insurance companies, you know, and they're getting pickier and pickier about authorizations. Hell, you don't even know if this girl's got insurance. It's a problem," he admitted.

"Oh well, at least we know that you guys are screwing up because of greed, not incompetence," Sally said.

The doctor glared at her. "You want my job?" he asked.

"Sorry," said Sally.

"I'm going back in there," said the doctor. "Thanks for the information. We'll get in touch with Mrs. Preston."

Sally waited for the doctor to leave. Then she pounced. "You said Billy had problems," she told Dickie. "What?"

Dickie shook his head. "You want to know something we see all the time? Stupid dumb-ass criminals who can't keep their damn mouths shut. Maybe they figure they're safe, because most of their friends are other stupid dumb-ass criminals who'd never run to the cops. Maybe they're so disconnected from society that they figure they're untouchable. Or maybe they're just friggin' out of it."

"You're saying Billy blabbed to somebody about Brad Preston?" Sally said. "Why would he do that? I mean, from the little Charlie told us, he was worried about her, trying to protect her."

"And since when would worrying be proof of innocence of a crime?" Dickie asked. "If we acquitted every defendant who ever admitted to worrying, the streets would be jammed with cutthroats and maniacs," Dickie pointed out. "Who's got better reasons to worry?"

"Yeah," said Hawk. "In fact, that worrying might have been what drove him to do the deed."

"Who came to you?" Sally asked Dickie.

"One of his sweet little roommates. Touching story—they met at church. Another pathological liar and thief. And where do these kids get those tats? My God, can you imagine sitting still while somebody turns you into a human pincushion, just so you can go around looking like something the circus left behind?" Dickie said.

"Do you mean to say that Billy told this kid he was going after Brad Preston?" Sally asked. She didn't know a lot of murderers personally, but if she were one, she didn't think she'd go around talking up her homicidal plans.

"Nah. He says he overheard Billy and his girlfriend talking about how they were going to rip off her old man. Said the girlfriend told Billy he didn't have to be gentle with the dad on her account. Said they were loaded when they had the conversation, and they didn't seem to care particularly who might be within earshot."

"What's this guy's name?" Sally asked.

"Alvin Sabble," Dickie replied.

"Like the singing chipmunk?" Sally asked.

Dickie considered. "Not quite. But there's definitely a rodent-like quality to him," he said.

"Roommates and vermin," said Hawk. "An all-too-common combination."

"Was the informant one of the kids who got evicted?" Sally asked Dickie.

The sheriff nodded.

"Where is he now?" Sally asked.

"Staying at the Waldorf Astoria. Why do you ask?" Dickie retorted.

"Consider backing off, Sal," Hawk said, putting his arm around her.

Sally gave him a look.

"Don't give me the stubborn look," said Hawk.

"Okay. You win," she conceded to Dickie. He clearly had his reasons for discouraging her from trying to get in touch with Alvin Sabble. But, she thought, she and Hawk were college professors, after all. They had plenty of students who probably did their share of partying. Laramie was a pretty small town. It shouldn't be too hard to find out a thing or two about the inhabitants of a recently evicted party house.

Her thoughts were interrupted by the clicking of heels on the linoleum. Bea Preston, grim and thin-lipped and perfectly coiffed, was coming down the hall. "Where's the attending physician?" she asked them, wasting no particular effort on giving them the time of day.

"He's in the ER," Dickie told her, and added, "I'm sorry, Mrs. Preston."

"You have no idea," said Bea, pressing her lips together hard. "I've been afraid it would come to this."

Sally had to tell her. "Charlotte wasn't here the day your husband was killed."

Bea looked at her. Nodded once. "I have to get in there," she said, and turned to go.

Hawk put his hand on Sally's arm. "Is there really any reason for us to stick around here? They're not going to let you in to see Charlie. Bea isn't going to decide you're her closest confidante. There's really nothing for us to do here."

Dickie put an arm around her shoulder. "He's right. Go on home. Don't you have things to do today anyhow? I sure as hell do. And much as I enjoy planting my ample fanny in this torture device of a chair, I've got to get to the office. Don't worry. I'm going to get a deputy down here. We'll have somebody around when the kid wakes up."

"When?" said Sally.

"She'll wake up," Dickie assured her.

*Click, click, click;* heels on linoleum. Melba Krich, the blond lawyer Sally'd met at the Dunwoodie reception, had arrived. "Howdy, Sheriff," she said, turning to Sally and adding, "I remember you."

Hawk introduced himself. They all shook hands. Melba sat down. "I'll take it from here," she told Sally.

Take it where? Sally had no idea. They walked on down the hall, *click, click, click.*

# CHAPTER 15

# VICTIMS AND STRANGERS

DICKIE WAS RIGHT. THERE were things Sally had to do, and there was absolutely nothing she could do for Charlie Preston at the moment. So she decided she might as well get her head out of her ass and spend some quiet time at her office. No one would bother her on a Sunday.

Her office was a mess. The place was a rebuke, stuffed with unread journals, unanswered mail, ungraded papers. She sighed. She had become one of those procrastinating professors she'd despised in graduate school. Worse yet, she couldn't bring herself to tackle any of the usual tasks.

So she cleaned. Threw out ancient mail. Dithered. Made a pot of coffee. Turned on her computer and read her online horoscope. Took a look at the *New York Times*.

Email.

Happily, the computer in her office hadn't caught the virus when she'd opened the attachment that had fried her home computer. The bad news was that she had forty new messages in her already out-of-control inbox.

One of which was from a sender she didn't recognize, titled "More Family Photos."

So much for the day job. She'd had to consider the likelihood that somebody was stalking her, but she'd tried to keep her mind away from the subject.

Sally called the cops.

An hour later, Scotty Atkins was sitting in the dilapidated easy chair, and the IT detective was running diagnostics on her machine. Sally had dragged the desk she kept in the hall into the office so she'd have a place to sit.

"Hmph," said Scotty. "I realize I haven't been here before. This is a pretty shitty office for the head of a big research center."

She didn't really feel like jousting with him. "It's cozy," said Sally. "And I kind of like it. It makes me feel like Jo March, scribbling in the garret."

"Who's Jo March?" Scotty asked.

"You've never read *Little Women*?" the IT tech asked, without stopping her clattering at the keyboard.

"The title never grabbed me," said Atkins.

"Was it the 'little' or the 'women'?" Sally asked.

"Your hard disk looks fine." The tech clicked some more keys, sat back a minute and waited. "Okay, now . . . I'm done scanning this message," said the tech. "Looks like it's coming up clean."

"Open it," said Scotty, climbing out of the chair just as Sally extracted herself from the desk. There was an awkward moment as they maneuvered around each other, moving to stand and get a view of the computer screen.

Sally felt like Pandora.

The message read, "Some recent shots."

"Not very revealing," said Scotty.

There were four photo file attachments.

"You're sure those are okay?" Sally asked. "I really don't want to screw up this machine."

"They're not infected," said the tech. "Should I go ahead?"

Scotty and Sally both nodded.

The first two were similar in content. Shots of Sally, Maude, and Aggie, cruising the mall in Fort Collins. The third was a solo shot of Aggie, looking coltish and innocent and gorgeous and very, very vulnerable.

"Fuck all," said Sally.

The fourth was a rather blurrier image. It showed Sally and Dave Haggerty, having dinner at The Bra. They were leaning toward each other. Sally was sipping her drink, listening intently as Haggerty talked. The quality of that photo was poorer than the first three. Sally tried to remember where they'd been sitting, and recalled that they'd had a table by the window. Someone could easily have snapped the picture as they passed by on the street. She hadn't noticed anybody with a camera, but then again, she'd been pretty absorbed in the conversation.

She could feel Scotty glaring at her. "What?" she said.

"Nothing," he answered.

For God's sake, she thought. She'd have enough trouble with Hawk when he got a load of that picture. The last thing she needed was for Scotty Atkins to be getting his bloomers in a bunch over her having some ordinary business-type dinner with a political ally and potential donor to her center.

Ordinary business? Hah.

The tech sent a copies of the message and the attachments to the sheriff's office, then suggested that Sally give them her password so that the sheriff's office could simply access any suspicious files she received electronically. Save time and effort. Sally declined. It might be useful, but she couldn't convince herself that it was a good idea to have cops pawing through her email. Her reaction was a little silly, considering that they'd already done so, and more. Dickie Langham and Scotty Atkins had once had occasion to go through her underwear drawer. But then, it wasn't as if they'd actually seen her modeling silk teddies and lacy nighties. When someone looked at your email, it seemed a lot more like being seen naked.

The tech left. Sally and Scotty spent another hour poring over enlarged images of the photos, along with prints of the first batch Hawk had received. Scotty pressed. Was there anyone she remembered seeing at all the places the pictures had been taken? Anybody at any of the places, taking pictures? If she thought about it a little harder, maybe she'd recall camera flashes?

Somebody had evidently been present, damn near everywhere she'd been recently. But she couldn't conjure up a stranger's face. As for people taking pictures, well, yeah. There'd been several people documenting the Dunwoodie reception, and plenty of people snapping away at the demonstration. What about flashes? She closed her eyes, searched for a visual memory, found nothing. She was by nature a singer and a player and a lover of the music of words. She tended to encounter the world through her ears more than her eyes. If there'd been a strange sound, she'd have remembered, but when it came to the sense of sight, she relied pretty heavily on Hawk, who could spot an English sparrow flittering in a bush a hundred yards away.

She tried hard, dredged up vague images of light changes here and there, but couldn't pin them down. It had to be one of those cell phone cameras. She said as much to Scotty.

"Yeah," he said. "That's a good possibility. So let's try this. Do you remember anybody using a cell phone any of those places?"

They both laughed.

It was an oddly comforting moment.

But there was no comfort in what he said next. "Somebody knows where you're going and what you're doing almost before you do."

It took her a minute to speak. "I'm not so crazy about that," she admitted. "But look on the bright side. All these pictures were taken in public places. Most of them were in crowds. Whoever took them isn't staking out my house, invading my private space."

Scotty inspected the photos. "Nope. Not yet, anyhow. Although you could say that this one"—he indicated the image of Sally and Haggerty, heads together over dinner—"conveys a certain intimacy."

"Or not," said Sally, declining to say more.

"That's none of my business, although if I were you, I'd be a little careful what I said around Mr. Haggerty," said Atkins. "He's a smart guy, with his own agenda. As for the photos, it could be we're looking at a trend, from public to private. The next time our photographer here decides to take a shot of you, or one of your pals, you could be at home, or alone, or both."

"Take a shot?" Sally said. "I'm not sure I like that language."

"It's precise. And yes, I am trying to induce caution here, Sally. It pays to plan for the worst."

She was still staring at the photographs, long after Scotty Atkins had departed.

Sally drank the last of her coffee, trying to unfreeze her brain. She needed a new angle on this thing. She was fighting off despair, trying not to think about Charlie Preston losing it and freaking out in her kitchen, now lying in a hospital bed, in God only knows what kind of shape. Fate preyed on women like Charlie from so many directions—physical violence, emotional abuse, poverty and loneliness and the weight of silence. Victims who got accustomed to their vulnerabilities, who adjusted and in the end, embraced their chains. Or as the hallowed Mary Wollstonecraft had put it, they learned to kiss the rod.

But they weren't entirely powerless, were they? Even the weakest had their weapons. They learned to avoid and manipulate, to undermine and sabotage. The abuser's power wasn't absolute.

Suddenly Sally realized what she'd been ignoring. Charlotte Preston was hardly the only victim in this situation. At least she was alive. That was a lot more than you could say for Bradley Preston.

How much did Sally really know about him? Charlie painted him as a deceitful monster. Delice had testified that she'd had to kick his ass when he'd gotten out of hand in her bar. Dave Haggerty and friends considered him a reactionary cutthroat, although Haggerty had been willing to concede Preston's talent as a lawyer.

Bea Preston considered her late husband a model husband and moral martyr.

And to most people, what was he? A solid citizen. A successful corporate lawyer. A political comer. Maybe it was time to pay a little more attention to Brad himself.

As an advocate for victims of domestic violence, Sally had done her best, and never felt as if it was enough. As a feminist, she'd managed to convince herself that every little thing you did had to count against the grand total. But as a professor, she knew the key to success lay in good research.

For Sally Alder, libraries were second homes. But law libraries were foreign turf. She needed a guide who spoke the language, so she headed straight for the reference desk.

The librarian was patronizing, but efficient. Within five minutes, Sally was seated at a computer terminal. She wanted to know what kinds of cases Brad Preston had taken, whom he'd sued and whom he'd defended, when he'd won and lost, what kinds of judgments he'd gotten. Much of that information wouldn't show up in easily accessible public records—most award judgments happened at the district court level, and those records weren't published. But she might find something in the State Supreme Court files. Cases from those courts, she'd learned, were published.

She found two cases from the last five years in which Bradley Preston had acted as counsel, both times coming in after plaintiffs had won judgments at the district level, and the insurance company had appealed. In the first, he'd represented Mammoth Mutual in what had ultimately turned out to be a strange case involving a sixty-two-year-old Laramie man who'd had a drink or two one cold winter night and slipped on the icy sidewalk in front of the bar, breaking his elbow. The guy had sued the bar owner in hopes of getting the insurance company to cover not only his trip to the ER, but six months of disability, claiming he'd been unable to perform his job as a cattle truck driver while he recovered from his injuries. He'd won, but the insurance company had appealed.

The report of the decision wasn't very revealing. So Sally ran a search on LexisNexis, found a couple of newspaper articles about the case. Brad had managed to prove that the plaintiff was a drunkard who had repeatedly hurt himself falling down outside bars, that he'd collected on at least one previous slip-and-fall injury, and that he'd evidently been well enough, only two months after the accident, to win a vacation for two to Branson, Missouri, in a horseshoe pitching contest sponsored by a bar two doors down from the one he was suing!

Sally had to laugh.

But the second case wasn't a laughing matter. A ten-year-old child had been brought into a hospital emergency room in Jackson Hole. The parents said they'd taken her skiing, and that she'd fallen off the chairlift. She had three crushed vertebrae, and the doctors had told the mother and father that their daughter might not walk again.

The parents didn't like that. They'd insisted on having her airlifted to a Denver hospital. When the news there wasn't any better, they'd sued the ski resort and the hospitals and everyone else, including the helicopter pilot, for negligence and malpractice. They alleged that the resort had inadequate safety on the ski lift, that the Jackson Hole doctors hadn't performed standard diagnostic and emergency procedures, and that the delay in proper treatment had been nearly fatal for their daughter, now confined to a wheelchair and in unbelievable pain.

The district court found for the plaintiffs, to the tune of three million dollars, including the pain and suffering. The hospital had appealed. Sally ran another Lexis search and found a *Denver Post* newspaper piece about the case, headlined "Defendants Bring in Big Gun in Paralyzed Child Case." Evidently dissatisfied with the attorney who'd lost the first round, the hospital and its insurance company, once again Mammoth Mutual, had brought in Brad Preston as head of their legal team.

Court decisions, written in legalese, weren't intended to be page-turners, in any case, but by the time she'd finally read the

Supreme Court decision, she realized that the court records weren't going to give her much. The Wyoming Supreme Court had heard the appeal, overturned the ruling for the plaintiff, and remanded the matter back to the district court. The judge who'd written the opinion didn't say much, but it took him thousands of words anyway. Sally found herself nodding off ten minutes into reading his decision. But she was a determined reader, and after all, a historian. She'd written a master's thesis, a dissertation, any number of books. If you wanted to find out anything interesting, you had to cultivate a taste for the boring. She pinched herself awake again and again, determined to slog through the decision before she indulged herself by searching for the newspaper coverage she was sure there must have been.

Lexis and Google searches turned up a raft of articles about the case. Brad had won the second trial by introducing new evidence, turning on two points. First, the kid had gotten the best possible treatment at each hospital, and the parents had been given very clear information at every turn. There was, in short, no negligence, no malpractice, nothing but professional, responsible care.

Second, Bradley Preston had convinced the judge that not only were the parents not being victimized by the doctors and hospitals, they were essentially evil people who ought to be facing criminal charges. Brad had been able to convince the judge that the victim had not sustained an accidental fall from the chairlift at all. There was reason to believe that the child might have been pushed by her mother, sitting next to her.

Jesus Christ.

The parents, it turned out, were the kind of people who made a habit out of living on what Sally's father used to call "if-come." They'd been playing the float on their credit cards, spinning out lines of credit on their home equity, paying a little on this debt, a little on that, for years. Their Cherry Hills mansion, their country club memberships, their Beamers and time-shares in Maui and Nantucket were leveraged to the eyeballs. They'd been desperate. And desolate. And the daughter had been adopted.

People sucked.

"Some people do," said Hawk, when she told him what she'd learned. "Not everybody. Not me or you. And from what you're telling me, it looks like even Bad Brad had at least one good point. Sure, he probably spent most of his time defending corporate greedheads, and from what we know from Charlie, he was a bastard and a brute of a father. But he didn't like fraud. He was relentless about tracking it down. You've got to admire that, in a way."

"I guess so. But it throws me. This guy's one big seething kettle of contradictions. How could he treat his own daughter the way he did, and then go out and tell the *Rocky Mountain News* that he'd felt he had to get to the bottom of what had happened to the kid in the case because 'sometimes, parents aren't very parental'?"

"Maybe it was guilt," said Hawk. "It's not impossible. He might have been trying to make up for all the terrible things he'd done in private by crusading in public. And it's not like his private behavior was all that consistent either. This was a guy who got out of control with his kid, then wept and moaned and bought her a sports car. He was all over the map."

Who wasn't? Nobody was only one thing. Everybody on the great green planet Earth had complicated feelings, secret urges, sudden desires to do something wrong or make everything right. Which meant that however much you might want to trust somebody, you were better off maintaining at least a grain of suspicion. It was the only way not to get hurt.

A person like Charlie Preston had plenty of cause to be more than a little defensive and cynical. The wonder was that she trusted anyone at all. She'd reached out to Aggie Stark, and to Billy. What did they have in common, Sally wondered, beside being kids? One seemed secure, well loved, confident. The other was pretty much a lost cause. They'd both accepted Charlie for what she was—that must be a big factor. But was there something else? Some hidden affinity? Some darker congruence?

Sally looked at Hawk. She'd never known anyone better. Nobody knew her better. And yet, she didn't tell him everything, didn't give him access to her whole soul. She'd never mentioned the buzz that she sometimes felt between Scotty Atkins and her, for example. And she was certainly giving him very skimpy information about her encounters with Dave Haggerty. She didn't want to wonder why.

Hawk was the straightest shooter she knew, but could she ever know him completely? What might he be hiding from her? The thought was disturbing. And arousing.

She looked at him again. What was he thinking? He reached across the kitchen table and took her hand. "Let's eat," he said. "I'm starving."

## CHAPTER 16

# MAKING A KILLING

"MONEY," SAID EDNA MCCAFFREY when she called at eight the next morning.

"Money's good," Sally said, yawning. She and Hawk had enjoyed a long, interesting night.

"More money's better," said Edna. "How's the donor cultivation going?"

Sally took the phone away from her ear, stared at the receiver. "Don't you ever think about anything else?" she asked.

"Nope," said Edna. "We live in the era of privatization, girl-friend. We used to pay for public education through taxes. Now we cut taxes so the rich can keep all their obscene profits, beg them to think of a basic service as a 'giving opportunity,' and then have to slobber all over them when they throw us a bone. The provost wants me to start selling classrooms as naming opportunities."

"Where will it end?" asked Sally. "Am I going to be writing on blackboards with the Rockefeller Memorial Chalk?"

"How about the Haggerty Reading Room of the Dunwoodie Building?" Edna replied.

Sally skirted the question. "I've been a little preoccupied."

"So I hear," said Edna. "You need some stress relief. Come to my yoga class this afternoon. The teacher's a genius."

Classic Edna move: an order in the form of an invitation. But she and Edna could have a nice glass of pinot noir after. "What time and where?" Sally asked.

Edna's yoga studio turned out to be in a strip mall on the eastern edge of town. The parking lot was full of gleaming SUVs and European sedans, disgorging well-preserved middle-aged people wearing spandex pants, carrying rolled-up neoprene mats and plastic water bottles. Edna met her at the door, carrying her own mat and a spare. She flashed a plastic ID card at an attendant, who scanned the card and pressed a button releasing the lock on an electronic gate. Edna pushed through, and they headed for the yoga room. Sally reflected on the quantity of petrochemicals and fossil energy and techno-gadgetry required to fuel Americans' desire to seek life on a higher plane than crass materialism afforded. Fill 'er up, bodhisattva.

They got to the door of the studio. There were dozens of pairs of shoes lined up outside. Edna slipped off her Cole Haans, setting them neatly against the wall by the door. Sally followed suit with her skanky old Rockport clogs. Looked like lots of people had discovered the genius of Edna's yoga teacher. Inside the room, the mats were lined up and jammed in so tightly, Sally bet the yogis and yoginis risked punching each other in the mouth every time they opened up for sun salutes. Nirvana on the assembly line.

Sally wondered where the hell she and Edna were going to squeeze in, but some yoga friend of Edna's beckoned them over, in a show of spiritual generosity, and then proceeded to harangue the people around her until they each moved an inch and a half, making room, just barely, for two more people on two more mats. Sally heard some grumbling, but most of them simply shifted and went back to their warm-up lunges and bends and downward-facing-dog poses. Sally was a little surprised to discover that, instead of giving themselves over to deep breathing, getting into the yoga groove, a lot of them were gossiping madly as they twisted and stretched.

"She's just furious," said the woman next to Sally, decked out in flared gray pants and a red halter top silkscreened with a color picture of Ganesh, the Hindu elephant god. "She bought that house and spent the next six months pouring money into fixing it up—you know the neighborhood. Right near the university, big old Victorians mixed right in with crummy little cottages and ranch houses and brick bungalows. Doesn't matter what. Some of them are in pretty bad shape, some of them chopped up into apartments, but people are snapping them up and the values are shooting through the roof. I just sold a place there for three-fifty."

Three hundred and fifty thousand dollars? In Laramie? What was it, the Taj fucking Mahal of Albany County?

"Yeah. That property around UW is really heating up. A client of mine got in just in time. Bought a shitty little clapboard bungalow on a funny-shaped lot around Fourteenth and Custer, gonna tear it down," said her neighbor, a woman with striking silver hair, talking very nearly to her own knees as she folded herself in three pieces. "Wants to build something about five thousand square feet. It'll fill up the lot, but she doesn't care. She's thinking Spanish medieval—wrought iron, tile roof, turrets, all that crap. She's used up three architects."

Yoga and real estate? Where did they think they were, California?

"There's a hell of a lot of money to be made just flipping the property," said the woman in the Ganesh halter. "But you've gotta be there when it's happening. It's like . . ." She darted a glance at Sally, who got very busy contemplating her navel. "The woman I was telling you about," she continued. "She gets this place all fixed up, and then her next-door neighbor goes and dies, and the son rents it to a bunch of students—students! With a twelve-month lease! So now here she is, sitting in her gazillion-dollar remodel, next to a rental unit with cars parked on the front lawn and rap music blasting out of the windows. They're building a huge pyramid of beer cans on the front porch, which is strange, she says, because what do they need with cans? They keep a keg out there on a permanent basis, so that all their pals can stop by and party any time. It's like living on the banks of Beer River."

"Can't she get them kicked out as a nuisance or something?" said the silver-haired woman.

"The landlord won't cooperate. Says they're paying the rent, and college kids have to live somewhere, and after all, they've got a right to a little fun. Says it's his property, and he'll do with it what he damn well pleases. But he said he'd try to get them to turn down the music, or whatever you call that stuff. I think he's broke and needs the rent money."

"That's so irresponsible," said her friend.

Yeah. Really irresponsible to be broke, thought Sally. And to offer students a place to live near school, maintaining the illusion that it actually might be a *college* neighborhood. All those frivolous and unsightly people, screwing up property values for the upright classes. It was a travesty.

"What can you do?" said the Ganesh woman. "She's not pushing it for now."

"She might as well back off," said silver hair. "Everybody with any cash to spare is trying to get in now anyway. In the next few years, those neighborhoods will be so overpriced, owners like the guy next door will be cashing out before they go bankrupt trying to pay the property taxes. The renters will be forced out. You've got to take the long view." She lay on her back, cradling her knees, rocking slightly and slowing down her breathing.

And where would the renters go? Would students have to start commuting from West Laramie, or maybe Cheyenne? The whole thing chapped Sally's butt. She'd moved to Laramie from L.A. precisely because it was a sweet little college town, an ideal place to get away from runaway greed and class warfare. Wyoming had its own problems, of course (livid rednecks, despoilers of desert and mountain), but at least they were homegrown. The old Gem City looked like it was about to get seriously Californicated.

"Let's get started," said a gorgeous, blue-eyed woman, standing on a mat at the front of the room, smiling very slightly.

It was probably horrible karma to start out a yoga session in a snit, but to Sally's amazement, her rotten mood didn't last long. An hour and a half later, she'd been put through the Triangle and the Warrior, prepared for the Pigeon, balanced on one foot with her arms in a knot, stood on her head, and spent a restorative ten minutes flat on her back in Corpse Pose. She'd gotten a hell of a lot more of a workout than she'd expected. By tomorrow, she'd be slamming ibuprofen and finding aches in muscles she hadn't known she had. But at this moment, she felt loose, strong, and completely blissed out. Edna was right—the teacher was a genius. Sally thought about getting some spandex clothes in Hindu god prints.

And then, to her amazement, the Realtors took up right where they'd left off as they rolled up their mats.

"Listen," said Ganesh woman. "I'm going to call you this afternoon about a property on Fetterman that may be available next month. There were renters, but they've gotten them out. It's a little run-down, but great location." She was about to continue when she noticed Sally. "We'll talk about it later," she said to her friend, tossing a glance in Sally's direction. Both women glared at her.

Annoyance turned to curiosity. Sally began to wonder about the eviction she'd witnessed. She didn't doubt that Billy Reno and company weren't the world's tidiest tenants. But maybe there was more to their getting kicked out than too much carousing in the place. Sally recalled group houses from her college days, where shifting crowds of people had come and gone for months and there'd been a pretty much constant party going on the whole time. Those places hadn't exactly been candidates for photo spreads in *Architectural Digest,* but the landlords had been content to collect the rent. She wondered who owned the place Billy'd vacated. A place, she recalled, with Charlie Preston's name on the lease.

What kind of landlord would rent to a basket case like Charlie Preston?

"How about a glass of wine?" asked Edna, still buzzing with relaxation. "I'd even feed you if you want. Call Professor Green and see if he's free too."

And so they ended up at Edna's, feasting on pasta puttanesca and Chianti. Edna and her husband, Tom, lived in the heart of the campus neighborhood, in a gracious two-story house full of Pueblo pottery, Navajo rugs, and Nepalese metalwork, reflecting Edna's years as a world-class field anthropologist. Edna told herself that it wasn't worth being a university bureaucrat unless you took advantage of the summer vacations. But her idea of a vacation was to go someplace remote and try to communicate with people who'd just as soon be left alone. The amazing thing was that often as not, the people Edna invaded ended up liking her. Sally bet she didn't let up until she'd wrapped everybody in the village around her little finger. Or perhaps compromised them beyond hope.

Probably some of both. The woman was plain relentless. "Have you got your hand in Dave Haggerty's pocket yet?" Edna asked Sally.

Sally nearly spit Chianti all over Edna's white linen tablecloth. Hawk cocked an eyebrow.

"Nope," said Sally. "It's not a good time. He's got a tough client."

"So I hear," said Edna. "Some little crackhead criminal who may have murdered Brad Preston. It's a damn shame about the daughter," she added. "I hear she's in really bad shape."

"Yeah," said Sally. "I went down to the hospital to try to see her this morning, but the nurse told me that only family were allowed to visit."

"Probably just as well," said Edna. "Look—I know you're worried about her, but there's nothing you can do. If she did have something to do with the murder, you're just going to have to accept it. And if she didn't, the police will take care of things. Give yourself a break and focus on what you *can* do," she advised.

"Like raising money," said Sally, forcing a grin. Time to change the subject—sort of. "Or maybe scouting a building Dave Haggerty can buy me for my center." Subtlety time. "Speaking of which, what in hell's going on with real estate in this part of town?"

"Great investment," said Tom, around a mouthful of puttanesca. "Even that itty-bitty house of yours has probably doubled in value since you bought it, Green."

"I'm a born real estate speculator," said Hawk.

"It doesn't make sense," said Sally. "I mean, it's not like Laramie's population is growing, or there's some big corporation moving in and setting off a boom. Why would property values be going up so fast?"

"Gentrification," said Edna.

"You mean, low interest rates on loans, and a few really rich doctors and lawyers wanting really big houses, willing to pay way too much, and suddenly everybody's scrambling for bigger loans, and pretty soon there's a bubble."

"And don't forget the trees," said Tom. "Some of them want big ugly mega-houses out on the bald prairie, but they'll pay a lot more down here in the tree district, where there's some shelter and some shade."

"And alleys," said Edna. "They like the alley access. This is Wyoming. If you've got an alley behind the house, you can pull your pickup right back behind the place, and leave the garage for the SUV and the front driveway for the snob car."

"Of course there's the reverse snobbery where you park the sporty model out back and leave the pickup out front so people will think you're a regular guy. That's a Wyoming move too," said Tom, who liked cars a lot. "That's what I do with my Alfa."

"Darling," said Edna, "you'll admit that you park the Alfa out back because you think there's less of a chance it'll be stolen. Which would be amazing in any case, given the alarm you've got on that thing. I swear, when it goes off, you can hear it in Colorado."

Sally took a sip of wine. Blackberries exploded on her tongue. "Is it possible," she wondered, "that just a few people could be driving up prices? I mean, a few investors with deep pockets, flipping properties until they've got enough to get out, and watch the bubble burst?"

"I've wondered the same thing," said Edna, "because if there is, we ought to be hitting them up, big-time. If they're making a killing on the university neighborhood, it seems only fair and proper that they'd give a little back to keep the mother ship sailing along."

Alleys and sports cars and real estate bubbles and making a killing. Now Sally's head was humming, and it wasn't just the yoga and the wine. "Maybe I'll do a little research," she said. "See who's doing deals and all."

"The college development office would know," said Edna.

"I think I've got a better source," said Sally.

Which was how Sally and Hawk ended up on the late shift at the Wrangler, sitting at the bar sipping club soda and waiting for Delice to finish reaming out a cocktail waitress for slipping too many free drinks to her sorry-ass deadbeat friends.

"This is her last chance," said Delice, glaring at the girl, who slunk away to tend to her tables. "I don't mind the occasional Budweiser for the boyfriend, but six double Chivases and a Baileys Irish Cream goes beyond my limit. Plus I'm not crazy about that fucking navel ring. But the cowboys seem to love it, so what am I supposed to do?" The bartender brought her a shot of tequila, a salt shaker, and a slice of lime. Delice licked her hand, shook salt on it, licked again, downed the shot, and bit into the lime. "What's up?" she asked, ritual over.

"Maybe we should go to a table," said Sally. "A little discretion."

"As long as we sit where I can keep an eye on things," said Delice. "I don't like the look of those guys who just sat down. They'll probably be okay, but then, they're more likely to behave themselves if I put the evil eye on them."

As they wove their way toward a table in the middle of the room, Delice made a pistol with her thumb and forefinger and pointed it at the young men she'd indicated, grinning as she passed by. Four guys with shaved heads, wearing football jerseys. They pretended to ignore her. Sally thought one of them looked familiar, but she couldn't place him. Then again, there seemed to be a whole lot of shaved-head punks in Laramie these days. Hell, half the male students on campus had gone in for the cue-ball look.

"Let's talk about real estate," said Sally as they sat down.

"You'd be better off talking to my sister-in-law," said Delice. "Or to Sam Branch."

Sally'd had plenty of conversations with the Realtors in question over the years. "I'm not in the mood to take their shit."

"I'm flattered that you're willing to take mine," said Delice.

Sally pressed on. "Property values in the U. area are blowing up."

Delice nodded. "And with interest rates the way they are, you can really make out. I just refinanced my house, and you wouldn't believe what it appraised for. Why? Are you thinking of getting a real job and making some actual money?" she asked.

"Sally? A real job? Not while they still pay people to pontificate," said Hawk.

"Speak for yourself," Sally answered. "Seriously, Dee, about those house prices. Do you know if there's somebody around town who's got the bucks to speculate in Laramie real estate?"

Delice thought about it. "A few businesspeople, a handful of doctors and lawyers—that's about it. I know a few people in town who've done pretty well in the stock market, but it's not like we're Denver, and there are people who own oil companies or microchip plants or big banks. Somebody local could have been squirreling money away for a while, and then started buying up property in a big way. But you'd have to have found some way to make a bunch of money without anybody in town noticing. And I'd have noticed, believe me."

"Which is precisely why I'm asking you," said Sally. "So do you think it's somebody from out of town? Some smart operator looking to play with his money in a sandbox nobody else had noticed yet?"

"Could be," said Delice. "But it'd probably be somebody with local connections. Otherwise, why bother? We're too far away from anywhere, the weather's too shitty, and we're just plain too insignificant for anybody to bother with, unless they have some reason for actually wanting to be here. Which suggests to me that it's somebody who lives here."

Sally's mind struggled through sludge, not quite fixing on a buried thought. Somebody who lives here. Somebody with a stake in the community. Somebody who'd made a bundle, and was now looking to make a real killing.

# CHAPTER 17

# MAY DAY

MAY DAY. TIME TO gather the blossoms of the field, festoon the big pole with streamers, put on the dancin' shoes.

Also the Workers' Holiday, the People's Holiday. Sally had an old friend, a sixties leftie turned Realtor, who'd sent her a card last year, a bright red square printed with the message "It's May Day. Time to think about private property."

After weeks of blustery winds, scudding clouds building into afternoon hailstorms, cold, thin sunlight at dawn and shivering silver dusk, isolated days of balmy false promise, the weather turned. Crocuses poked their heads up. Daffodils ventured out timid blooms, nodded their yellow heads with growing confidence. Irises and tulips speared forth, lilac bushes budded out. In all likelihood, there'd be one more monster snowstorm, but for now, Sally stretched in the sunlight, shook out her legs, and welcomed the first morning in months she'd run without gloves and a hat.

She needed thinking music, so she'd chosen jazzy guitar/bass duets by Hot Tuna and set off at a lope, seeing the familiar street scenes, the very houses along her route in an entirely new light.

Here, somebody was adding on a second story, with vaulted ceilings and custom wood windows out the wazoo. There, workers were hauling plumbing pipes and fixtures, a china sink, a porcelain toilet, into what had once been a detached garage, now being transformed into a luxury cottage for the proverbial mother-in-law. And there . . . something else again. A huge Victorian with peeling yellow paint, gravel driveway packed with a VW van painted with clouds and graffiti, a superannuated Buick Century with a broken taillight, flying the Jolly Roger from its radio antenna, and a light pickup sporting a "Go Pokes" bumper sticker; two motorcycles parked on the front lawn. On the huge, inviting front porch, someone was huddled in a sleeping bag on a dilapidated couch. An empty Southern Comfort bottle lay on its side, halfway down the front steps.

A mud-spattered brown Chevy Suburban with University of Wyoming logos painted on the front doors sat at the curb. Sally sidled up to the passenger side, peered in at the front seat. A sweat-stained feed cap with a "King Ropes" logo lay on the bench seat. In the plastic slot on the inside of the driver's door, someone had stuck a curve-headed rock hammer and a yellow-backed waterproof notebook, the kind geologists used so they could take notes on rainy days in the field.

She glanced back at the porch, and now she noticed a pair of crusty boots sitting on the deck next to the sleeping bag–shrouded figure on the couch. The mud job on the boots matched the one on the Suburban. Hmm.

And something else caught her eye. A "For Sale" sign in the middle of the lawn. Sally mentally noted the name and phone number of the listing Realtor, then spent the rest of her run reciting the phone number to herself, over and over, until it had become the lyrics to the Hot Tuna instrumental jam. She kept up the repetition, even as she decided to take a detour past the apartment that had once housed Billy Reno and his roommates. She was not at all surprised to see a "Sold" sign out front.

The minute she got home, she wrote the real estate agent's number down, did a few stretches, and then picked up the phone. "I'd like some information on a house for sale at Tenth and Kearny," she began.

"Oh yes, that's a fantastic property," said the Realtor, who'd answered the call herself. "I could meet you there in an hour and a half. I've got another appointment right now, but if you're interested, you're going to want to move fast. You understand, of course, that the place has been a student rental, so it's going to need some updating and a touch of TLC."

Which was supposed to stand for "tender loving care," but in this case, Sally suspected, probably meant "tremendous load of cash."

Think fast, Mustang. "Um, actually, I can't make it this morning. But for now, could you just tell me about the place?"

"Five bedrooms, one and a half baths, farmhouse kitchen, detached two-car garage. The tenants have a lease until August 1, but we could get them out sooner if absolutely necessary. We're listing it at three-seventy-five, and if you move quickly, you can probably get it for that. But once there's a bid in, a war could start."

Real estate war? Sally swallowed. "That sounds like a lot, frankly. I mean, there'd be plenty of expense just repairing what the tenants have broken. Not to mention putting in another bath, updating the kitchen and appliances, paint, landscaping . . ."

She was taxing the agent's patience, and she knew it. "Look, it's entirely up to you. I'd be delighted to show you the place, if you're really interested." Sally was beginning to think "interested" was a code word for "rich enough."

"But to be honest, for this neighborhood, you're looking at a seller's market. My most recent listing sold the day it went on the market. Either you jump on what you want, or it's gone. And as far as this property goes, the owner is in a position to demand the asking price, or more."

In a position? Meaning, again, "rich enough"?

Might as well go for it. "So who does own the place?" Sally

asked, knowing that Realtors really weren't supposed to divulge that kind of thing, but what the hell.

"Sorry," said the Realtor. "I'm getting a call on my other line." She hung up.

Sally called the development office at the university. "This is Professor Sally Alder," she said.

"Oh yes, Dr. Alder. One moment, please."

The receptionist connected her with a development officer, a man Sally had met several times socially, and once for a business lunch at which they'd agreed that nothing mattered more than having a first-rate university. It wasn't the greatest deep-thinking moment of her life, or for that matter, his, probably, but he'd seemed like a nice, intelligent guy.

"Ted," she said, "have you heard about somebody snapping up a lot of real estate near campus lately?"

"I put down a bid on a house on Custer," he said. "Asking price. They came back later and said somebody had offered twenty K more. And then I heard they'd turned right around and sold the place for fifty more. It's obscene. And of course, whoever has the bucks to do that kind of stuff ought to be giving giving giving to their friendly neighborhood institution of higher learning. But are they? Nooooo. We can't even find out who it is."

"Really? Why not?" Sally asked. "I'd have thought you guys would have a line on every dollar in this town."

"Maybe that was possible ten years ago," said Ted. "But it's a new world. One of our attorneys did a title search on some of the properties that have changed hands in the last six months, and you know what? About a dozen houses in this town have been bought and sold at least twice during that period, with big price jumps. In every case, the first buyer, second seller turned out to be a corporate blind with offices in Longmont, Colorado. When you call them up, you get an answering machine."

"What's the name of the outfit?" Sally asked.

"Just letters. WWJS. Probably the last initials of the partners or something. We're still pursuing it, but in the meantime, we're focusing on the people who're ending up with the places. We have this foolish idea that they might actually be planning to live in the houses, and they've all shelled out a big chunk of change, which suggests to us that they might want to show us some love. Frankly, we don't see it as all that fruitful to go chasing after some money-grubbing Coloradans who've probably got about as much interest in Laramie as a community as they do in saving the whales."

Did anybody care about the whales anymore? What about saving the students, or at least their chance of living in something remotely resembling a campus neighborhood? Sally thanked the development guy, then hung up.

Hawk came into the kitchen, damp from his post-basketball shower.

"Who do you know who drinks Southern Comfort?" she asked him.

He made a face. "Students," he said. "They'll drink anything."

"Okay," she said, "let me narrow it down. Who do you know who drinks rotgut and might have checked out a university truck yesterday?"

"That doesn't narrow it down much," said Hawk. "But it's easy enough to find out. Why? Have you joined Professors Against Drunk Driving of University Vehicles?"

"No. But tell me what you think of this," Sally said, and related what she'd seen on her run.

"I don't get it. What's your point?" Hawk asked.

"Think about that eviction I saw," said Sally. "Consider the fact that Charlie Preston's name was on that lease. I mean, the slum-lords probably make more money evicting deadbeat tenants than they do renting to them, but still. She was barely of age, she had a long history of mental illness and run-ins with the law, she was a mass of facial piercings and, not to put too fine a point on it, she's a *girl*. Who the hell would rent to her?"

Hawk thought about it. "Somebody real stupid, somebody real cynical, or somebody who knew her and thought they were doing her a favor."

"My theory," said Sally, "is that the somebody was her father. Try this out. Let's say he owned some rental property, and she knew it. Her boyfriend needed a place to live. In one of their make-up moments, maybe she told Daddy she'd come back home if he'd rent sweet misunderstood Billy an apartment, and he said he couldn't take the risk, and she talked him into it somehow by offering to sign the lease herself."

Hawk was following closely.

"Then things went to hell between them as they always did, and Brad ended up deciding to kick them out. Maybe he was watching the market and figured it was time to sell anyhow. It took the rental management company a few days to get around to actually evicting them, and in the middle of all that, somebody got pissed off," Sally finished.

"Pissed enough to beat him to death?" Hawk asked.

"I don't know. There I lose the thread," said Sally. "But as I told you, I ran by that place, and it's been sold. I really want to know who's buying and selling these party houses. I've hit kind of a dead end with the real estate side, so maybe it's time to start talking to the tenants. Maybe make a few subtle inquiries with our students."

"Yeah. You specialize in subtlety, I've noticed," said Hawk.

"I can be subtle when I need to! But why not? Maybe there'll even be somebody who could tell us more about Charlie's situation. Anybody who parties a lot in this town probably gets around to all the usual places," Sally said.

Hawk gave in. "I can drop by the motor pool this morning and see who signed out a van. And then I'll go talk to the guy."

"Call me. I'll come with you."

"Sally," said Hawk, "let me handle this one thing. For all I know, it's one of my own students. And if it is, and he's been drinking and driving in a university truck, we'd surely have to have a few words. One way or another, I can check it out, maybe work the conversation around to the party scene, see what I can dig up. For once, I can give you some cover."

She grinned at him. "I really like it when you give me cover."

Meanwhile, she'd practice patience.

It was a beautiful Friday morning, not a teaching day. She had, remarkably, no meetings, no appointments until the afternoon. She futzed in their little garden, planting lettuce and spinach and beans and peas, things that would survive cool days and cold nights and be lush and delightful by the end of June. She fiddled with her next lecture for women's history, took care of lagging correspondence, deleted a couple of hundred outdated emails. By then it was time for lunch, and she decided she'd just mosey over to Hawk's office on the way to her own. Just, she told herself, to see whether he felt like grabbing a bite.

To get to Hawk's office, you had to navigate the wonderful old geology building, a mazelike cabinet of curiosities. The hallways were lined with display cases full of rocks and maps and scale models of oil wells, and, of course, photographs of windburned, hearty geologists grinning their heads off in scenic places. Hawk's office was around about fifty corners, and she'd been known to lose her way.

". . . budget crunch time, son," she heard him say as she came around the last corner and spotted him sitting at his desk, addressing a young man who looked very much as if he'd been ridden hard and put up wet. "If you had a mishap with that truck, how long do you think it'd be before the university had the bucks for another one? In case you've forgotten, you checked out that van to do a little something we call fieldwork. We can't be put in the position of getting jerked around when we need vehicles, and trust me, they'd hold it against us at the motor pool if one of our drivers was irresponsible enough to screw up one of their trucks. Am I getting through to you, Mike?"

The guy looked absolutely miserable, and not just because Hawk was tearing him a new one. His jeans were muddy, his boots a mess, and he appeared not to have combed his lank, shoulder-length hair in a week. He slouched so low in the chair, he seemed in danger of sliding right out of it and onto the floor. His eyes were slitted nearly closed, and he was working his mouth in a way that made her suspect he was badly in need of a toothbrush.

"I'm really sorry, Dr. Green," he finally managed. "I know what you think. But I didn't drive drunk, I swear it. I was out in the field all day yesterday, and on my way back to the motor pool when a friend called up and asked me over for a beer. Uh, well, you know how it is. Sometimes you have one beer, and sometimes you have two . . ."

"And sometimes," said Hawk, "you have six. And a couple-three shots of tequila, maybe, or was it Southern Comfort?"

The kid groaned softly.

Hawk looked sympathetic. Sally felt the same way. It wasn't as if they were unfamiliar with the feeling of having nails pounded into your skull. And it wasn't as if it hadn't taken them both years to learn that you could avoid that unpleasant sensation merely by, well, not drinking until you lost the use of one or more senses.

"Well, at least you showed good judgment in not driving after you'd started drinking," Hawk conceded. "But you're sixteen hours late turning in the truck. You're my frigging student, not to mention the fact that I need you as a field trip driver. You're a candidate for the doctorate in earth sciences, a grown man. What, may I ask, were you thinking?"

"I dunno. I'm a jerk. I have no self-control. It wasn't supposed to be a party, but you know how these things go. First it was just a few of us sitting around. Then somebody started taking up a collection to get a keg. Then everybody started making calls, and more people started coming around, and the next thing I knew, the cops showed up and busted a bunch of kids for MIP. People were screamin' out of there, tryin' to get away before they got popped."

"MIP? What's that?" Sally asked, deciding she'd lurked in the hallway long enough.

"Minor in possession," said Hawk. "So it wasn't just grad students, or even college kids?"

"Not hardly. Some of those chicks looked like they were still suckin' on pacifiers," said Mike.

Sally frowned. "How old would you say the youngest are?" she asked.

"I don't hang with them. I'm not interested in jailbait," the boy answered. "But lots of guys are. And they're not asking for IDs, if you know what I mean," he finished.

"I bet that's a big reason the cops show up," said Sally. "Sounds like a perfect setting for date rape."

Mike shook his head. "I'd hate to say what I've seen on a couple of occasions."

"Have you been to a lot of these parties?" Sally continued.

Mike shrugged. "A few. Fewer and fewer. After last night, never again."

She laughed and asked him if he'd ever been at a party at the building where she'd watched the eviction.

He scrubbed his face with his hands. "Who hasn't? That place was notorious. Of course, they were only there a couple of months, but by the time they got booted, they'd acquired, uh, a reputation."

"But that'd hardly be your crowd, Mike," said Hawk. "You're a fine upstanding student in an advanced degree program. You're a scientist, for chrissake. What the hell are you doing hanging around with a bunch of little thugs and thieves whose idea of upward mobility is bigger bling-bling?"

"Not that I'd know anything about it," said Sally, "but I'm guessing somebody in that household might have been dealing some weed."

Mike looked uncomfortable.

"Look," said Hawk, "I don't give a damn if you smoke a splif every night before the evening news. I don't actually care if you wake up every morning and fire up a big one. But if there's somebody at that house selling dope to little kids, that's another story. A really bad one."

The boy squirmed in his chair.

"What'd you see, Mike?" Sally asked.

He bit his lip. Rubbed his face some more. Made his decision.

"Okay. Remember I said I'd seen some things I wasn't crazy about? Well, I was there exactly once. I was just stopping off to, uh, I mean, stopping off with this friend of mine."

"Uh-huh," said Hawk. "Everybody's got a friend like that."

"Er, yeah. So, uh, they had a big scene going on when we went to see this guy, just, you know, to purchase a very small amount for personal use, as they say. And when we found him, he was, like, getting all these little chickies baked on this bomber stuff, and his buddies were putting the moves on a couple of them. Shit, those girls looked like they couldn't have been more than fifteen or something. And then one of the housemates comes in, this chick with all this face hardware, and she starts getting all freaked out 'cause she knows one of the little girls. So she ends up hauling off and belting this one guy, and she's, like, screaming that he'd better get the fuck out of the house before she gets his ass thrown in jail. The guy told her to fuck off, and the little kid just sat there staring—I guess she was wasted by then. The girl with the piercings was pretty out of it herself, but she just kept yelling, and then she starts hitting the guy, and finally this other guy came in and pulled her off and grabbed the little girl too and got them both out of there. So, um, yeah. I guess you could say there was some dealing going on."

"How do you know that the girl with the piercings was one of the housemates?" Sally asked.

"She said so. She was all, 'This is my fucking house. And what I say goes.' Like they gave a crap," said Mike.

Charlie Preston. To the rescue. Of at least one young girl. Maybe Aggie Stark.

"Did the dealer live at the house?" Hawk asked. "How about the guys who were hitting on the girls?"

"I don't know. Maybe. I had the impression people were in and out." Now he sat up, leaned over, put his head in his hands. "Fuck. I feel like somebody ran over me. Can I go home and get some sleep?"

# CHAPTER 18

# CREEPING JENNY

BOY, LARAMIE. THE BOOSTERS liked to think of it as an all-American hometown. They weren't wrong. Inside of a month, Sally had encountered domestic violence, murder, drug dealing, runaway real estate speculation. How much more all-American could you get?

And how much more cynical? But that wasn't really her nature. As she made her way home from campus, Sally bounced from cynicism to worry, anguish, and fury. And in the background, all the time, was that pinprick of a feeling that she already knew something that mattered. That, at least, ought to be reassuring. But it wasn't. Recent experience had taught her that knowing something without knowing what it was, or why it mattered, could be a very dangerous thing.

There was a Toyota 4Runner parked in front of her house. Scotty Atkins leaned against the driver's door. He was wearing a salmon-pink polo shirt, khaki Dockers, and his usual poker face. "It's a beautiful day in the neighborhood," he said as she approached. "Let's go for a ride."

She eyed him warily. "Where?" she asked.

"Get in," he said.

Of course, she knew. When they pulled into the alley where she and Hawk had found Bradley Preston, she was not in the least surprised. Scotty Atkins believed that returning to the scene of a crime was a real good way to jog a witness's memory. He didn't give a damn about the feelings of the person he was dragging along. In fact, he wasn't above exploiting strong feelings of all kinds to get answers to questions. And in fairness, why shouldn't he? He was a cop, not a kindergarten teacher.

Scotty pulled the 4Runner to the side of the alley, shut off the motor, got out, and walked to the place they'd found the lug wrench, now trampled down by investigators, at the least, and who knew who else? What could she do but follow?

And now, despite the trembling in her chest, the visceral response to the place she'd seen violent death, she *was* surprised. She didn't feel hysterical or horrified or overwhelmed. Instead, she experienced a weird combination of detachment and passionate curiosity.

Why?

Maybe it was the change of the seasons. The last time she'd stood in that alley, trying very hard not to look at a body, it had been cold and windy. Blowing dust had stung her eyes and lodged grit in her clothes, coated her teeth. Today, by contrast, was a purely gorgeous spring day. There weren't all that many such days in Laramie, and she'd come to treasure them in a manner so bone-deep that such weather, after the long, dark winter, was simply delightful. She could very nearly feel the ice cracking in her chest, the thawing of her heart. She couldn't help it. The return of the sun, the warmth, the green made it impossible not to feel a trickle, then a gush of hope.

Even that trashy alley bore signs of the awakening season. Where brown stalks had crackled and shaken, tufts of patchy green broke the surface. New shoots of a viny plant twined around and sprouted among the garbage can frames. She knew the vine would bloom in early summer, with delicate pink-white trumpet-shaped blossoms. She'd always thought it pretty, even though Hawk told her that the common name for it was "bindweed," and that it was a bane to cattle ranchers and lawn lovers. But she couldn't quite hate the plant. She'd looked it up in the Audubon wildflower guide Hawk had given her, the first Christmas they'd known each other, so very many years ago. And she'd discovered another common name for the vine, one she'd used ever since: creeping Jenny.

Despised and weedy, hardy and stubborn, sending out tentative, defiant, and all too fragile pale flowers. People did what they could to kill it. They yanked it out, sprayed it with poison, cursed and kicked, but here it came again. Creeping Jenny had something in common with Charlie Preston.

Sally thought of Charlie, still, she'd been told, under heavy sedation at Ivinson Memorial. She hoped the girl was half as tough as the creeping vine.

Sally walked up and down the alley, Scotty at her side, pretending he wasn't staring at her, willing her to talk. She wanted to observe and to think. The feeling was familiar to her. Similar emotion came to her every time she sat down in an archive or library amid books and files and boxes of documents. She was preparing herself to search and examine and rearrange facts and impressions, to try to make sense of random things, to construct a convincing explanation.

Detectives and historians had a lot in common, that way. And of course, both were in the business of dealing with the dead.

Most of the backyards bordering the alley were hidden behind wooden fences. Here and there, a loose slat revealed a glimpse of greening lawn, of bedded daffodils, a barbecue grill, a flock of plastic flamingos, a Tuff Shed festooned with antlers. Laramie homeowners, feathering their domestic nests. The fences marked the edge of order and family and prosperity, separated from the utilitarian, dirty public space of the alley.

Well, maybe not all the fences. About halfway down the alley, one homeowner had gone in for chain link instead of wood, the obviously cheap option, revealing a yard that was the picture of neglect. Once there had been a lawn, judging by the presence of a rusting push mower in one corner. But the ground had mostly been reduced to bare dirt, dotted with aged car parts, festooned with cigarette butts and cans and bottles, a couple of rotting tennis shoes tied together and thrown over a carousel clothesline that looked as if it would topple over the next time the wind blew.

The house didn't look so great either. Dirty windows, one cracked and patched with cardboard, flanking a sagging back porch.

The scene made a statement: rental.

"Hey, Scotty," said Sally, "what do you know about Laramie real estate?"

He inspected the barren yard beyond the chain-link fence. "Judging by the state of that lawn, the landlord isn't paying the water bill. Or maybe the tenants are just dead lazy."

"Or maybe there aren't any," Sally said.

He looked at her. "There were when we went to talk to all the neighbors after the murder," he said. "College kids."

"But there's no sign of life here. Let's go around front," said Sally, "and knock on the door."

She watched him wipe momentary annoyance off his face. "I've already talked to these people, Sally. I don't usually knock on a door unless I have a good reason," said Scotty. "In case you hadn't heard, people don't like to have police officers come knocking. Especially kids."

"Fair enough," she said. "Let me try to give you a reason. I've got this theory."

"You and Charles Darwin," said Scotty. "Plenty of people in this town wouldn't give either of you the time of day."

"How about you?" Sally asked.

"I brought you here," he answered.

"Okay. Think about that eviction. Think about the fact that Charlie's name was on the lease. Can you imagine any landlord, or landlady, for that matter, within their right mind, who'd rent to somebody like Charlie?"

"People who become slumlords don't care if the properties they rent are maintained. They just care that somebody's paying the rent," Scotty said. "Did you see that place? It'd take a pretty desperate person to want to rent a hellhole like that. Or somebody so out of it, they wouldn't even expect things like safe electricity, no gas leaks, a toilet that worked."

"That's enough—I don't need the details. But look, Scotty. It's more than that. Lots of renters in this part of town are being kicked out, because property values are exploding. Somebody's manipulating the real estate market. And I've got this theory—"

"You already said that," said Scotty.

"This theory," said Sally, "that maybe Brad Preston was involved. There's a whole lot of money changing hands in this town right now. I can't imagine anybody who'd rent to Charlie, except, maybe, her father. I admit, there are a few loose ends, but what if he was here for reasons having nothing to do with her, but something to do with property?"

"How do you explain the lug wrench?" Scotty asked.

"I don't have this all nailed down," she shot back. "Humor me. Let's see if we can roust a tenant at that place."

No one there. The blinds in the front windows were closed, pulled down to within an inch of the window sash. Sally went to the window closest to the door and peeked in. No furniture. A pile of trash on the floor.

Scotty joined her. "No tenants," he said, "but no 'For Sale' sign either."

"That doesn't mean it hasn't been sold lately," Sally observed, thinking back to the discussion between the yoga Realtors. "Sometimes they do deals before the house is listed for the public. In a hot market like this, I bet that happens a lot. Don't you think it's worth finding out if Brad had some connection to this place?"

Was that a glimmer of grudging admiration in his eyes? If so, it was gone in a second. "I'll check it out," he said.

They walked back around to the alley and got in his truck. But he didn't start the engine. He turned to face her. "I also came by to let you know about those family photos of yours. They were taken with a camera phone."

"How do you know?" asked Sally.

"The quality. Compared to other digital images, they're pretty horrible. That won't be true for long, I'm told, but for now, at least, there's a big difference," Scotty said.

"But they're easy to take," said Sally. "I mean, it's getting to the point where everywhere you go, somebody's taking a picture. Jesus, sometimes I think camera phone pictures could replace writing. I'm pretty much a throwback when it comes to technology. Every other college professor in the country has gone to websites and PowerPoint and all that stuff, or at least overhead transparencies, and I'm still scribbling all over the blackboard. But my students make up for it. Last week I did a lecture on the history of abortion in America, in my women's rights class. I noticed one student pretty much slept through the whole thing, which bugs the shit out of me, naturally. But then, at the end of class, she woke up, took out her cell phone, and took a picture of the blackboard. She can probably Google every term I wrote down, and get enough information to pass a test on the subject."

"Those camera phones can send pictures anywhere in a second," Scotty said.

"I hadn't thought about it," said Sally. "Hawk finally got a digital camera, and he has to plug a chip into the computer in order to send photos to his dad. But you're saying you don't need that extra step with these phones?"

"Nope. And that makes them even more of a problem for us. Whoever took the pictures can just send them out, with messages, from a car, or a gas station, or sitting on a park bench. They're completely mobile. Virtually impossible to track, if they don't want to be found."

Sally frowned. "You'd think, by now, I'd have noticed somebody taking a pictures of me, even with a cell camera. But then again, I guess if they wanted to be sneaky about it, they wouldn't make a big deal of holding out the phone, framing the shot, all that. They'd just act like they were making a call."

"Take another look at the pictures," said Scotty. "They aren't exactly award-winning shots. They're framed all crooked, off center, like that."

"And the photographer's purpose," said Sally, "isn't to make art. It's to let Hawk and me know we're being watched. It's to intimidate us."

"Especially you," said Scotty.

"It works," said Sally, "but it pisses me off too. I mean, whoever it was followed me down to the mall in Fort Collins. I was looking for Charlie, and they know it. They want me to stop trying to help her."

Scotty was silent.

"I guess you know about the drug dealing that was going on at Billy's place," Sally said.

Scotty's eyes narrowed. "How do you know about it?" he asked.

"Let's just say that since I'm a university professor, certain information comes across my path now and then," she replied. "Which one of the tenants was in the business?"

"Which of your students was looking to score?" Scotty asked in turn.

"Somebody who had nothing to do with anything, Scotty. Don't hammer at me for a name—he's not involved. He's just a guy who's trying to stop being a slacker and start being a grown-up, and along the way he happened in on one of the parties at that place. He described the scene to Hawk and me—lots of drink and drugs, predatory older guys, and underage kids there, getting drunk and stoned."

"As your slacker students would say, duh," Scotty said. "Why do you think we bother busting parties? It's not because cops hate fun."

"Right," said Sally. "Take you, for instance. You practically invented fun."

"You'd be surprised," said Scotty, and their gazes met and glanced off each other, and she managed not to let him see her shiver.

"Um. Yeah. So anyway, this guy told us he'd seen Charlie pitch a fit when one of the guys started hitting on some young girls in a very aggressive way. Sounded like Billy dragged her away before she got herself punched or worse," Sally told him.

"You never know," Scotty mused. "Girls who've been treated like shit sometimes respond by leading other girls into bad situations. Sometimes they want to play savior. Sometimes both. They swing back and forth. It's part of the pathology that leads them into trouble. And make no mistake, Sally, Charlotte Preston is in big trouble."

"When hasn't she been?" Sally asked. "Poor Charlie. Even if—when—she comes to her senses, she's way too fucked up to be able to defend herself. It's a good thing she's got a smart lawyer."

Scotty looked at her. "She does?" he asked.

"Yeah. Dave Haggerty's associate. I called him right after they took Charlie to the hospital, and he got in touch with the lawyer. I saw her myself."

"I was at the hospital that afternoon," said Scotty. "I wanted to see if the kid was conscious enough to give us a statement. She wasn't."

"And she shouldn't have, even if she had been," Sally said. "That's what lawyers are for."

"There wasn't any lawyer there," said Scotty. "The only person there was Bea Preston. And she'd given the doctors strict instructions that nobody was to be allowed to see Charlotte. Nobody."

Bad, bad news. "She must have fired the lawyer. I talked to Bea, Scotty. And Charlie too. Those women hate each other. What if Charlie needs to be protected from her?"

Scotty's lips pressed together. He gripped the steering wheel, stared straight ahead, and then looked over at Sally with as much intensity in his icy green eyes as she'd ever seen him display. "We have a deputy at the hospital all the time, and we've let the doctors know we're to be kept informed on the girl's medical condition. When she's able, we'll talk to her. This is a murder investigation, Dr. Alder," he said. "Even somebody who's got a direct line to Jesus can't mess with us."

# CHAPTER 19

# THE RING OF FIRE

HAWK STOOD AT THE kitchen counter, sorting through the day's mail. "There's a message for you on the machine," he said.

"Oh?" she said. "Who was it?"

He began leafing through the new *Mother Jones* magazine, not even bothering to look up as he said, "Dave Haggerty."

"Uh, okay," she said, a flush of embarrassment washing over her face.

And now he did look up, and then said in a very even, very quiet voice, "What's the deal, Sal?"

She met his gaze. "I just saw Scotty Atkins. He said Bea Preston had gotten rid of Charlie's lawyer. It's probably about that."

"I don't think so," he said, looking back down at the magazine, turning a page. "Listen to the message."

"Hawk," she began.

Now he looked at her straight, a furrow of pain between his eyebrows, lips pressed tight. "Later," he said.

Dave Haggerty. He was one for crossing lines. What was on that message? Whatever it was, something had put hurt and distance in her lover's eyes. She could feel Hawk stepping back, withdrawing. The fear of losing him seared through her.

She touched his arm.

"Go listen to your message," he said.

"Don't, Hawk. Don't do this. Dave Haggerty cares about those kids. He's also a potential donor to my center," she said. "Edna's putting on the pressure."

He took a breath. "This isn't about Edna. It isn't a work thing," he told her, putting down the mail and walking to the refrigerator. "I think I'll just have a sandwich for dinner and then go to my office. Got a lot of work to do."

"Hawk," said Sally. "Please. Don't pull away from me. You care about this too."

"Right now, actually, I don't, Sally," he answered. "It's eating you alive, and I can't compete. I don't even want to."

"You don't have to compete," said Sally. "You saw Charlie. For God's sake, you saw Brad Preston's body! Somebody sent those pictures to you. We're both in this."

"And wouldn't it be better, in pretty much every way, to leave this to the cops?"

"It would be easier," Sally admitted. "I'm sorry. I don't know why Dave called."

His eyes bored in on her. "The man's hitting on you, Sally. What are you going to do?"

"Nothing," she said.

"You'd better do something," he told her, opening the fridge and turning his back on her.

She went to the phone and punched up the message.

"Hello, beautiful woman. Dave here." His hypnotic voice. "We've got a problem. I need to see you as soon as you can get away."

Yeah. That crossed the line.

The last time she'd seen that kind of hurt in Hawk's eyes, he'd been standing by her bedroom door, covered with snow. It was the middle of a winter night. And she was naked in bed. With somebody else.

She'd never expected to regain his trust, let alone his love. Years and years had passed before she'd seen him again.

Even a man as sane and strong as Hawk Green had a fragile side. How could she hurt him again?

But what could she do?

She heard the front door slam.

She could call Haggerty back, but she was hardly in the mood.

She could try to find out more about the parties and the drugs. Aggie Stark doubtless knew a lot more than she'd been telling.

The idea of pounding on a fourteen-year-old didn't have much appeal.

She could call Bea Preston and ask why she'd gotten rid of the lawyer. Now there was a really pleasant prospect.

Sally was out of gas.

She poured herself a glass of sauvignon blanc. A big glass. Then she went into the bathroom, opened the tap, dumped in enough lilac bath potion to submerge the entire bathroom in perfumed bubbles. She got a steamy suspense novel and, after a minute, her cell phone. If a long and very indulgent soak didn't make her feel better, she could call Delice and vent. Or maybe, when she'd relaxed a little, she'd call Hawk and see if she could coax him into coming home to talk it out.

The combination of warm, fragrant, foamy water, cool wine, and Hollywood writing had her dozing in no time. She awoke with a start, just in time to save the book from following so many of its best-selling predecessors to a watery grave.

But it wasn't just the weight of the downward drifting paperback that had wakened her. Had she heard the front door open and close?

Her spirit lifted. Maybe Hawk had decided on his own that it wasn't a good idea for them to spend an evening by themselves, getting madder, or more defensive, at least farther apart. Maybe, any minute, he'd open the bathroom door, give her a pleading smile, propose joining her in the tub.

Footsteps in the front hall. Damp as she was, the hair on the

back of her neck stood up. She knew the sound of Hawk's footsteps, and these were different. Unfamiliar. Oddly tentative, as if
the person who'd entered was tiptoeing, trying not to be heard.
And nobody was calling out to see if anybody was home. Something was very, very wrong.

She leaped out of the bathtub, sloshing water and bubbles on
the floor as she hurried to lock the door.

Not a moment too soon. Her splashing around let the intruder
know she was there. Running footsteps, pounding, and in no time,
the terrible noise of somebody strong trying to wrench the bathroom door off its hinges.

Sally lunged to the floor for her phone. Standing naked and drip-
ping, as far from the door as she could get, she called 911. "This is
Sally Alder. I'm locked in my bathroom and there's somebody trying
to break in. Listen!" She held the phone out so that the operator
could hear the banging. "You've got to get out here right now!"

The dispatcher asked for her address.

Sally gave it. "They're on the way!" she shouted, hoping the
prowler was paying attention. Then she went nuts. "That was the
sheriff's office, you fucking creep, and they're going to be here in
about ten seconds!"

The pounding stopped.

Sally froze. She desperately hoped the guy—a guy, surely?—
was half as scared as she was now, but wouldn't that set him running as fast as he could? Maybe she should have tried to stall him
until they came, so they could catch him in the act of breaking
into her goddamn bathroom?

Silence. She waited a fraction of a second, listening hard for
the sound of footsteps moving away from the door. Nothing. She
was shaking so hard her teeth were rattling. And she was still
bare-ass naked. She wrapped a towel around herself, working for
a little warmth.

Still nothing.

And then a clicking noise, followed by the clunk of metal on
the wooden door. Stop. Hey. What was that sound?

Terror struck. She dived behind the toilet. The door splintered. The full-length mirror next to the bathtub shattered, glass spraying everywhere.

Her ears were ringing so hard, she almost didn't hear the siren.

She did, at last, hear the footsteps running away, as she squeezed herself into the space between the toilet and the wall.

That was how Dickie Langham found her when he surged in, minutes later. He hauled her to her feet, held her at arm's length. "Are you hurt? Anything? Anything, Sally?"

She burst into sobs.

"Come on!" he said. "If you can tell me, spit it out. Sally . . ." He began to run his hands down her arms, eyes moving over her body to check for injury.

She clung to the towel, knotted under her arms. "I-I-I-, I'm f-f-f-f-f-f-f . . ."

"Oh fuck," said Dickie, ascertaining that she wasn't bleeding, nothing was broken. "Oh Jesus, oh God, oh fuck, oh Christ," he said, pulling her into a crushing, incredibly comforting bear hug. "Oh God, Sally. How the fuck . . ."

She hugged him back, the towel hanging in there, partly due to the lack of space between them.

And then Hawk was there, and Dickie let her go, and Hawk wrapped her up, and there was quite a bit of crying going on.

By the time Scotty Atkins and the crime scene team arrived, she was bundled up in sweats and wool socks and felt slippers, shivering at the kitchen table while Hawk put on the kettle for tea, and then came back to sit down and hold her hand. "It's my fault," he kept saying. "I shouldn't have left. This wouldn't have happened if I'd stayed."

"This isn't your fault," Dickie said, unwrapping a stick of gum and chomping down. "The responsibility belongs entirely to whoever fired that gun. Now, Sally, you have to stay calm here and tell me everything—every single living thing—you can remember about what happened."

"How the hell do I know?" she said. "I was nodding off in the bath when somebody came into my house. I locked the door and called 911 while whoever it was did his best to rip the door off."

Dickie's lips curled upward. "It's not everybody who takes their phone into the bathtub," he said.

"It's not like I can't go anywhere without it," Sally said. "But, well, Hawk and I had a fight. I was thinking about calling him from the tub."

"Too much information," said Dickie.

"You asked," Sally shot back.

"Well, anyway, maybe it's good you had that fight. So can the guilt," he told Hawk.

Hawk just shook his head.

"Now give me the details," said Dickie.

So she went over it for him, trying hard to recall the sound of the footsteps, of first the clicking, then the thunk of the gun against the door. And when Atkins emerged from the bathroom, leaving the crime scene guys to complete their meticulous work, she recounted every detail all over again.

"We found the slug," said Scotty, "embedded in the Sheetrock behind where the mirror was. It's messed up, but judging from what it did to the door and the size of it, it looks to me like a three-eighty."

"Nice," said Dickie. "Very nice."

"What does that mean?" Sally asked. Everything she knew about guns could be put in your eye.

"You say you heard a click first, before the sound of the gun on the door?" Scotty asked.

"Yes," said Sally. "I'm sure."

"There's a kind of gun called a three-eighty, very popular with the street punk crowd," said Scotty. "Nice little death machine you can put in your sock. The bad little kids love 'em because they're cheap and small with a lot of stopping power."

"Stopping power?" Sally said.

"Yeah. Like about twice as much as a small caliber weapon of about the same size," Scotty explained. "That's why they're so well liked."

"Oh," she said weakly.

"But they're not real reliable, and that appeals to the kind of moron who gets a rush out of wondering if he'll blow his hand off when he pulls the trigger. Lots were, and are, sold illegally," Dickie added. "People generally refer to this kind of cheap gun as a 'Saturday night special.' There are a bunch of gun manufacturers, in a kind of ring surrounding L.A., that specialize in making cheap handguns for gang-bangers. Cops called it the 'Ring of Fire,'" Dickie said. "This one company, Bryco, used to make a hell of a lot of three-eighties."

"What's a lot?" Hawk asked.

"Couldn't say for one company," Dickie said affably. "But I heard one estimate that the Ring of Fire companies make a million handguns a year, and more and more of them are three-eighties."

"You say used to?" Sally asked.

"Yeah," said Scotty. "But Bryco went bankrupt a couple years ago. Some kid got shot by his babysitter and ended up a quadriplegic. Faulty safety on a Bryco three-eighty. By the time the courts were done with it all, the company owed the plaintiff, like, twenty-five million dollars. Naturally, the owner scooted."

"Where to?" Sally asked.

Scotty almost smiled. "Florida," he answered. "Land of Sunshine. But the point is, there are still plenty of guns coming out of the Ring of Fire, and hundreds of thousands of these little sweethearts floating around on the market. You could buy one off the Internet this afternoon and have it here by tomorrow, and nobody'd pay any attention."

"Until you shot somebody," Hawk said.

A moment of silence.

"How much do they cost?" Sally asked.

Dickie snorted. "A working model, at a legal dealer, maybe one hundred and fifty dollars. For the less fastidious purchaser and seller, maybe fifty dollars and a bag of weed. And of course, there are websites where they ask no questions, make no guarantees about whether the fucker will shoot, and the price goes down to something any kid working a pizza delivery route could easily afford."

"And easily buy, no questions asked," Scotty added.

"Jesus Christ," said Hawk.

"Hey," said Dickie, "you'd be surprised how many pizza boys are packing. They never know, when they come up to somebody's front door, what kind of lunatics might be inside."

"I'll remember that next time I complain that they didn't put the anchovies on my pie," said Sally.

"You might think about getting yourself a nice heavy wooden door for that bathroom," Scotty said. "That thing blew a hole the size of a golf ball in your piece-of-shit hollow core door."

Sally sagged.

Hawk took a breath. "Enough. Why would some little scumbag come into my house and shoot at my girlfriend? She's currently on a crusade to save every punk and punkette in the Rocky Mountains."

"We'll find out," Scotty said.

"Emphasis on *we*," said Dickie, aiming a look at Sally that she was sure he used on his kids, probably with excellent effect. "Not you. Not either of you. You're through. You will not go tearing around town looking for assholes. Consider yourself extremely lucky to have survived this encounter with one of them."

The teakettle whistled. Hawk brought Sally a mug. She put her hands around it, warmed her icy fingers. She nodded. "I take your point."

"About those pictures," said Hawk. "There has to be a connection. And there are other people in them. Maude Stark. Aggie Stark." He hesitated almost imperceptibly, though Sally noticed. "Dave Haggerty. All kinds of people in crowds."

"We're on it," Scotty said.

"So what do you do?" Sally asked. "Go around looking for some little shit in big saggy pants with a camera phone in his pocket and a fucking gun in his sock? And let's see, maybe a sweet little Palm Pilot so he can schedule his robbing and shooting and terrorizing and pick up text messages from his homies? Man, these days you can carry enough high-tech gear to run a small war without even maxing out your pants pockets. Especially considering the size of the pants."

"The pants," said Dickie, "are functional."

"Well, one thing's for sure," said Sally. "We know that Billy Reno wasn't the one. He's in jail, right?"

"Sure," said Scotty. "But he has friends, you know."

"And enemies," said Sally.

"Don't concern yourself," Dickie said, warning in his voice.

"What about Charlie? Doesn't she have enemies?" Sally asked. "Doesn't she need protection?"

Dickie slumped in his chair. "You have no idea," he said.

"What are you talking about?" Sally said.

Dickie and Scotty exchanged a glance. "Bea Preston took her out of the hospital. It happened about an hour ago, when my deputy was down in the cafeteria, getting a cup of coffee and, unfortunately, taking the time to flirt with the girl who was working the steam table. Just like that. The floor nurse called right after they left. Said she tried to stop them, but Bea wouldn't listen."

"Was Charlie conscious?" Sally asked. "How did they get her out?"

"Seems she woke up," Dickie said. "She'd been in and out, according to the nurses, and Bea barely left her side the whole time she was there. They took her out in a wheelchair."

"How could they?" Sally's voice rose, tinged with a hint of a shriek. "She's a witness in a murder investigation."

Dickie looked down at his hands, then looked back up. "The nurse said Bea told her she wasn't satisfied with the care her daughter was getting in the hospital. Said she was taking her to a private facility where she would get what she needed."

"I just bet," Hawk said.

"Was it just Bea, or were there more people with her?" Sally asked.

"Just Bea," said Dickie. "And the nurse said it looked like Charlie was going along with it. But then, if it was me zoned out on horse tranquilizers and nerve bombs, I don't reckon I'd put up much fuss when somebody told me they were springing me from the hospital. I guess, whatever else might be, I'd be grateful for that."

"Maybe," said Sally. Or maybe not. Brad Preston had, after all, died a well-to-do man whose immediate family consisted of his daughter and his second wife. The terms of his will might affect how much gratitude Charlie had toward her stepmother.

# CHAPTER 20

# FACING THE STRANGE

IT SEEMED AS IF it took the police forever to finish up, scouring the house for evidence, checking Sally over for injuries and shock, asking the same million questions a billion times. By the time they were finished, Sally was drained. Dickie suggested that she and Hawk get a motel room for the night, just in case the intruder had some plan to come back, but Hawk took one look at Sally and declared that they weren't going anywhere, and he'd take responsibility for dealing with anybody who came around, for any reason. Dickie didn't like it, but Hawk stood firm.

So when at last the cops departed, Hawk swept up the last of the mirror shards and wood splinters, wiped down the tile and mopped the bathroom floor, methodically made a list for a trip to the hardware store to get things to repair the damage.

The property damage. How in hell would they recoup the emotional cost of the day?

Sally barely moved. She got up from the table once, to make more tea, but mostly she sat still, staring at nothing. Her brain, usually so jumpy and quick, felt swollen and sluggish, as if some-body had injected it with molasses. Was that how shock felt?

"How about some food?" he asked. "You barely ate anything at lunch."

Lunch? Oh yeah. They'd had lunch at El Conquistador, right after they'd finished up talking to Party Boy Mike. Before her use-less Friday afternoon meeting. Before she'd gone into the alley with Scotty Atkins. Before the quarrel, and the bath, and oh Jesus, the rest. Could you really live through all that in one day?

"Food. I probably need some food," Sally replied dully.

Hawk peered into the fridge. Watching him, Sally recalled their earlier conversation. "I'm sorry. I'm so sorry. I don't know how I get myself into these things."

He turned and sat down at the table with her. "I don't either. I mean, I understand why you care when people get hurt. I do too. I want to help out where I can. But why, really darlin', why do you constantly put yourself at risk?"

She drank a little tea while she thought about it. At length, she said, "It's about being alive."

"Being alive?" His voice began to rise. "You were damn near shot in your own bathtub, Sally! Being alive?"

She took a moment to choose her words. "It's hard to explain. It has to do with the lure of the unknown, with the spark that comes from things being unpredictable, edgy, risky."

Hawk got up, got the Jim Beam out of a cabinet, and poured himself a shot. "Keep talking," he said.

She held out her mug. He poured a little whiskey in her tea. She took a sip, nodded. "When I first started playing music with bands, everything was brand-new. The best of them were like get-ting a new life every night. We practiced a lot, did a lot of new material, played new places, saw new faces every single night. We traveled all over the place. Half the time we gigged in clubs and bars and halls we'd never played before.

"You never knew what was going to happen. Sometimes it wasn't so good. Sometimes there were fights, and a lot of people ended up getting bloody or even getting busted. Sometimes guys hit on me in really disgusting ways. Sometimes I even felt threatened. But that element of the unknown was what kept it, well, exciting. It was . . . stimulating. You know that line in the David Bowie song 'Changes'? The one about facing the strange? Well, that's what I liked about it. Seems I'm a sucker for the strange."

"You still play music," Hawk said.

"Yeah. I play in a hobby band full of geezers who still sound pretty good. We play in the same old places. We know everyone in the room. Hors d'oeuvres are served. We haven't learned a new song since 'Don't It Make My Brown Eyes Blue.' It's fun, but it's hardly living on the edge," said Sally.

"Let's run the Colorado on a raft," suggested Hawk. "Let's climb in the Wind River. Let's go to the Galápagos and see giant tortoises."

"All good ideas," said Sally.

"Better than doing shit that gets you shot at," Hawk pointed out.

"No doubt. But . . . what about puzzles, Hawk? What about the fascination of seeing things that make no sense, and worrying them until they do?"

He inspected her with utter seriousness. "Puzzles. People get killed, and you're thinking about puzzles?"

"Of course not. Neither are you. Murder isn't just a mind game. Neither is the kind of abuse Charlie Preston's had to deal with most of her life. But getting to the bottom of these things—I don't know. It's compelling. It's about starting with chaos and finding order, and some kind of reason for the ordering. It's, well, it's just a rush."

He reached over and took her hand. "You crave the chaos. I get that. But what really freaks me out is that you're attracted to the danger of the strange. And I know it's going to sound like nothing but jealousy—there's some of that, I grant you—but this Haggerty guy bugs me. There's something about him that doesn't add up."

"You might be right. I don't know. And I'm sorry to give you cause to be jealous. I can be a real jerk sometimes," said Sally.

"I give up. I love you anyway. I'm gonna make us some eggs," said Hawk.

Dr. Josiah Hawkins Green, eggs-over-easy expert, offering the comfort of the reliable. She accepted, and was glad.

But at two A.M., she lay staring at the ceiling, heart pounding. She'd barely slept a wink. She couldn't stop worrying about Charlie Preston.

Maybe she'd seen too many documentary exposés, read too many horror stories about the treatment of the mentally ill. Sure, there were places where people with serious psychological problems found sympathy and therapy, the right combination of human and pharmaceutical care, whatever might be suited to their particular problems. Charlie Preston was clearly a deeply disturbed young person, and Sally didn't begin to think she understood the causes of Charlie's disease.

She tried to give Bea Preston the benefit of the doubt. She'd said she was taking the girl to a place she'd get good care. Why wouldn't she be telling the truth? When Sally had visited her house, Bea had expressed at least some sympathy for the kid, right?

Not much.

And how had she treated Charlie's earlier episodes? From what Bea had said, and what she'd learned from the Starks, Bea's answer to Charlie's problems had been to have her locked up.

Where? Some cushy clinic where they'd pump her full of Thorazine until she seemed docile enough to release, suggestible enough to be persuaded that acting out and bursting out was what bad girls did? To be convinced to keep taking the meds and leave the management of her life and her desires to the experts? Some remote retreat where they'd mix in group therapy, keep in touch with her after she left, take a real interest in her well-being?

The Prestons had the bucks to send Charlie to the most luxurious, spa-like psychiatric resort, if they wanted to. But would they? Wouldn't people who believed in an angry God, people who clearly believed that sparing the rod spoiled the child, go for something more boot camp than Broadmoor Hotel?

Or worse than boot camp?

What about state hospitals? Had Charlie spent time in the care of the Wyoming mental health authorities? If she had, there would be some kind of government records about where she'd been treated before, maybe a clue as to where she was now.

Right. Like some state mental hospital records clerk would just hand over the files when Sally came marching in declaring that she was a concerned professor. Whoever heard of a concerned professor? She wasn't even a friend of the family. She was just some schlepper off the street. Hospitals didn't generally play loose with medical records in any case; juvenile psychiatric records were probably harder to pry loose than Scotty Atkins's smiles.

But of course, Scotty would try to get them. Was probably doing so even now. And unlikely to accord high priority to keeping Sally in the loop.

Maybe the Starks would know something. As Charlie's former foster parents, wouldn't they have been privy to certain kinds of information about their charge?

And what about Aggie? What might Charlie have confided? What might Aggie have seen for herself?

Teenagers were a lot more complicated than most people gave them credit for being. From appearances, Aggie Stark was a model kid, an athlete who did her homework and obeyed her parents and loved her little doggie. But there was that story about the girls in the dope house, with Charlie Preston playing the part of out-of-control rescuing angel. Aggie must have been involved.

Sally worried the questions, like a whole mouthful of sore teeth, through the black hours of a blustery night. She pulled Hawk close, needing more comfort, but tried not to wake him with her restlessness and fear. She'd never been a very accomplished sleeper. Hawk, on the other hand, believed that seven hours of sleep belonged to him by birthright, and averaging eight hours was the mark of a truly successful life.

It wouldn't be long. It wouldn't be polite, of course, to call Aggie's house before, say, seven-thirty. She could call Maude at six.

The phone rang at five forty-five.

Trying not to wake Hawk, she got out of bed and went into the kitchen to answer. But it wasn't Maude. It was Aggie, and she was crying.

"They took Charlie away!" she said. "They're going to do something terrible. You don't know what they've done before, Sally. We've got to find her. You've got to help."

"I'll do everything I can, Aggie. Take a deep breath," Sally said.

Sally heard the girl inhale, exhale. Then fumbling noises, the sound of a nose being blown. "I'll be okay," Aggie said, still shaky.

Sally took her own deep breath. "Look, Aggie, we need to talk. I heard about some parties at Billy's place. I think you know what I'm talking about."

Silence.

Sally pushed on. "Your mom and dad are going to find out about this stuff eventually. I won't be the one to tell them. I won't even tell Maude. You've got to make your own decisions. But if I'm going to help, you have to tell me what you know."

A pause. "Okay."

Sally thought a moment. "Do you want to come over here now and talk?"

"I don't know," said Aggie. "I need to get a run in."

What a kid. The world going to hell around her, secrets Sally was only beginning to imagine, but at fourteen, she had the discipline to keep to her workout schedule.

There was the possibility that Mr. Saturday Night Special might be crazy enough to shoot somebody in broad daylight on the streets of Laramie. Then again, it might be more dangerous for Aggie to come to Sally and Hawk's house, where there'd been some actual shooting. Everything had risks. And they might as well burn some calories. "Give me your address and I'll come to your place," she told Aggie. "We can run and talk, as long as you're willing to take it slow."

"I like running with a partner," Aggie said. "I don't have to kick it every day."

Aggie was waiting, with her little dog on a leash, when Sally arrived. The dog barked joyously and ran circles around his own tail, leaping on Sally's shin. She reached down to pet him and sent him into ecstasy. "Hey, Beanie, hey, good dog. You're a friendly one, aren't you?"

"He's the best doggie in the whole wide world," the girl said as the dog pranced on his tether. "He remembers all his friends, don't you, good boy? You even know how to keep up and not have to pee until we get to the park, right, Beanie boy?" She reached over to rub his back and scratch him under his whiskers, looking up at Sally. "And if anybody bugs us, this little schnauzer will bark like a mad dog."

Sally gave him another pat. He licked her hand and wagged his stumpy tail so hard, he nearly fell over sideways. Great. If someone attacked them, he could wag the bastard to death.

They set off at an easy pace, Aggie clearly watching out for Sally's comfort. The kid was a peach. Sally wished they could just jog around and gab about the weather and the virtues of miniature schnauzer dogs. But time was running out.

So she got to the point. "Somebody came in my house last night, while I was taking a bath," she told Aggie. "They shot at me through my bathroom door."

Aggie screeched to a halt, yanking Beanie's leash. The dog gagged and hacked. "No."

Sally nodded.

"And you're out running around this morning?" Aggie said, gaping.

"I'm not thinking about it. I don't have enough brain cells. So you have to help me."

Aggie began walking again, slipping into a lope. Sally kept pace. "Do you know anything about people with guns, Aggie? People who might have drugs too?"

The girl stared straight ahead, picking up the pace.

Sally panted to keep up, then gave up and took charge. "Slow down. In fact, let's walk. Talk to me."

Aggie stopped and turned to face Sally head-on. "Okay. Yeah. You promise you won't tell my parents or my aunt Maude?"

Sally crossed her heart.

"They had a lot of parties," she began, assuming Sally knew enough to follow along. "I don't know why I went. I mean, lots of girls from Laramie High did, but it wasn't really that much fun. I mean, if you like to get drunk and stoned and all, I guess it's fun, but I don't like it all that much. It's scary. Those parties were always at least a little scary, and sometimes really bad."

Beanie was pulling on his leash, eager to walk. Sally touched Aggie's arm, and they headed on. "I heard about one in particular. Some guys were hitting on underage girls, and Charlie went crazy. You were there, weren't you, Ag? She was trying to protect you."

Aggie sniffled, tried to suck back the tears, and in the end, gave in. "I shouldn't have been there. It was only the second time I went. Charlie told me before to stay away, but I just had to see what was happening. And there was this guy who wouldn't let me alone, Sally. I couldn't make him go away."

Sally chose her words. "Aggie, don't blame yourself. I'm going to guess that you might have been a little loaded at the time, and you're not sure whether you did something that made him think it was okay to hassle you. No matter how drunk or stoned you were, nothing gives him that right. Guys don't get to decide that 'no' doesn't really mean no. I'm sure you were frightened. I heard as much, from somebody who was there."

"Charlie?" Aggie said. "Charlie couldn't have told you about it. She wouldn't. She swore."

"Not Charlie. Somebody else, a college student. And he was appalled at the guy's behavior. So don't ever think that you did something that made the guy think he had the right to treat you that way. I mean, you know where your error in judgment came—that was in being there, in drinking or smoking. You can make different and better choices, and you know it. But getting jumped on by some dickhead, well, that's *so* not your fault. Forget about it. Next time, maybe you'll know enough to say no when people try to get you to go to a party like that."

"Are you kidding? Like, never, never again," Aggie said, unconsciously speeding up until Sally was panting again.

"Slow down." The girl slowed. The dog changed his gait, toenails clicking on pavement. "Okay. Now tell me about the guns and dope," Sally said.

Aggie looked around. They were on a side street, heading for the park, but not yet there. Nobody else was on the street. "Well, there were lots of both," she admitted. "A couple of the guys who lived there were dealing."

"Guns or drugs?" Sally asked.

"Both," said Aggie. "They'd go in a back room to do business, but it was obvious. People would come back into the living room stuffing things in their pants, or wiping their noses."

"Was Charlie involved?" Sally asked.

"Not in the dealing. I mean, she does drugs and drinks. I tried to get her to stop, but she couldn't. I told her that if her stepmother caught her, she'd use it as an excuse to put her away again, but she told me to shut up and mind my own business. She said she needed something to kill the pain."

Sally just bet she did. "What about Billy?"

"He didn't touch anything—not liquor or weed or blow or anything. He said his body was a temple, which you have to admit is kind of a riot, when you think about the fact that the guy's covered with ink."

"Maybe he's a Hindu temple," said Sally.

Aggie smiled faintly. "Whatever. He hates drugs. But I guess you know he's got other problems. He just can't help himself. He's been stealing since he was a little kid. He can't stop. And he carries a gun, pretty much all the time. But I'll say one thing for Billy. He loves Charlie so much, he'd do anything for her. He tries to talk her out of getting high. I've seen him take a beer out of her hand, and make her leave a party even when she gets mad at him. I've seen her haul off and slug him while he's trying to get her out."

"Did you ever see him hurt her?" Sally said, the question sticking a little in her throat.

"I've seen him grab her arms pretty hard. But she was trying to slap his head off at the time."

"Do you think he could have killed her father?" Sally asked.

"I don't know. I can't stop thinking about it. Her father was terrible to her, Sally. He beat her. They said it was for her own good. That it was God's will."

"That's not a God I can believe in," Sally said.

"That's what my mom told Charlie. I mean, she asked my parents why they didn't ever hit me."

Jesus. "What about when the Prestons sent Charlie away, Aggie? Where did she go?"

Aggie shuddered. "She couldn't talk about it, not really. She'd mention being locked in a little room she called 'the hole,' nothing but a cot that was bolted to the floor and a toilet and sink. It sounded like jail. She said it was all kind of fuzzy. I guess they kept her on some pretty heavy meds. They told her they had to do it, because when they cut back on the medication, she got violent and she tried to hurt herself and other people. Sometimes they tied her down."

Aggie took a ragged breath. "You know the worst part, Sally?" Aggie said. "They started putting her in that place when she was just a little kid. And nobody ever went to visit her. She'd be there awhile—I guess until the zookeepers, or whoever, decided to let her out. Then her stepmother would come and get her. She said she'd promise to be good, so they wouldn't have to send her back. But I guess she couldn't keep it up. Sooner or later she'd snap, and it would start all over again."

"And it was always Beatrice who came to get her out?" Sally asked.

"Uh-huh," said Aggie. "That was one big reason Charlie hated her dad so much. I mean, when she'd get out and go home, he'd be all, 'Oh honey, I love you, I hope you can behave this time, be a good girl for Daddy.' And like that. But I guess he didn't think it was his job to take her to the slammer, or whatever it was. According to Charlie, her father and stepmother talked all the time about what God ordained for women and for men. The husband's job was to earn the money and rule the household. The wife's job was to keep the place clean and deal with the children. I guess they thought that locking up their kid was women's work."

# CHAPTER 21

# THE FIFTH COMMANDMENT

WHEN SHE GOT BACK home, she found Hawk sitting at the kitchen table, cleaning his Smith & Wesson. The whole house smelled like gun oil. He didn't look up when she came in.

"Want some coffee?" she asked.

Now he did look up, with an expression in his eyes she hadn't seen in a long time, and had hoped never to see again. Cold. Remote. Nothing there to hang on to, much less touch. "I've had some," he said.

She moved to the stove, twisted around to address the back of his head. "I guess if you've got a gun, you just have to clean it now and then."

He didn't turn around when he finally answered. "True," he said. "But I also figure that there's not much else I can do. I mean, you don't even bother to get me up before you go waltzing off, the very morning after some fucker came in here and shot up our house. I'm becoming convinced that you'd rather get yourself killed than be my partner. I'm not quite sure what to do about that, but in the meantime, I'm going to take precautions."

She tried to make a joke of it. "Guess somebody around here has to."

Hawk put the gun down on the newspaper-covered table and wiped his hands carefully. Then he exploded to his feet, and before she knew it, he was gripping her upper arms and shouting in her face. "You've got to stop, Sally! I can't stand this! We can't stand this! I love you, damn you, and I swear to God, I'm about ready to give up on you."

The distant look in his eyes was gone. Now there was anguish.

She threw out her arms, broke his grip. "Let go!" she said. "You're hurting me."

He looked at his hands. He hadn't realized how hard he'd been holding on to her. "I'm sorry."

"I'm sorry too," she said. "But I'm in too deep."

"You sure as hell are," he shot back, turning to clean up the table.

She wanted to go to him. To put her arms around him. To tell him he mattered more than anything, even a troubled girl whose life, sad as it was, might be running out on her. She could feel Hawk slipping away, slowly and painfully, and she wanted to pull him back, with all her strength. She'd just taken the first step toward him when, goddamn it, the phone rang.

"You get that," he muttered. "It's probably for you."

So she answered. "Dave Haggerty here," said the voice on the wire. "Are you free this afternoon?"

No flirtatious preamble, no outrageous come-on. To Sally's vast relief. She hesitated. "Why?" she asked.

"Billy Reno insists that he wants to see you," he said. "When I told him that Bea Preston had fired Charlie's attorney, and then taken her out of the hospital, he freaked out. He said Charlie told him she'd come to you, and you'd given her all your money and the coat off your back. He says that makes you his homie."

She thought about that. To her knowledge, she'd never been anybody's homie. But she didn't think Scotty Atkins would be excited about the idea of her chatting with his murder suspect.

"I'd like to talk to him," she told Haggerty, "but wouldn't he talk to you about anything he'd tell me? You've known him since he was a baby, and after all, you're his lawyer."

"Yeah," said Haggerty. "Well, I don't know. Our relationship is . . . complicated."

Sally looked at Hawk, who was stuffing oily newspaper in the trash, grimacing hard. Everything about this situation was complicated. "Okay. You think you can get me in to see him this afternoon?"

"Can and should," said Haggerty. "It could be pretty important for Charlie."

Nothing more needed to be said. But he did say one more thing. "I heard about what happened at your house. I'm really sorry."

"Not your fault, Dave," she replied.

"We'll get this fixed, Sally," he said.

And so, for the first time in her life, Sally found herself going to visit somebody in jail. It didn't surprise her that her level of anxiety built as she walked across the parking lot toward the squat, windowless building, or that once she was inside, the place smelled like a combination of dust, sweat, old smoke, and disinfectant, or that she had to go through a metal detector and submit to a body search before they let her into the waiting area. She'd expected all that.

But she'd found herself profoundly unsettled by, well, by the vibe of the place. Despite the echoey hard surfaces of yellow ceramic-fired brick walls and gray tile floor, there was almost no noise. And yet, beneath the quiet, the place seemed to roar inside her head, to shriek with the rage and desperation of those who'd been confined there, of whoever was even now locked up beyond the walls. The place pulsed with the fury.

She wished she'd worn a warmer jacket, even as she felt sweat begin to trickle between her shoulder blades.

She'd become accustomed to thinking of Albany County law enforcement in personal terms. Sheriff Dickie Langham was one of her best friends, and if her relationship with Scotty Atkins was testy, well, that was personal too. But there was nothing intimate or individual about the Albany County jail. Doubtless, having Dickie or Scotty there would have made her feel more secure, more herself. But she hadn't called them about the visit, and didn't care to examine the motives for her reticence.

And surely it would have been easier if Dave Haggerty had met her there, smoothed the way. But Billy was allowed only one visitor at a time. Haggerty had explained that he had other pressing matters to attend to, even on a Saturday. As she went through the process of being screened and admitted, she'd never felt so alone.

Imagine how Billy Reno must feel.

She was led to a cubicle partitioned by Plexiglas, with a chair, a Formica counter, a phone. The other side of the partition featured an identical setup. She took out a notebook and a pen. She'd made a list of questions, and now she added more. She had half an hour. She hoped they'd make it count. A few, very slow minutes passed before Billy Reno was brought in to face her.

He was tall and thin and deadly pale, with immense, liquid brown eyes, like a doe or a child. His orange jail jumpsuit seemed to hang from wide, sharp shoulders. The dragon's head twined around his neck, and when he picked up the phone on his side, there was a crudely done, fresh tattoo between his thumb and forefinger. It said, "Charlie."

"We didn't do it, Mrs. Alder," he said, without preamble.

Mrs.? A title of respect, she guessed. "Call me Sally, please, Billy. And let's be serious here. I'd like to believe you. But your fingerprints are all over that lug wrench," Sally said, beginning to write.

"Big whoop," Billy replied. "Charlie's a shitty driver. She's always running over curbs. We changed a lot of flat tires. Somebody planted the wrench."

"The police have an informant. Somebody who says they heard you two plotting to kill Charlie's father."

"Yeah, we're that fuckin' stupid. I mean, if I were going to commit murder, I'd definitely want to talk it up in front of everybody I know. Fuckin' Munk."

"Munk?" Sally said, looking up from her notes.

"Like Chipmunk. I know who ratted us out. Alvin fuckin' Sabble. Wonder what charges against him they dropped in return?"

Sally thought a minute. "Billy, is there any chance that he did it himself and set you up?"

Billy tapped a finger on the counter. "Yeah. Sure. I mean, I couldn't tell you what that fuckin' guy might be capable of. I mean, he's not your Eagle Scout." More tapping. "Then again, I don't see him using a wrench, if you know what I mean. He's more of a gun man."

Sally shivered, cold sweat springing up with a vengeance now. "A Saturday night special kind of gun man?"

Billy nodded slowly. "Among other things. But yeah, the man likes a little piece he can keep handy in case of emergencies."

Her teeth had begun to chatter. She clamped them together and ordered herself to stay focused. "What does he look like?" she asked.

"Like a fuckin' chameleon," Billy answered. "I mean, he's G'd up from the feet up, but then again, he can blend in. He's got a lot of ink, but nothing that shows in a dress shirt, if you get the picture. He says it helps in his line of work."

"And what is that line of work?" Sally said.

"Whatever anybody pays him to do," Billy responded. "Fuckin' bastard."

"So why did you agree to be roommates with him?" Sally asked.

"You don't always get to choose the company you keep," Billy explained. "And what makes it worse is, he thinks it's all okay because he fuckin' goes to church all the time and God forgives him. Of course, a lot of that goes around. Shit, my mom took me to church every Sunday after she got born-again, and look at all the good it did us!"

"You grew up going to church?" Sally couldn't control her amazement.

"Hey, I believe in God and everything—who doesn't? But going to church doesn't guarantee anything. I mean, the first time I ever saw Charlie, she was at that church with her parents, pretending to be one big happy freakin' family. I fuckin' met Alvin Sabble at the church, and look at him. Look at my mom. You'd be surprised how many dope addicts think Jesus is going to come in and save them. You know how many times she told me God was watching out for me? Charlie heard the same crap from her old man and the stepmother, and then again every Sunday. Shit, if He was watching out for us, He was the only one, I can tell you that. And he sure isn't payin' very close attention now, is he? Kind of like the cops."

"Give them some credit. I'm sure they're working every angle?" Sally asked.

Billy snorted. "It's be easier for the cops if Charlie and I did it. They like to make it easy on themselves."

"I bet you don't," Sally told him, looking him square in the eye.

He laughed at that, a strikingly sweet sound. She looked up from her notebook. And at that moment, Sally realized why the crusading attorney had called his relationship with the boy criminal "complicated." When Billy Reno laughed, he looked a hell of a lot like Dave Haggerty.

"Listen, Billy," she said. "I have to ask. Why did you want to talk to me?"

He gazed back at her through the glass, intent. "You helped my girlfriend. She went to you when she was in deep shit. You listened to her, and you gave her money, and you didn't call down the cops on her. You gave her the fuckin' coat off your back. That's enough for me."

Maybe most people wouldn't be flattered by praise from somebody like Billy, but Sally blushed. And pressed on. "Tell me," she said, "about Charlie and her father."

"They had that love-hate thing," said Billy. "Like most kids and their fathers."

"Most fathers don't beat their kids until they're bloody and bruised," Sally said.

"He didn't, usually," said Billy. "Mostly he tried not to hit her where it would show."

"It showed a lot the last time," said Sally.

"That one," Billy said, "wasn't Brad."

Sally leaned closer. "Who was it?"

Billy shrugged. "This guy the bitch brought around. Fuck, coulda been that guy who did the old man."

"You mean Bea Preston had someone else beat her stepdaughter?" Sally asked, writing rapidly.

"Who else?" Billy replied. "I guess the old man had decided he didn't want to be the enforcer anymore."

"What do you mean, the enforcer?" Sally said.

"They had a deal. Brad was one of those fathers who thought raising kids was the woman's job. He was so busy, making money and all, he barely fuckin' saw her. I mean, he pretty much left everything up to the wicked stepmother, where Charlie was concerned."

"But sometimes, of course, he had to do his duty, as a father," Sally prompted.

"Oh yeah. Yeah. Bea would tell Brad when Charlie was—what did they call it—breaking the Fifth Commandment. The one about dishonoring thy father and mother. Then Brad would, as they said, chastise her. It was pretty rough."

Sally tried to think how to ask the question. "Was Bea present for those, um, chastisements?"

Billy shook his head. "She made it a point not to be there. But you know what? I think old Bea liked knowing he was doing it, a whole lot. What she didn't like was seeing how sorry he'd be about it. According to Charlie, Brad always cried afterward. And then he'd buy her something expensive to try to make up for it. The problem was, Charlie never knew when it was coming. Sometimes it seemed like he beat her for no reason at all."

Keep it together, Sal. Limited time, lots of questions. But she was quaking inside, on the verge of exploding. "What a horror" was all she said.

He looked back, resolute. "Oh yeah. And that wasn't even the worst of it, because after the beatings, they'd decide that they couldn't handle her anymore and ship her off to the crazy house. But you know what? Charlie Preston's made of iron. I mean, that girl is so fuckin' strong, you wouldn't believe it. Think about it. If she wasn't a fuckin' brick house, she'd be dead by now."

Yes. She would. Sally prayed that she wasn't, took a breath, asked another question. "Was Brad your landlord at that place you all got evicted?"

"Yeah," said Billy. "Landlords don't exactly love my record. The other guys weren't in any better position. Charlie hooked us up."

"And when he rented her that apartment, was that one of those make-up presents?"

Billy cocked his head, thinking. It made him look very, very young. "Yeah. She said he wanted to prove to her that he trusted her. That's what the Miata was about too."

"I can see the car," said Sally. "Parents like to bribe their kids with cars. But what about the apartment? It seems to me he was begging for her to screw up."

"I don't know. I got the impression he hadn't owned the building that long. From what she said, he was new in the real estate game. Charlie said the stepmother was really ticked at him for renting it to her."

"That doesn't sound very motherly."

He laughed again, this time without a trace of mirth. "You're fuckin' kiddin' me."

"Was he planning to evict you?" she asked.

"Charlie said he'd promised not to. But how do I know? All's I know is, after he got killed, the management company kicked us out. End of story."

"Okay," said Sally, writing rapidly, then looking up and once again into his eyes. "Do you have any idea where Bea might have taken Charlie now? Would she take her back to wherever they treated her before, for instance?"

"Treatment!" Billy exclaimed. "Yeah, right. Like getting thrown in a hole and shot full of elephant tranqs is some kind of fuckin' treatment. They didn't give a flying fuck about treating her. Charlie's got some problems. Don't we all? But whatever they were doing, it wasn't to make her better. It was just to get her the hell out of the way or something. Can you believe she didn't just off herself when she was in there? Shit, who wouldn't?" he said. "Hey—fuckin' jail's better than that."

Sally swallowed hard. "I heard that Brad never went to see her in those places," she said.

"That place," Billy corrected. "According to Charlie, after the first time, when she was nine years old and they sent her to the hospital in Denver and did all kinds of tests on her, it was always the same place. Shelter Clinic. How do you like that? Some shelter! And the same doctor, bald dude, thick glasses. She'd have nightmares about him. Can't remember his name. Same fuckin' drugs. Fancy reception area and all, but once you're inside, BAM, they hit you with the needle and next thing you know, you're in the hole. You don't see daylight again until it's time to let you out. And no. Daddy never went to visit."

He looked down. Drew figure eights on the counter with his fingertip. "You know what kills me? He did all that shit to her, and she still loved him to his dying day. Probably still does."

"Don't we all love our parents, in spite of everything? Don't you?" Sally asked.

Billy's warm eyes went cold. "This isn't about me."

"Sorry," said Sally.

"And she doesn't love Bea, I'll tell you that. The bitch'd come get her out of the clinic, or whatever it was, and she'd talk all about how she hoped Charlie had finally forsaken her wicked ways, and all shit like that. It's a fuckin' miracle Charlie never killed her!"

Sally could see his point. "But it's strange. Brad Preston obviously had misgivings about the way he was treating his daughter. Don't get me wrong. I'm not letting him off the hook. But it does sound as if he let Bea call a lot of the shots. As if he had no clue how to be a father."

"Like that's some big news," said Billy. "You think a lot of fathers do?"

Sally smiled, very sadly. "Actually, I think a lot of fathers do. And it's really, really tragic when they don't."

Billy bit his lip. It took him a moment to control his breathing. "Yeah. Well. I don't know all that much about fathers. But you know what Charlie said? She said she thought he might have been about to change, right there at the end. It wasn't just that he decided to rent her the apartment. He told her that he'd begun to think they'd made some mistakes with her upbringing. He told her that it was time they turned over a new leaf."

"And what did you think about that?" Sally asked.

Billy Reno didn't look young and innocent now. He looked blank and cynical and sneering. "He'd said all that stuff before. People will say all kinds of shit. How much do you think anybody ever really changes?" he said.

"I think," said Sally, "that nobody is only one person. I think everybody has all kinds of people inside them, and as we live our lives, different people come out, depending on what happens to us, what we learn, what we regret, what we want. Who we love."

And now Billy looked like he was about to cry. "Well, I love Charlie Preston." He began to say more. The receiver went dead. A guard appeared behind him, gestured for him to get up and move out.

No sound now. But as he rose, and the guard took him by the arm to lead him away, Billy looked over his shoulder and mouthed words plain for Sally to see. "I love her," he said into the silence. "Find her. Find her now."

## Chapter 22

# THE COUNTRY CLUB

SHE WALKED OUT OF the jail back across the parking lot, unlocked her car, and drove around for fifteen minutes, utterly numb, completely blank.

Then she pulled into a convenience store parking lot, shut off the engine, put her head down on the steering wheel, and let the pain roar through her. When that was over, she looked up, shook her head, and gave herself a stern lecture.

Okay. So she'd felt sorry for the guy. She'd liked him, in fact, found him beguiling, orange jail jumpsuit, skin ink, potty mouth, and all. She'd found herself believing every word he said.

But Billy Reno was, after all, an incorrigible thief, a pathological criminal, a con artist. Who'd be better at gaming her?

She could think of one person. Billy, after all, had more of Dave Haggerty in him than a pretty smile. And now fury began to smolder. Dave Haggerty. Doing a number on her all along, it seemed. And now she thought she had some idea why.

Unlikely intimacies. Strange connections. Odd estrangements.

People who seemed to have no relation to one another, densely entangled.

She turned the key in the ignition. The Mustang came to life. She headed straight for the offices of Haggerty, Hebard, and Bright.

The law firm had two floors of efficient, cozy space in a building that had been a hotel, back at the turn of the twentieth century, catering to passengers moving through on the Union Pacific. The building façade was red brick and Victorian gingerbread, the waiting room deep carpet and comfortable chairs. The receptionist, in Saturday casual jeans and sweater, told Sally that Mr. Haggerty was in a meeting. Sally told the receptionist that she really needed to talk to Mr. Haggerty, and that she'd just come from seeing one of his clients in the jail. That did get the woman's attention. Sally added that the matter really couldn't wait, but she would. She was getting used to sitting around in waiting rooms, amusing herself with magazines she'd never otherwise read. She picked up a brand-new issue of *Prevention,* thinking that she probably needed to start subscribing. If there was one thing Sally Alder needed help with, it was prevention.

Less than five minutes later, she was told that Mr. Haggerty would see her.

The man must specialize in speed meetings.

At least he met her eyes when she walked in, glaring. "Hi, Dave," she said, sitting down in the wingback chair across from his desk, tossing her shoulder bag on the floor. "Looks like you've got more in common with Brad Preston than just being a hotshot lawyer. Are you proud of the job you've done as a father?"

"Now that you mention it," he said, "no. No. I'm not."

"And of course, Bea knows, doesn't she? Did she guess from the resemblance? Or maybe God told her?"

Haggerty shook his head. "No. Billy's mother told her. Bea, of course, is very big on traditional families. When she sees a single mother in the congregation, she does everything she can to find out who the father is. Beatrice Preston's a charismatic woman. She can be very persuasive."

"And then what happens? She lets the old runaway daddy know that he can demonstrate his paternal virtue by giving a contribution to the Traditional Family Fund?"

"Something like that," Haggerty admitted, now avoiding Sally's gaze.

"Does Charlie know about you and Billy?" Sally asked.

"I can't say. It's not common knowledge. We don't exactly run in the same circles. I gave Billy's mother plenty of incentive to keep it quiet."

"Cash incentives," Sally said.

"Yes. Which she needed very badly, given her difficulties with staying employed. She claimed Bea was the only person she ever told. Something about seeking forgiveness and saving her soul."

Could Bea Preston really be that big a hypocrite? Sally had nothing per se against Christian devotion. Bishop Tutu was a Christian. Bruce Cockburn was a Christian. William Sloane Coffin was her favorite Christian.

What kind of person used God as a reason to prey on the weak?

"Do you pay Billy too?" Sally asked.

"I would, if he'd take it. But he won't. He's got his own kind of scruples. The only thing he'll let me do is help when he has problems with the law, which seems to be happening with increasing frequency. It might surprise you, but he doesn't want people knowing he's my kid, any more than I do. He blames me for his mother's problems." Haggerty pursed his lips.

Sally was almost sympathetic. Almost. "Did you know what the Prestons were doing to Charlie?" Sally asked. "Could you possibly have been that callous?"

"I'm not proud of this, Sally. But no. I didn't know until Billy was arrested. He doesn't exactly confide in me."

"But you knew Brad and Bea. You knew they had a troubled daughter. Didn't you guess?"

"It wasn't my business to guess. I've had plenty on my plate without getting involved in that sort of stuff. I've tried to be a good citizen, support the right causes, help where I can."

"And you've stayed out of politics. Boy, I can just imagine what it would have been like for you and Brad to run against each other for Congress. Talk about dueling skeletons in the closet!"

"Please, Sally. I did what I could. Brad's murder opened up a lot of doors I've tried to keep closed."

She stood up, put her hands on his desk, leaned in close. "And you've got plenty of ways of doing that, right? I mean, just consider the way you've 'misdirected' me—everything from cash bribes for my center to crass come-ons. It makes a woman wonder who else you've been jamming and scamming, Dave. You are a piece of work, you know that? You've even been having me tailed, haven't you? Those pictures actually did come from you—you even went to the trouble to get whoever you hired to take a picture of you with me! You harassed my boyfriend! You fried my fucking hard disk!"

"Didn't fry it very hard. I knew you'd get it fixed. It was for your own good anyway. I do regret wasting police time, but hey, those guys are good at their job, and I doubt they'd be too pissed at me for trying to pull you off this thing. It really is up to the sheriff to find out who killed Brad Preston, right, Sally? And no, I don't think Charlie and Billy did it. I'm a pretty good defense lawyer. I figured I could take care of them myself."

"But then Charlie freaked out, and Bea took her away, and somebody came into my house and shot up my goddamn bathroom door! Was that part of your plan too, Dave?"

"No. I swear, I had nothing to do with that. And to be honest, Sally, I never had a very good plan. I was just, well, reacting to circumstances. Improvising."

"Improvising. Great. You son of a bitch. Your son's in jail, charged with murder, and Charlotte Preston may be dead. Don't you think it's time to come clean? Give me one reason why I shouldn't call Dickie Langham right this minute." She leaned over, dug in her shoulder bag, pulled out her cell phone, and brandished it like a weapon.

"Main reason: You wouldn't be telling him much of anything he doesn't already know."

"He knows about you and Billy?" she asked.

"Yes. And he knows that Bea's been squeezing me. He even questioned her about it. She claimed to know nothing about Billy's and my relationship, and to be shocked and insulted at the idea that I'd accused her of blackmail, although she did think that I'd be better off owning up to my sins rather than deceiving myself that I could hide from the All-Seeing-All-Knowing. I'm guessing that she'll go public with it pretty soon. I'll deal with that when I have to. Makes me wish I'd never given her a cent," he added ruefully.

"Does the sheriff know that you had me followed, hacked my computer, and sent Hawk and me harassing photos?" Sally was aghast.

"Okay, maybe he doesn't know everything," Haggerty acknowledged. "Give me five minutes," he said. "There are a few things you ought to know first. I owe you that much."

She stared at her phone. Made a decision, snapped the phone shut, and sat down again. "Talk," she said.

"Okay. In my own defense, let me say that I first started having you followed because Billy asked me to keep an eye on you. Charlie was, as you've heard, having some problems down in Colorado, and he wanted to know what you were up to, without tailing you himself. It started out pretty informally. I took the pictures at the reception myself."

That really gave Sally the creeps.

"But Billy does things on impulse too. That morning Sheriff Langham came to your house, before the demonstration," said Haggerty, "I had some things I wanted to ask him about. I called him and woke him up, and on the way to my office, he happened to drive by your place and see the sheriff's truck parked out front. He freaked. That was when we got serious about surveillance. I called a guy I know."

"Naturally you'd know a guy," said Sally.

"Any good criminal lawyer does," Haggerty replied.

"I still don't get it. Why would Billy worry about me?" Sally asked.

"I don't think you or I can begin to understand how his mind works, Sally," Haggerty pointed out. "And Billy doesn't particularly care about anything but helping Charlie, which he's trying very hard to do, in his own way. Which was why I was right on the scene the day they got evicted, and which is what led me to some very interesting information, in connection with helping them fight the eviction and the damage claims."

"I've been thinking about that," Sally said. "If Brad Preston was the owner of the building, and he was no longer living, who'd be doing the suing and collecting the damages? In other words, who owned the building at the time of the eviction? That information would have been in his will, right? But it wouldn't have been probated yet, would it?"

"Not even close," Haggerty said. "Not only not probated, but contested. You wouldn't believe how many lawyers don't have their own affairs in order. I'd never have pegged Brad as the kind of guy who'd let things slide, but hey—we never really know anybody, do we?"

Sally glared. She wasn't about to let Haggerty cajole her. The lying bastard.

"Anyhow, Brad didn't practice what he preached. He'd made a will right when he first married Bea, and then never got around to updating it. And it was what you might call an unbelievably blunt legal instrument. For reasons I'll never understand, he simply stipulated that everything he had be split right down the middle between his wife and his daughter. Bea was to act as guardian and trustee until Charlie came of age. If that will were enforced, of course, Charlie, being of age now, would have half interest in the building—she'd be suing herself!"

"Good grief. That's the kind of situation that must have you lawyers licking your chops and phoning your Porsche dealers," said Sally. "I assume Bea's contesting."

"Naturally. Not only on the grounds that the will is out of date. She's trying to have Charlie declared incompetent."

"Oh boy," said Sally. "This latest breakdown plays right into Bea's hands."

"It does, of course," Haggerty said. "But Bea's way ahead of the game. She's already filed a brief loaded with evidence of Charlie's lifelong mental instability, including records of seven different instances of inpatient psychiatric treatment between the ages of nine and eighteen, some lasting for months."

"So there are records? From the Shelter Clinic, I presume?"

"Billy did tell you a lot," Haggerty said. "Yes. A church-affiliated facility, very posh, mostly catering to rich born-agains backsliding into the bad habits from their previous profane lives. Big drug and alcohol rehab clientele. A much smaller program catering to children and adolescents whose parents want their kids to have a dose of spiritual medicine along with the Thorazine."

"Very posh?" Sally asked.

"I've heard the place referred to as the Crazy Christian Country Club," said Haggerty.

"Doesn't sound like the kind of place Billy described," Sally pointed out.

"They've got detox rooms that aren't quite so cushy," Haggerty explained. "And then again, it may be that Charlie Preston spent most of her zoo time someplace else, and got trotted over to the Country Club only when the social workers and state investigators came around. The rest of the time, well, out of sight, out of most everybody's mind. In fact, it's beginning to look like the Shelter Clinic did a fair business in so-called off-campus institutionalization of children and adolescents who'd become, shall we say, embarrassments to their parents?"

Warehousing mentally disturbed children? Sally looked at him, intent. "How do you know this?" she asked.

"It turns out," said Haggerty, "that the last time Charlotte Preston was a patient at the clinic, the insurance company contested the claim for her medical bills. By that time, it seems, several insurers had begun to suspect that the clinic was billing, and billing big-time, for services never rendered, from luxury suites and hydrotherapy to outrageous gouging prices for designer drugs. One of the companies suing the clinic was—"

"Mammoth Mutual." Sally finished his sentence. "And they

called in their favorite fraud specialist, Bradley Preston. What a shock for him to find out that while he'd been busy climbing the pyramid and getting his name in the paper, his daughter had been a victim of the very kind of scam he'd made his bones exposing. But Bea must have known, right? I mean, maybe she was even in on the deal."

"A very distinct possibility," said Haggerty. "In which case, the confrontation between the Prestons could have gotten ugly. Especially considering their traditional family values and all."

"But she couldn't have killed him," said Sally. "She was at the demonstration. I saw her with my own eyes." Then it dawned on her. "Unless, of course, it happened earlier that morning. And the protest at the abortion doctor's office was a very convenient alibi for her."

"Or perhaps even a particularly dramatic bit of misdirection, to keep the cops occupied," said Haggerty. "Consider the car bombing."

She was considering that when another thought intruded, infuriating her anew. "You said Billy saw the sheriff's truck parked in front of my house that morning, on his way to your office? And you woke him up shortly before that? Let me put this another way. How much time did you spend with him? I've got this appalling idea that you're in a position to give him an alibi for the morning of the murder."

"I think," said Haggerty, "my five minutes are about up."

"I cannot fucking believe you," Sally exclaimed. "You're so goddamn determined to keep people from suspecting the truth about you and him that you'd let your own son rot in jail, when you could spring him with a freaking phone call!" She flipped open her cell phone now, speed-dialed Dickie Langham's cell, got voice mail. "This is Sally. I've just been talking to Dave Haggerty at his office. Can you come down here now?" she told the machine, and rung off.

"Okay," she said. "Now I'm going to call Scotty Atkins. And you and I are going to sit here until the sheriff or Detective Atkins shows up. And then you're going straight down there to the jail and get that kid the hell out of there."

"Before you damn me to hell again," said Haggerty, "just think about one thing. I've learned, over the years of representing quite a few clients who've been guests of the country, that Sheriff Langham runs a tight, tidy, professional little jail. I realize that it seems pretty hard of me to leave Billy there for now."

"Pretty hard!" Sally said.

"But ask yourself this. Somebody came into your house and shot at you. Bea Preston's stashed Charlie God only knows where, but if it's a place she's kept her before, she might think Charlie had told Billy about it. I may be a candidate for world's shittiest father, but it's occurred to me that right about now, Billy might be a whole lot safer in Sheriff Langham's jail than running around Laramie."

# CHAPTER 23

# SIN CITY

SHE HAD TO HAND it to Dave Haggerty. While she told Dickie and Scotty everything she'd learned that day, from Billy Reno's revelations to the lawyer's admissions, Haggerty kept his cool. Even in the face of Dickie Langham's exasperation and Scotty Atkins's icy disdain, he remained genial, relaxed. In fact, by the look of him, you'd think Haggerty was in control of the situation. Even as Scotty was explaining that he was inclined to pursue criminal charges against him, in the matter of the computer hacking and harassing pictures, not to mention withholding evidence pertinent to a murder case, most particularly including the alibi for Billy Reno, Dave Haggerty nodded, half smiled, took a few notes on a yellow pad but otherwise sat peacefully behind his big cherry desk, hands loosely folded in his lap.

And when Scotty finished, Haggerty pointedly ignored him and addressed Dickie, who stood leaning against the wall, more stone-faced than Sally had ever seen him, "I hope you gentlemen will reconsider taking action against me. After all, I did connect the dots for you when it came to the insurance fraud. You're this

far away"—he put his forefinger and thumb a millimeter apart—
"from figuring out exactly where Bea Preston fits into all this, if
she does. And when you get Bea, you'll get the girl. Let's be honest
with each other."

"Hah!" Sally couldn't help saying. All three men gave her the
same dyspeptic look.

"I can be of some further use to you," Haggerty continued, "if
you'll permit me to do my work and not hassle me with frivolous
criminal charges."

Sally took a page out of Haggerty's book and looked at
Dickie. "Do you guys have any idea where she might have taken
Charlie?"

Dickie pulled a bandana out of his back pocket, took off his
cowboy hat, wiped his forehead, stuffed the bandana back in the
pocket, put the hat back on. "She's not at the Shelter Clinic. They
are, by the way, under a court order to shut down pending the
outcome of a criminal investigation. You don't want to get on the
wrong side of the insurance companies. In the meantime, we've
had the Fort Collins police search their facilities, including what
they refer to as their 'off-campus' sites."

Sally closed her eyes. "I keep imagining self-storage units," she
said, "with kids sitting by themselves in the dark and cold."

"You've got a good imagination," Scotty Atkins said. "The
kids who were there have been taken to a real hospital. Charlotte
Preston wasn't among them."

The good news and the bad. "So where do you look now?"
Sally asked. "Where's Bea?"

"She called us this afternoon, to say that she didn't want us to
worry about Charlotte. She insists that what the girl needs is quiet
and seclusion, a chance to grieve for her father and seek health
and spiritual guidance."

"You guys are buying that line of crapola?" Sally asked,
amazed.

"We're being cautious. The last time anybody reported seeing
Charlotte was when Mrs. Preston took the girl out of Ivinson.

We've been watching the Preston house. Nobody's been there. There's a little consolation in the fact that Charlie probably isn't walking under her own power. From the moment Mrs. Preston took the girl out of the hospital, we've had people watching the regional airports for a girl in a wheelchair," said Scotty, "probably accompanied by an attractive woman. So far she hasn't turned up."

"Great. At least she isn't on a plane to Paraguay," said Sally.

"Yeah. At least," said Dickie. "I want that girl, Sally, but we have to treat Mrs. Preston with some caution. At this point, we don't have anything specific to implicate her in the fraud." He turned to Haggerty. "It's time to stop fucking with us, Dave. If there's anything else you can possibly do or say that would help, I reckon you'd better do or say it, before we head down to the jail to release a suspect we no longer have any reason to hold. And I should warn you. By the time you get down there, we'll have called the *Boomerang,* to let them know what's up. You might be thinking about what you want to say to the media. And once you've thought about it, you might consider flying it by Scotty or me."

Haggerty nodded, then looked down at his desk, visibly disturbed for the first time. He drew figure eights on his desk blotter with his index finger.

"Charlie might not even be with Bea," said Sally, feeling sick with the realization. "Bea might have stashed her with one of her people. Maybe the guy who beat Charlie up the last time, for example. Maybe the fucking asshole who shot up my house. From what Billy told me, I'd think that Alvin the Chipmunk is involved."

Haggerty cleared his throat. "Um, as a matter of fact, I've had a guy on the Chipmunk, ever since he fingered Billy and Charlie for the murder. He wasn't exactly laying low. I could show you pictures of him all over town"—and now he opened his center desk drawer, extracted something, and laid it on the blotter pad—"including this one, taken at the Wrangler Bar and Grill that has, would you believe it, Professor Alder here in the background, sitting at a table with her friend Delice Langham and her boyfriend, tight there."

Scotty gave him a sour half smile. "You're a resourceful guy, Haggerty. Make sure we get electronic copies of everything," he said.

Dickie walked over to Sally, pulled her up out of the chair, put his arm around her shoulder, and looked down into her face. "Look, Mustang. I know you're upset. I can't tell you how I felt when I heard about the kids in that place. They're out of there now. We're doing absolutely everything we can to find Charlotte Preston, and we haven't forgotten about her stepmother. We will get to the bottom of this, I promise you. I'm grateful for your help. In fact, you done good. But there's nothing more you can do. You look like shit. Go home and take a nap or something. I'll call you as soon as we know anything."

She did need to go home. She needed to talk to Hawk. Put it more honestly. She needed him in just about every way. God knows, she owed him. Explanations. Attention. Maybe just affection.

It was the magic hour of the day. Off to the west of town, sunlight gilded the Snowy Range, lit up the waves of prairie. As Sally drove through town, toward home, the setting sun touched everything with a warm glow. Such beauty in such a hard world.

She found him sitting out on the back steps, drinking a Budweiser and gazing at the distant mountains. She couldn't count the number of times she'd seen him just that way. Hawk knew how to stop and watch at sunset.

She sat down beside him, put her arms around him, put her head on his shoulder. He stiffened, then sighed, put the beer down on, and put an arm around her. Then the other arm. They sat like that as the sun melted down, sliding behind the mountains. They watched the sky, pink and blue, red and gold, graying to dusk.

"I love you," said Sally. "I'm sorry."

"I'm sorry too," he said. "And you know I love you. That's exactly what makes it so damn hard. I admire you for what you've been trying to do for that kid. I try to help in the ways I can. But there comes a point where the price gets too high, Sally. I'm not saying you're wrong for getting involved, for caring. But I get to where I feel as if I can't ever care enough, do enough, protect you enough, goddamn it. I feel like you need more than I can give. And in the meantime, I start feeling like you're shutting me out, like you don't want to be bothered with me or how I'm feeling. I don't know what to do."

"I think I'm the one who has to do something. Or maybe do nothing. I've been obsessed with this Preston thing, but it's clear I'm not doing a damn thing to help. I need to back off and leave it to Dickie and Scotty. And more than anything, I need to pay attention to us, to you. Nothing matters to me more than you. You are the most important thing in my life. Everything else can go to hell."

He looked at her, brown eyes huge and intense. "Are you sure?"

She stroked his hair, tears coming into her eyes. "God, there's so much meanness in this world. I can't believe it."

"Tell me about it, if you want," he said, rubbing her back.

She poured out everything she'd seen and heard as dusk gave way to dark, and stars winked on. He listened, until she had nothing more to say. "That's it. I'm exhausted. I'd like to go plop in the bathtub, but the thought of it gives me the shakes," she said.

"Come on," he said, rising, helping her to her feet. "Back rub time."

She found a little smile for him. He smiled back. Her smile spread. "That's fine," she said, "if you'll let me drive."

Arms still around each other, they went inside. They passed the bathroom on the way to the bedroom.

"You fixed the door!" Sally exclaimed.

"Needed fixing," he answered.

She slid a hand lower down, really liking the way his soft old jeans covered his fine ass. "You need fixing."

"I bet you'll fix me good," he said.

She pulled his head down for a kiss as an answer.

In the bedroom, she lit a candle, wanting only soft light.

"I think," said Hawk, "that this would be a good time for us to remove our clothing. If you're going to give me a massage, I would prefer that you use your entire body, please."

Hawk was a fan of almond oil. Sally was a devotee of the way he responded to being rubbed, very slowly, deeply, and thoroughly, with the stuff. She started with his shoulders and back, working her thumbs along the creases between his shoulder blades, sliding her fingers along his backbone, working the tight muscles all up and down his neck. Eventually she got around to the backs of his legs, working her way all the way down to give careful attention to his feet, making him giggle once at a ticklish spot, more often making him sigh, even once producing a satisfied groan.

And as she began to work her way back up his legs, he flipped over, leaving her straddling him from above. In the process of working on his back, her own front had become somewhat slippery with massage oil, due to a certain amount of sliding along him to get at sensitive places. He took the oil off the bedside table, poured it in one hand, rubbed his hands together, and reached up.

"Hey," said Sally. "If this were a professional massage, you'd be way out of bounds doing that."

He kept on doing it. "Do you want me to stop?" he asked.

"Mm. No. I believe this is an amateur massage."

"I'll show you who's an amateur," he said, sliding his slick hands around and over her until he had her exactly where he wanted her, and exactly where she wanted to be.

Somewhat later, showered, dressed, and holding hands, they walked into the Yippie I O café. It was Saturday night, not the best time to try getting into the best restaurant in town without a reservation. But then again, it was after eight, and Laramie wasn't Barcelona. The tables were full, but they found seats at the bar. The regular bartender had called in sick, so Burt Langham was tending bar, gorgeously decked out in his usual crisp Wranglers, a body-hugging suede cowboy shirt in a shade of turquoise that exactly matched his eyes, and a belt with a PRCA champion belt buckle.

"I didn't know you rodeoed," Hawk said.

"I didn't," said Burt. "Had a friend who did. Don't ask," he added before they could. "I'm a married man now."

Now she remembered. Burt and John Boy's wedding reception was less than a week away. He and John Boy were doubtless hip-deep in last-minute crises of the type that Sally could barely imagine. Things like what to do if they couldn't find organic arugula or wild salmon. She imagined John Boy's reaction to the thought of serving farm-raised salmon to anyone he didn't hate, and smiled. But then again, obsessing about what you ate, and what *it* ate, was a pretty good way to avoid thinking about people who, for no good reason, hated you. People whose hostility raised potentially larger issues, such as whether there would be a mob of self-righteous bigots banging on the front door of the Yippie I O the night of the reception, threatening to break in and wreck the joint in the name of—what else?—family values.

"A couple new items on the menu," Burt told them. "John Boy's on a retro kick. He's got this spinach salad with a warm bacon dressing that has a little touch of curry in it. A little something he picked up back when he was waiting tables in the eighties. Very decadent. How about a cosmo to go with that?"

"I never drink clear booze," Sally told him.

"Cosmos are pink," Burt said, but they ordered the spinach salad and capellini con gamberetti and a bottle of a New Zealand sauvignon blanc.

As Burt went over to the cooler to fetch the wine, Sally began to explain to Hawk her plan for becoming a normal person who had a regular job and a nice, satisfying relationship with a boyfriend, in a quiet Wyoming town. Suddenly, she heard Burt say to a woman three seats down the bar, "I hear they've signed a contract with some firm that did the newest casino on the Las Vegas strip! Can you imagine? I mean, a theme tabernacle?"

And the reply: "Well, at least it'll be an architectural improvement. I mean, even if it's a scale model of the enchanted castle at Disneyland, at least they won't be holding services in something that looks like there ought to be corrals for shopping carts in the parking lot. And after all, it's great for business. There's no such thing as bad publicity, right?"

"I've heard they're even thinking about a university," said a voice Sally recognized: one of the yoga Realtors, now sucking down one of those famous cosmos and signaling Burt for another. "I've got a couple of clients who are looking to unload a big parcel north of town. I think that'd make an ideal campus, don't you?"

"Ummm, sure. Yeah. I guess," said Burt, bending down to pull the wine bottle out of the cooler and averting his face, ever careful not to alienate a customer.

"It's incredible. Laramie could be the next Colorado Springs!"

Sally's blood froze.

Burt emerged with the wine, smiled charmingly at the Realtor, said he'd be right back to freshen her drink, and returned to open the bottle.

"What's all that about?" Sally asked him, keeping her voice low.

Burt spoke quietly. "It's the latest. That Inner Witness church is part of some Christian consortium that's talking about starting an evangelical university, either here or in Fort Collins, to combat the evils of secular public education. It's a multimillion-dollar project, and if they decide on Laramie, it'll bring an ungodly amount of money into town."

"Odd choice of words," Hawk told him.

"I'll stick by 'em," said Burt, expertly uncorking the wine. "I mean, what is that woman thinking? Having those people taking over the town might be great for her business, but I'm not so sure about mine, right? I'm pretty happy with Sin City just the way it is."

A thought struck Sally with the force of a blow. "Where would a church that's been holding services in a discount warehouse get the money to hire big-time architects, let alone bankroll a university?"

"Maybe they're doing big business with the collection plate," Burt said, pouring their wine and moving off with a wave.

Hawk frowned. "I know what you're thinking."

Sally put her hand on his wrist, speaking very softly. "She's the link, Hawk. I mean, even if she didn't know, at first, what kind of crap they were pulling at that clinic, she had to have found out eventually—at least when she got her paperwork back from the insurance company. And she kept sending Charlie back. She had to have been getting a cut, and I bet that cut kept getting bigger. It would be like an addiction."

"Yes and no. From what we've learned about Bea Preston, she'd tell herself that she was putting the kid in the hands of people who understood what she needed, spiritually and medically. Remember, this is the woman who talked her husband into thinking he had to beat his child to be a good father. She probably chose that clinic because she thought Charlie wasn't getting enough discipline," Hawk said. "I grant your point about the paperwork. But I can't believe that every parent who sent a child there would have been endorsing fraud and torture. The bastards who ran the place had to be pretty good at deceiving people, if they'd been getting away with it for years."

"But the kids would talk, wouldn't they? They'd tell their parents what had been done to them."

"And a lot of those parents wouldn't believe a word they said. Or at least they wouldn't want to. People can be incredibly good at deceiving themselves. Look at Brad Preston. For years he told himself that he was doing right by his daughter, even though it made him weep every time he hurt her. What the hell gets into people?"

"It's mind-boggling," Sally said. "I mean, here was this man whose enemies, even, admit he was brilliant and tough-minded. And when it came to his own flesh and blood, he ignored the evidence of his eyes and his ears and his heart, and went on hurting her, until the lawyer in him found out what the father had been doing, what he'd permitted. It makes you wonder if he'd ever have owned up to what he was doing and stopped, if his job hadn't forced his eyes open.

"But how would he have felt about Bea at that point? Wouldn't he have wondered how a woman as smart as she is couldn't have suspected that something was rotten at that clinic?"

Hawk shook his head and swallowed some wine.

Sally leaned close and whispered. "She had to have known. She must have been involved. She killed Brad, or had him killed. She may have killed Charlie already. Oh God."

"God has nothing to do with this," said Hawk, pulling out his wallet and tossing money on the bar. "I've lost my appetite."

"Me too," said Sally, signaling to Burt. "Sorry, Burt, but we'll have to take a rain check on John Boy's retro specials. We've got some things to do. We'll see you at the reception."

Burt blew them a kiss.

## Chapter 24

# CHURCH ROCKS!

"DO ME A FAVOR," said Sally, as they walked down Ivinson Avenue toward Hawk's truck. "Would you mind driving out to the Sanctuary of the Inner Witness?"

Hawk's eyes narrowed. "Why? Why now?"

"I don't know. It's a long shot. Maybe Bea's got Charlie stashed out there."

"Sally," Hawk said patiently, "she could be anywhere. In a motel room. In the back of a minivan. Why would Bea take her to the church?"

"She has to have accomplices. The blond guy, for one. Alvin the Chipmunk. I can't think of anything that ties them together outside of the church. I know it's lame, but what else have we got?" Sally asked.

"What happened to your plan to live a normal life?" Hawk said wearily.

"It starts tomorrow. Just humor me."

"Okay. I admit it," he said, "all that talk about universities and warehouses got me thinking too. I doubt we'll see anything interesting, but I'm willing to take a look."

He opened the passenger door, helped her in. It struck Sally that she took his fine manners for granted. That, and his loyalty, his wondrous mind, his lovely body, a whole lot of his other fine points. Then he climbed in the driver's seat, leaned over, opened the glove box, and slid out his pistol. Keeping it in his lap, below the level of the window, he checked to make sure it was loaded, put it back in the glove compartment.

In the past, she'd have given him a load of grief about schlepping guns around. Tonight, Sally said nothing. Being shot at, in her own bathroom, had somewhat altered her views on Hawk's tendency to go armed.

So they drove out Grand Avenue, passing by the university and the football stadium, past strip malls and fast-food joints, past new housing developments on scraped-off prairie, to the giant parking lot surrounding the big tin box with the neon cross on top.

"Wow!" said Sally. "This place is rocking!"

Cars were jockeying for parking places in the packed lot. And what an array of cars! Fully loaded SUVs, minivans, reconditioned Volkswagen Beetles, Jaguars and Beamers. You name it, it was parked there.

"I think I see a space in the next row," Sally told Hawk. He drove around, approached the space, was about to pull in when they heard the deafening boom-boom of blasting bass notes from some overamped car stereo, accompanied by the hoarse roar of an engine coaxed into continuing service, long past its prime. A Cadillac Seville, late eighties vintage, lowered and dolled up with flashing rims. One side panel gleaming metal-flake purple, the rest of the exterior awaiting the removal of a deep coat of rust before repainting. A work of art in progress.

The driver cut Hawk off and slid into the space.

Hawk said a really bad word.

"Can you go to hell for cussing in a church parking lot?" she asked him.

He said three more terrible words, glaring at the Caddy.

"I don't think," Sally said, "that you want to get into it with whoever's driving that thing, over a parking space."

The driver got out. Shaved head. White ribbed tank T-shirt. Jeweled cross around his neck.

"Oh Jesus," said Sally.

The passenger opened the door, unfolding himself upright. Big guy. Blond. Dressed in a designer polo shirt and khaki pants. Clean-cut.

"The guy with the cross? That's the Chipmunk," she whispered. "And that blond guy. He's got to be the one who works for Bea."

The pair were plainly engaged in a heated conversation as they headed toward the building.

"Stop the truck!" she told Hawk. "I'm going after them."

"The hell you are, without me," Hawk said. "Let me park this thing."

An empty spot materialized between a monster truck and a Mercury Marquis.

Miracles did happen.

She was about to leap out when he put a restraining hand on her arm. "No running," he told her. "You don't need to be drawing attention to yourself."

He leaned toward the glove box.

"No guns," she said firmly. "There are too many people in there."

"You think that bothers the Chipmunk?" Hawk asked her.

"It bothers me," she insisted.

"Sorry," he said, taking out the gun and slipping it into the waistband of his jeans, in the back, hidden under his jacket.

"Great. I hope you don't shoot your own ass off by mistake," she said.

"Me too," he said. "Let's go."

And then he laughed.

"You aren't exactly dressed for the Lord's house," Hawk observed.

Sally looked down at herself, taking a minute to register what she was wearing. Snug black sweater, black leather skirt, fishnet stockings, high-heeled boots. "I didn't start out this evening thinking we were going to end up in church."

"Nope," he said, grinning. "You were expecting to end the evening where we'd begun, and dressed accordingly. I love that about you. The fishnets send me, by the way."

"If only they went with running shoes," Sally said, limping a little in the too-tall boots.

The marquee trailer out front proclaimed "Saturday Night Sing-Out, Featuring the Praise!"

Now Sally heard the swelling sound, hundreds of voices joined in a rousing rendition of "Rock My Soul in the Bosom of Abraham." She gave in to it, just a little, let it sweep her up, just a touch. She couldn't help it. Gospel music did for her what fishnet stockings did for Hawk. She swayed a little, humming along.

"Steady now, Mustang," said Hawk. "Not time to sign up for the choir."

She refocused, just in time to see the Chipmunk and the blond man disappear inside the entrance. Hawk took her arm and hurried her along.

The place was jammed. Elsewhere in Laramie, on a Saturday night, crowds gathered to drink whiskey and whirl on a dance floor while guys in black hats banged out shit-kicking redneck tunes. Some got laid. Some got in fights. Some ended up in the wrong place at the wrong time. But the music got it all started.

It wasn't that different at the Sanctuary of the Inner Witness, Sally realized. If the band at Brad Preston's memorial service had been less than inspired, the group they had tonight (the Praise?) was ripping the place up. You'd never know from the looks of them that they were a Christian band. The guitar and bass players had enough hair and leather and studs to play in any thrash metal group on the planet. The singers, in baggy cut-down pants and sideways baseball caps, did dance routines. The drummer had a Mohawk.

They'd segued from "Rock My Soul" into some kind of hot, hip-hop rendition of "Swing Low, Sweet Chariot," a little something for everyone in that arrangement, that tune. Young and old, rich and poor, were out of their seats, swinging and clapping. If the folding chairs had once been in neat rows, they'd now been shoved back haphazardly as people got up and got into it. Little kids on their parents' shoulders, groups of teenage girls moving in synch, old people banging their canes. "Man!" she said. "Church rocks!"

She caught herself grinning. And realized she'd lost sight of the Chipmunk and the blond man.

"Shit!" she exclaimed, drawing amazed looks and frowns from people nearby. "I can't see them!"

"I can," said Hawk. "One of the advantages of not being a shrimp."

"Okay, big fella," she said. "Let's get closer."

He grasped her hand and pulled her along, slipping and squeezing his way between people and chairs, through the crush. Unable to see past the people around her, she was feeling a little claustrophobic amid the sweaty, rocking worshippers. Hawk was holding tight to her hand, but sometimes someone would get between them, stretching them out. Finally, when her arm was nearly wrenched out of its socket, she yanked back and pulled him closer. "Slow down," she yelled, over the din. "I need this arm."

Hawk craned his neck, trying for a clear view. "Oh crap. It looks like they've split up. I can see the blond guy, but I can't . . . no, wait. There's the Chipmunk. And would you believe, he's talking to your good friend Bea Preston?"

"Come on!" said Sally, abandoning all pretense of politeness now, and elbowing her way through the crowd, dragging him along. A little voice in her head told her she wasn't thinking clearly. The adrenaline rushing through her drowned the little voice. She kept moving, kept pushing.

And ran smack-dab into the hard wall of Scotty Atkins's chest, Hawk piling up behind her.

"I thought you were Jewish," Atkins said.

Sally took a deep, steadying breath.

Scotty looked her up and down, biting his lower lip. "Guess they dress differently for synagogue."

Now she scowled at him.

"You can stay right here," he told her. "We've got everything under control."

They were close enough that she finally had a clear view of the area in front of the stage. And now she saw Dickie Langham walk up and say something to the guy running the sound board. The sound guy gestured to the lead guitarist, who turned to the other band members, made a circular motion in the air with his hand, musician-speak for "Take it around one more time, and then wrap it up." One more chorus. Then the singer announced a break.

Dickie got up onstage, walked to the microphone, and said, "Sorry, folks, but we're going to have to call it a night. Everyone go on home now."

"What's going on here?" said a woman nearby.

"That's the sheriff," someone replied. "Looks like he's closing us down."

"The police can't just come in here and shut down a worship service! I demand my right to freedom of religion!" the woman shouted.

"Freedom of religion! Freedom of religion!" the crowd began to chant.

"Just relax here, people," said Dickie in his most genial, Gene Autry voice. "We're not trying to interfere with anybody's rights. But in the interest of your own safety, we would appreciate it if you'd exit the building in a quiet, orderly fashion."

"They're busting somebody in our church!" somebody shouted.

Sally realized that Scotty Atkins had left her side. And now she saw a uniformed deputy, hand on Bea Preston's shoulder. Scotty was in the process of putting handcuffs on the blond man. The Chipmunk was nowhere to be found.

Most of the crowd, eager to avoid trouble, streamed toward the exit. But some, visibly angry, began to close in on the police. "What's going on here?" a man demanded. "How dare you invade our sanctuary? This is police brutality!"

Dickie had a careful arm around Bea. Aside from cuffing him, Scotty had barely touched the blond guy. It wasn't exactly Selma, with dogs and fire hoses. But Sally had to admit, a bust in a church, maybe the fastest-growing church in Laramie, wasn't going to spell great PR for the sheriff's department.

Bea looked up, an expression of noble sacrifice on her beautiful face. "Brothers and sisters, be comforted," she said in a voice that carried, clear but sweet, without benefit of microphone. "The sheriff and his men are simply doing their job." She looked up at Dickie, admiration and gratitude in her gaze. "Praise the Lord," she said, brimming eyes now turned to the blond man in the handcuffs, "they've got the man who murdered my husband!"

## CHAPTER 25

# IN THE TALL WEEDS

IT TOOK THE POLICE some time to clear the place out, but the band did them a favor, turning off the PA system and packing their gear. In the meantime, the deputy and the blond man disappeared. So did Bea Preston, much to Sally's dismay, and Scotty Atkins. Dickie and another deputy remained, the deputy to watch the door, and Dickie to supervise, listen to complaints, keep things cool.

"This thing in my waistband is digging a hole in my sacrum," Hawk told her. "Let's get out of here."

She could see his point. Maybe not the best thing to be hanging around a church with a gun in your pants. "Give me a minute. I need to talk to the sheriff," she told him.

Hawk looked at Dickie, who was pretending not to notice either of them. "I don't think he wants to talk to you," he observed.

"Too friggin' bad," Sally said. "He's going to talk to me."

"Watch your language," Hawk whispered.

"I am," said Sally. "And he's still going to talk to me, whether he likes it or not. Why the hell would they bust these guys at a big church thing? There's something really screwy going on here."

Finally, everyone had left, and the sheriff walked out into the parking lot, still acting as if he was unaware that Sally was right behind him. She actually had to grab his arm and turn him around.

"Why, Mustang," he said, faking surprise in the least convincing manner. "I had no idea you'd been born again."

"What's going on here, Dick?" she asked.

"I thought I told you only this afternoon that it's time for you to give this thing a rest," he said, clearly exasperated. "And here you are, one more time, Miss Bad-News-in-Fishnet-Stockings. Get out of here."

She wasn't backing off. "Listen, Sheriff. Somebody in this town who thinks they're on first-name terms with God is putting together the Laramie real estate deal of the millennium, probably using insurance claim funny money. Hasn't it occurred to you that Bea Preston's in a position to have been on the inside of whatever's going on? Where'd she go?"

Dickie avoided eye contact. "Mrs. Preston's gone on home. She's been very helpful with our investigation. We'll be talking with her again tomorrow. Don't worry about it."

She reached up, grabbed his face, made him look at her. "What in the hell are you talking about? Where's Charlie?"

He looked at her because he had to. But she couldn't believe her ears. "Mrs. Preston says Charlotte's doing well," Dickie told Sally. "She's been recuperating in a private treatment center. She'll be released tomorrow. If she's able, we'll talk with her too."

"A private treatment center! I can't believe this. Think about what happened all those other times Bea put her in a nice, quiet, private place!"

He looked her in the eye. "Don't worry about it, Sally. Bea has assured us that she'll produce the girl tomorrow, and we have every reason to believe she's in decent shape, at least as decent as it's possible for somebody that messed up to be. And the most important thing is that we've got the guy we've been looking for."

"And how long have you been looking for him, might I ask?" Sally said.

Dickie got busy, patting his pockets for his cigarettes. "Oh, I guess ever since the Fort Collins police found a partial thumbprint on the trunk of that Miata," he admitted. "We sent them to the federal registry, and it turned out that the print matched up with a guy named Wesley King, who'd been a suspect in an abortion clinic fire in the state of Washington. We got the information back yesterday, just so you don't think we've been holding out on you."

"Oh no. I'd never think that. I mean, just this afternoon we had a nice conversation in Dave Haggerty's office, at which you mentioned not one word of this. So why would I ever think you're holding out on me?"

Dickie didn't bother to answer.

"So let me guess," Sally pushed on. "You asked Bea Preston if she'd ever encountered this King character, and she said, well, yeah, as a matter of fact, he's in my Bible study group, and if you like, I can get him to meet me at church tomorrow night?"

"Something like that," Dickie said, lighting up, taking a desperate drag, blowing smoke. "Seems Mr. King also worked for some time as a medical technician at the Shelter Clinic. You never know how a case is gonna break."

"I presume you're aware that he showed up with the Chipmunk," Hawk said.

Dickie stared at Hawk, noted the way his jacket was hanging in the back. "Yeah, we're aware. You developing dowager's hump there, Hawk?"

Hawk shoved his hands in his pockets and started whistling.

"The Chipmunk," Sally pursued. "He slipped out while you were busting Wesley King. Don't you need to talk to him?"

"We're not complete idiots, Sally," said Dickie. "We've actually managed to have a word or two with the man. We've advised him to stay in touch. He's a slippery one, but we're not done with him yet."

She puffed out a breath. "So was this King guy involved in the insurance fraud? Is that why he killed Brad Preston?"

"Looks that way. Mrs. Preston is helping us put those pieces together. She's appalled at what that clinic evidently did to Charlotte and the other kids."

"I can't believe this. Bea Preston has basically been torturing her kid for years! Why in the name of God are you believing her now?"

Dickie took a long drag of his cigarette, regarded the glowing tip, exhaled slowly. "Let's get serious here, Sally. How do you know that? I mean, exactly who are your sources of information?"

She thought a minute. "Charlie. Billy Reno. Aggie Stark."

"Great. Two sociopaths with criminal records and a gullible little kid."

"You'd be a sociopath too, if you'd been through what those kids have. It's the worst. You've probably even been too busy kissing up to Bea Preston to let Billy out of jail, huh, Dickie?"

"Below the belt, Mustang. He was released late this afternoon. Don't ask me where he's gone. Probably somewhere stealing a police cruiser, if I know Billy. Go ahead and feel sorry for those two, but don't be fooled. They have only the most casual acquaintance with the truth, and that only when it's easier than lying."

"Better an honest sinner than a canting hypocrite," Sally shot back. "What about Bea blackmailing Dave Haggerty?" Sally insisted.

"Dave's not exactly an unbiased source on that question, now is he?" Dickie said. "We haven't found a shred of evidence that what he told you about that is true."

"How about checking the donation records of the Traditional Family Fund? If they've been cashing checks from a leftie like Dave Haggerty, wouldn't you think that'd be pretty good evidence?"

Dickie looked at the sky, then back at Sally. "I guess you would, at that. And we will take a look, as soon as their lawyers stop fighting our subpoenas. But look, Sally. You'll note that nobody, not one single soul, has accused Beatrice Preston of laying a hand on her stepdaughter, ever. In fact, if you look at the evidence another way, it might appear that all Bea Preston has done is to try to take care of an extremely disturbed girl, to protect her from a violent father and get her some treatment. This is a deeply religious woman, a community leader. Who you gonna believe, Sally, her or the crazy kids?"

Sally looked him right in the eye. "I know who I believe."

He looked right back. "Believe who you want. My job requires me to look at things from all sides. And right now, it looks like we've got the guy who murdered Bradley Preston. If it makes you feel any better, Charlie and Billy are in the clear on that one. We can take our time sorting out the rest of it."

Sally kept staring at him. "This is disgusting. Somebody's squeezing you. I'd never have thought you'd cave in to pressure."

Something came and went in his eyes, but he didn't look away.

"Who's stepping on your unit, Sheriff?" she asked. "What's going on? Did Bea call up some big-time buddy of hers? Did you get a phone call from Washington, D.C., maybe, telling you to watch yourself around upstanding Christian ladies with powerful friends? Or maybe suggesting that you might want to do what you can to accommodate people who might bring a lot of money into Laramie, say in the form of an evangelical university?"

He dipped his head now, flicked his cigarette butt in the parking lot dirt, ground it out with the heel of his boot. "Sometimes I hate this job," he said, looking back up.

"We're not done," Sally told him.

"You certainly are," he said. "Not one more step, Sally. You've gone far enough. I've got about all I can handle, without having to get into a cluster fuck with you pissing off the people who rule the world. I am not kidding. Give it a rest."

Hawk snorted.

Dickie and Sally looked at him.

"You've got to be kidding, Sheriff," said Hawk. "You think you can just throw her a big piece of red meat like that, and not expect her to take a bite?"

"If she does, she'll be the meat," said Dickie. "Look at me, Dr.

Alder. I swear on the graves of John Lennon, Bob Marley, Janis Joplin, and Hunter S. Thompson, I am doing everything I can to get to the bottom of this, to take care of Charlotte Preston, and to keep the peace in my town. But we're in the tall weeds here. There's big money involved, and lots of people who think they're doing God's work, probably even including you. I'm just taking it day by day, trying to mind the people's business. I thought I had you convinced this afternoon that it's time for you to back the very hell off. I can't be worrying about you and doing my job. Please, Sally?"

Sometimes you could see the whole world's pain in Dickie Langham's eyes. "You promise me?" she said.

"I just did," he answered.

"I'm on her," Hawk told him.

"Okay," said Dickie, giving her a hug. "I'll be in touch."

# CHAPTER 26

# DISTURBING THE PEACE

HER INTENTIONS WERE GOOD. Really, they were. She couldn't help sympathizing with Dickie, who'd found himself in the middle of a bigger mess than he'd ever seen. Plus there was the element of fear. The cops might have captured Wesley King, the presumed murderer. But she didn't have much confidence that King was the one who'd shot her bathroom door. It took more than one person to cook up a conspiracy, right?

She felt like ten miles of bad road as they headed home. Hawk was doing all he could to console her. "He can't help what he's doing, Mustang," he said, holding her hand as he drove. "He's an elected official. If guys with big bucks and a grudge decide to go after him, he'll not only lose his job, he could end up being the target of a national smear campaign. They wouldn't have a bit of trouble digging up a mountain of dirt on him. Imagine the headlines: 'Alcoholic Coke Dealer Now Sheriff of Cowboy Town.' They'd run him out of office, maybe drive his kids out of school, who knows? For all we know, they have the power to fuck up his credit rating, maybe even get him thrown in jail himself. When you think about it, they could do the same to any one of us."

She'd always said that if she ever decided to run for president of the United States, she'd have to do so on the "Yes, I Did" ticket. You could start an agribusiness on the dirt they'd have on her. But she'd never seriously considered the idea that anyone would bother. For all her bravado, she'd felt safe in the academic cocoon. "I get the point. It's incredibly depressing."

Hawk drove slowly, as if he was afraid to disturb the peace of the quiet streets of Laramie, late on a Saturday night. Downtown, the bars might be hopping, but up by the university, there was almost no traffic. It was a cool night, but not cold. Even out on Ninth Street, there was nobody out, except one young couple walking a dog.

"Hey, wait a minute," said Sally. "Is that who I think it is?"

Hawk pulled to the curb just ahead of the dog walkers. Sally rolled down the window. The little dog, recognizing her, yipped happily, tugging at his leash.

"Hey, Aggie," she said. "Do your parents know where you are?"

Aggie Stark tossed her mane of hair, pouted, and said saucily, "Of course they do. I'm walking my dog."

Beanie wagged his stumpy tail, still barking.

Billy Reno stood watching them, legs splayed apart, head cocked in wariness, or defiance. Hawk narrowed his eyes, measuring the boy. "You're Billy," he said.

"This is Hawk," Sally told him. "He helped me with Charlie when she called me from the bus station."

Billy remained silent.

"When'd you get out?" Hawk asked.

"This afternoon," said Billy, giving nothing away.

"He made the evening news," said Aggie, gaining steam. "That's how I knew. So I called him up."

"You called him up?"

"They took my cell phone when they busted me," said Billy. "They gave it back when they let me out. Dave made sure of that." He stuck his hand under his shirt, revealing a hard belly and several inches of striped boxer shorts above his sagging jeans. "My old man. He's a goddamn prince." Billy smiled bleakly, looking very young in his backward baseball cap.

"So where are you headed?" Sally inquired, as coolly as possible.

"We're going to find Charlie," Aggie told her, "even if it takes all night."

Sally and Hawk shot a look at each other. "Maybe that's not such a good idea," said Sally.

"If you feel that way," said Billy, "maybe it's none of your fuckin' business."

Sally found herself granting his point. "What makes you think you have any chance of finding her, Billy?"

A long pause, while he considered his answer. "Put it this way," he said finally. "I gotta figure that whoever's got her has either killed her"—he hesitated, gulping, forging on—"or is keeping her close by, since they couldn't take her to that so-called clinic. And if they're keeping her alive, they must figure they'll have to let her come out sometime, after they've got her so scared or doped up or hurt or whatever that she wouldn't get in their way, at least for a little while.

"If they've killed her, shit, I can't do anything about that. But if she's around here somewhere, I gotta say that the assholes who have her are so fuckin' arrogant, they'd make it easy on themselves. They'd want to be able to move her around if things got hot."

"You probably haven't heard," Sally told them. "They got the guy who killed Brad Preston. The blond guy. His name is Wesley King."

Billy looked at the sky, threw his hands out in a gesture of reverence. "Hallelujah," he said, "and fuck that."

"Why do you say that? You told me he was the one who beat up Charlie that last time. He worked at the Shelter Clinic. Bea helped them get him."

Billy laughed without mirth. "I bet. I just fuckin' bet. You know what? Old Wesley, he was one of their success stories at that clinic. I mean, he first went there just like Charlie did. She told me his parents put him in there because he was the kind of little kid who couldn't help hitting other little kids. He was always bigger, so he had a tendency to really hurt the littler ones. I guess that made him useful to those bastards at the clinic. After a while, they told him his treatment was working, and they kind of made him a trusty of the other kids, kind of like they do in jail. He's one sad, scary motherfucker." Billy shook his head. "And you know how he finally got out? Bea got him out. She said she'd help 'mainstream' him—I love that word—kind of keep him close, keep him walkin' on the Jesus road, all that. He's her fuckin' enforcer. And now she's hung him out to dry. What would Jesus think?"

Sally knew that Dickie was right. Billy wasn't the kind of reliable source you could take to the bank. But despite his bad mouth, his tattoos, his rap sheet, his tough pose, and his lifelong intimacy with lying, she felt certain that everything he was telling them was true.

She looked at Aggie. Aggie shrugged. "I don't know this Wesley King guy. Charlie never told me about him. But she did say that one of the worst things about the clinic was that they didn't protect the little kids from the big kids."

What made it all plausible, Sally was sure, was the real estate connection. Brad had been a landlord. The evictions had started after he'd died, and the only heir who'd have been interested in evicting was Bea. Her actions exactly matched those of whoever else was buying up houses, evicting tenants, and flipping the properties at a huge profit. The transactions seemed to go through a Fort Collins management firm with the name of WWJS. Why not believe that Bea and her well-heeled, well-connected Traditional Family Fund were in the middle of it all, especially now, with plans seemingly going forward for an evangelical college in Laramie?

What *would* Jesus think?

Or do?

Or sell?!

"It stands for 'What Would Jesus Sell'!" she exclaimed.

"What?" said Hawk.

"That Fort Collins real estate firm, WWJS. Get it? What Would Jesus Sell!"

Hawk's eyes grew wide. "I had the impression that it was Jesus who drove the moneylenders out of the temple."

"That's the beauty of the Bible," said Billy. "You can pick and choose what parts you feel like ignoring."

Hawk went on. "There are a lot of empty houses around here, right about now. Former party houses, where people coming and going are pretty much par for the course."

Billy inspected his fingernails. "Yeah. Pretty much."

"I bet you know all those places," Hawk observed.

Billy hesitated again, nodded.

Hawk put his hand on Sally's arm. "Maybe we'd better go with you," he said. "And Aggie'd better go on home."

Aggie stuck out her lower lip. "I'm the one who came up with this idea," she said. "You can't make me go home."

"No?" said Sally, pulling out her cell phone. "Why don't I just call your parents and see about that?"

"You can't reach them. They're in Denver at the symphony with my aunt Maude," Aggie tossed back. "They said they might stay over if they didn't feel like driving back."

"So . . . they don't exactly know where you are?" Hawk said, eyes boring a hole in the girl. "And they left you alone overnight? That seems a little hard to believe."

Aggie realized she'd been caught. She squatted down and got busy petting Beanie, for comfort, and to avoid Hawk's gaze. "I'm supposed to be at a sleepover. It got canceled."

"I bet," said Hawk.

Billy grinned cynically. "Don't try to bullshit a bullshitter, Aggie," he advised.

Sally knelt beside her, letting the dog lick one hand, patting Aggie's back with the other. "You can come home with us. Both of you," she added, looking up at Billy.

"Um, no thanks," he said. "Sorry."

What would a parent do at this moment? Sally looked at Hawk. He looked back. Neither of them had a clue.

"Come on, Billy," said Hawk. "You're not going to do Charlie any good, and you're just going to get yourself in a big heaping pile of trouble."

"I been in trouble my whole fuckin' life. It don't mean shit to me. If I don't try to find my girl, all's I am is a fuckin' ten-time loser with nothin' to show. So don't think you can change my mind. And just in case you want to try, I'd advise you not to."

He reached into the pocket of his baggy pants, pulling out a small handgun with a short, large-bore barrel, and pointing it at Hawk.

"What the fuck would you want to shoot me for?" Hawk said, unconsciously adopting Billy's manner of speaking.

"He wouldn't." Sally turned to Billy. "You wouldn't, would you? You don't shoot people. That's not your thing."

"It's my thing with anybody who wants to fuck with me tonight, when it comes to Charlie Preston. Don't call the cops. Don't do a fuckin' thing. I'll see you later," said Billy.

"Wait! We're coming with you!" Aggie said, rushing to his side.

If they called the police, Billy would probably end up back in jail. Aggie Stark might even find herself in trouble for the first time. And when the system got hold of a kid, that was never a good thing.

They probably wouldn't find Charlie anyway.

"You're rationalizing, Sal," said Hawk, reading her mind.

"We'd better go with them," she told him.

"I know," he said. "Give me a minute."

He got the Smith & Wesson.

Sally forced down the panic in the pit of her stomach, made an effort to convince herself that what they weren't doing wasn't asinine, dangerous, illegal, futile at best. She failed miserably. But when Billy turned to start walking, she said, "Wait a minute. We might as well take my car."

Sally Alder had done plenty of creepy things in her picaresque life, but driving slowly down Laramie's empty streets, stopping at empty, dilapidated houses, getting out, prowling around, and getting back in the car ranked among the creepiest. Billy, of course, knew where every party house in Laramie was. To Sally and Hawk's dismay, Aggie seemed familiar with a good many of those places. The girl was clearly too much of an athlete to be disabling herself with drugs and alcohol, but it seemed to Sally that if even such an all-American girl knew so much about how to sneak out, and where to go to get wasted and raise hell and meet the most disreputable punks in town, parents these days had the hardest job in the world.

Billy had a plan. At each dark, rickety house, Hawk, Sally, Aggie, and Beanie would stay well clear of the building, but walk around looking for signs of recent disturbance. "I've done my share of B&E," he told them. "If anyone goes in, it's me."

Aggie protested, but Billy held his ground. "This ain't for you, kid. Just hangin' around won't get you busted. I got a lot less to lose."

He didn't bother with the first three places. "Nobody's been here," he said, inspecting dusty doors, windows, basement dormers. "No footprints in the dust. No smears anywhere on the windows."

"You're a regular Inspector Columbo," said Hawk.

"I know my business," said Billy, flashing a grin that was gone, replaced by a grim expression, in an instant.

And so it went. House after house. Some had once been solid two-story buildings, now subdivided into scummy apartments. Others were not much more than clapboard and shingles slapped together into boxes, now falling apart, but in good campus neighborhoods. Future tear-downs, Sally bet. By the time they'd visited seven places, Sally and Hawk were more than ready to give up and try to convince the kids that it was time to call it a night.

"One more," Billy insisted. He looked hard at Aggie. "Maybe you better not come. You never been to this place. Ain't nobody there now, but it used to be a little rougher than anything you've seen. A real hellhole. It's out in West Laramie."

Hawk was puzzled. "I can't imagine that real estate speculators would be buying up West Laramie hellholes."

Billy just looked at them, grim-faced. Clearly he was debating with himself, wondering whether he owed them an explanation. Finally he reached his decision. "Yeah, okay. I doubt your land grabbers would give a fuck about this place. But Alvin the Chipmunk used to live there. He did a lot of business there. Put it this way. It wasn't a very safe place to be."

"Aggie," Hawk began.

"Forget it," she insisted.

"I've had enough of putting you in danger," Hawk shot back.

Billy snorted. "She's in a lot less danger tonight than just about any other Saturday night I can remember," he said. "You never been to some of those parties. And it's not just the kids. One time, I remember, the cops came in with their guns drawn, yelling and screaming, and made everybody get down on the floor. They were freakin'."

Aggie bit her lip. "Well, I guess I could see why. I mean, how do you think the police feel about walking into a place where half the people are sixteen years old, toasted out of their heads and packing heat?"

"You were at that party?" Sally asked her, aghast.

"I'm going to tell my parents everything tomorrow," she told Sally. "So don't worry."

Great. That would take care of everything. Clearly they couldn't turn the girl loose, knowing that her parents were out of town. Who knew where she'd go, or what she'd do? If she went out on her own and stumbled across Charlie Preston, Sally didn't want to think about what might happen.

"We'll stay in the car," Sally said. "We'll call the police the minute things get weird."

Hawk drove. Billy rode in front, giving directions. Sally, Aggie, and the dog sat silent in the backseat. Laramie had been quiet. West Laramie felt ghostly. The moon was out, and the night had turned cold. Sally wished she was wearing a sweater and jeans. She was shivering in her leather skirt and fishnets, and her boots pinched. Maybe it was the cold. Maybe it was the tension. Hawk reached over the seat, grabbed her hand, felt her trembling. He might have smiled reassuringly. But he didn't.

They turned off on a dusty side street, pulling up in front of an aluminum siding–clad ranch house, surrounded by a sagging chain-link fence. Sally was paying attention, noting the name of the street, Blueberry Lane, and the number, 66. Wasn't that cheery? The siding had once been painted Rust-Oleum red, but most of the paint had peeled off. The yard was littered with smashed cans and broken bottles. Party-house landscaping. It didn't strike Sally as evidence of great merrymaking.

Beanie the schnauzer, who'd been more or less quiet all night and was now half dozing in Aggie's lap, suddenly jerked to attention, ears cocked, and set up a racket barking.

"Shhh, Beanie," Aggie said, to no effect. The dog was bred for barking at trouble.

"Something's definitely fucked up here. I'm going in there," said Billy, opening the car door and reaching in his pocket for his gun.

"Hold on, kid. I'm going with you," said Hawk, getting his own weapon out of the Mustang's glove compartment and opening his own door.

"Wait a second!" Sally said, stroking the dog. Between her and Aggie, he'd quieted down a little, but was still growling low, barking intermittently. "You've got your phone, right, Billy?"

He narrowed his eyes. "Yeah."

"Aggie's got hers, right?"

The girl nodded.

"Give it to me." She punched in the menu for calls, selected the "outgoing," and said, "Which number is Billy's?"

Aggie told her.

Sally scrolled to the number and hit "send."

Billy's other pants pocket exploded in a tinny version of the William Tell Overture.

"Answer it," said Sally, "and leave the connection open. I've got my phone too. If there's trouble, we'll hear it, and we'll call the cops." She dug in her bag, pulled out her own phone, turned it on, and set it in her lap.

Billy looked skeptical, but stuck the phone back in his pocket, leaving it connected. Then he and Hawk slipped through the unlatched gate of the chain-link fence, disappeared around the side of the house.

The dog whimpered, making it plain that he wanted to get out of the car. Aggie held him tight. At least he'd stopped barking. Sally held Aggie's phone to one ear and plugged her other ear with a finger. She was having a hard time hearing what was on the other end of the line, getting a lot of interfering noise from the rustle of Billy's saggy trousers. She heard what sounded like footsteps. Then a hushed voice. "There," the voice whispered. "That base-  · ment window. It's open. I think I see light."

"Let me go," said a voice she knew almost as well as her own.

"Fuck that," came an adamant whisper. "Stay out here and watch my back. Get help if you need to." Followed by a scraping sound and a thump. Sally imagined Billy crawling in the window, jumping down.

Footsteps.

And then, "Okay, Munk. Drop it. I mean it. Right fuckin' now."

"You're shitting me, Reno. You just go ahead and drop that piece of shit. I'll shoot her in the head, you know I will."

Now Hawk ran around the front of the house, yelling to Sally. "Call nine-one-one! They've got her in there. Call the police, now!" he said, running in the front door of the house, Smith & Wesson drawn.

Before Sally knew it, Aggie sprang out of the car, the dog leaping out and sprinting ahead of her.

Sally was hot on Aggie's heels, hanging on to both phones, dialing 911 on her own. "Tell the sheriff to get out here right now!" she told the dispatcher, giving the address. "They've got Charlie Preston!"

Aggie was halfway down the basement steps by the time Sally

caught up with her, nearly ran into her. The dog was barking hysterically, while Aggie struggled to hold the leash, breathing hard. Sally could see why.

They were all staring at the sight of Charlie Preston, bound and gagged on a filthy mattress, eyes wide with terror. The basement stank of cat piss and mildew. Alvin the Chipmunk, jeweled cross glinting bloodred in the beam of a tiny reading light, was holding a gun to Charlie's head. In his other hand, he held Billy Reno's nearly identical weapon, aimed at Billy himself.

Hawk stood by helplessly, his own gun useless.

"Welcome to the party," said the Chipmunk, smiling nastily. "Say your prayers."

"The cops are on the way," Sally said.

That stopped him for a moment, but the hand holding the gun to Charlie's head and the other one aiming at Billy remained steady. "We'll be gone before they get here. Don't mess with me, Reno. I got the Lord's work to do."

"If I know you, Munk, it's the Lord and a whole fuckin' lotta green. What's the bitch paying you, anyway?" Billy yelled over Beanie's barking.

"Watch your language, Reno. Mrs. Preston's saved a whole lot of souls, including your own mother. She's practically a saint, and she's just trying to clean up this town. What's a loser like you know about anything?"

"I know I'm not a murderer, Munk. Or did you give that up when you gave your life to the Savior?" Billy asked.

"Sometimes you have to take one for the Lord. But you wouldn't know about that. You're nothing but a second-rate thief. Too bad for you, Reno. Breaks my heart to think of you burning in hell for eternity."

"But you'll be singing in the heavenly choir, right, Alvin?" Sally said, taking a chance. "After all the help you've given Bea. Like when you put the bomb in that car at the doctor's office. Like when you shot at me through my bathroom door. You're a real angel, you know that?"

The Chipmunk scowled. "You've got nothin' on me. Can't you shut that dog up?" he asked, fury rising in his voice.

The dog was beyond human intervention, all his instincts kicking in, snarling, snapping, bellowing shrilly, a schnauzer recognizing a rodent, his natural enemy.

The Chipmunk swung Billy's gun toward Beanie, taking aim.

"No!" Aggie screamed, lunging toward her dog.

"Aggie!" Sally yelled. "Don't!" She dived at the girl and dog.

The Chipmunk grimaced, tensed, pulled the trigger.

And blew his own hand off.

# CHAPTER 27

# ROUNDERS AND LOVERS

HER HEARING WOULD NEVER be the same. For days after, Sally had ringing in her ears. She went to see an audiologist, who did tests and shook her head. That ballistic event in a closed room, coming not that long after the explosion at the doctor's office, the gunshot in her bathroom, on top of all those years of playing in loud bar bands, was bound to take a toll.

But at least the blast had distracted everyone from the hideous bloody sight of Alvin Sabble, as the police charged in, as the ambulances took Charlie Preston and Alvin off to Ivinson Memorial, as paramedics checked out the rest of them and let them go. Sally had a nice gunpowder burn on the back of her leather skirt, and one of Beanie's eyebrows had been singed half off, but amazingly, everyone was okay. That is, if you didn't start thinking about how the whole experience might have affected Aggie Stark, let alone what kind of recovery Charlie Preston had ahead of her.

Eventually the ringing went away, and Sally reflected that a little hearing loss was a reasonable price to pay for saving Charlie and seeing Beatrice Preston brought to justice. When the police went to question her, Bea professed to know nothing about Alvin Sabble's holding Charlie prisoner in an abandoned basement. She speculated that the same people who were behind her husband's death had kidnapped her daughter from the private facility where she'd been receiving treatment. But Bea refused to divulge the name or location of that private facility. And within days, Scotty Atkins had rooted out financial connections between the Shelter Clinic, WWJS Realty, and the Traditional Family Fund, enough that he now had grounds to dig deep into Bea's own affairs. They were holding her on everything from fraud to child abuse to conspiracy to commit murder.

Bea released one public statement, through her attorney, a high-priced woman who'd once been on O. J. Simpson's legal team. The whole thing, said the lawyer, was nothing but a case of religious persecution by a sheriff who had a long history of criminal activity and liberal politics. She was confident that Beatrice Preston would be exonerated.

In which case, thought Sally, Bea shouldn't have betrayed her henchman. Wesley King was opening up like a can of corn. According to King, everything he'd done, he'd done at Mrs. Preston's orders. Early on the morning of the murder, Bea had called Brad to say they'd found Charlie's car in the alley, and that he should go to pick it up. When he got there, of course, King was waiting for him with the Nut-Buster lug wrench he'd taken from the Miata. The same wrench he'd used on Charlie herself, before she'd taken off.

By the time King got done talking, they'd have plenty on Bea. And by the time Alvin Sabble recovered enough to move from the hospital to jail, minus a hand, he might be feeling a little less loyal to the woman who'd brought him into the mess, then left him to swing in the breeze.

"I never thought I'd say this," said Dickie Langham, slugging down Coca-Cola and tugging at his tie, "but thank God for unsafe, unlicensed, shitty little Saturday night specials. Not that I'm not sorry for Alvin the Chipmunk, but all that stood between somebody getting killed and what did happen was that gun being as badly made as it was. It's a plain damn miracle that your precious Billy Reno didn't blow himself up before."

Sally took a sip of some very decent champagne from—where was it? New Mexico? But then, it would be excellent champagne. Burt Langham and John Boy Walton wouldn't have anything less at what they were calling the "Wyoming Wedding Reception of the Century." The Yippie I O was festooned with flowers and abuzz with guests dressed to impress. Was that the famous lesbian daughter of one of the most powerful politicians in America, sporting an Armani suit and smooching with her honey?

"You know what, Dick?" Sally said. "I don't think Billy'd ever fired that gun before. In fact, I wonder if he just went somewhere and bought it the minute he got out of jail."

"For a criminal," said Hawk, snagging a bacon-wrapped prawn from a passing server, "he's pretty bush-league. But the kid's got a brain. He ought to get out of the crime racket and put his energy where it'll do him some good."

"Like where?" asked Dickie.

"From what you've told me, he's a genius at hot-wiring cars. Sounds like he'd be a pretty good auto mechanic," said Sally.

"Or maybe he could go to the vo-tech school and become a dental hygienist. Then again, anybody who had his hands in their mouth would have to worry about him snatching their fillings," said Delice, jangling her bracelets and munching a morsel of rare, seared ahi. "Which is why I decided I'd better hire him on as a dishwasher when he came in yesterday, looking for work. There aren't too many places you can fence coffee cups."

"Didn't matter a bit that you had another dishwasher quit on you, did it, Dee?" said Sally.

"Call it fate," said Delice, gesturing with her glass of Patrón and setting more bracelets clattering. "I told him to let Charlie know she could have her old job back when she's ready."

Sally smiled, and sighed. She'd been down to Denver to see Charlie at a world-renowned clinic, where the girl was receiving treatment intended to cut through layers and layers and years and years of trauma. It would be a while before Charlie was back slinging a coffeepot at the Wrangler. But at least, Charlie told Sally, she had moments where she actually felt safe, maybe for the first time in her life.

Burt and John Boy, clad in perfect white linen shirts, black leather jeans, shiny black cowboy boots, and matching custom belt buckles featuring their linked initials, were circulating with gardenias for the ladies and gracious greetings for all. They were both absolutely glowing. She watched them exchange air kisses with Edna McCaffrey, who spotted Sally and Hawk's group in mid air kiss.

Sally had been feeling pretty elegant in her black Donna Karan, but Edna was a showstopper, all sapphire-blue satin and miles of legs. "Well, Dr. Alder," she said brightly, striding up to them in a way that proved she knew a lot more about walking in spike heels than Sally ever would. "Seems you guilt-tripped Dave Haggerty into a frenzy of check writing. Ivinson Memorial Hospital will soon have a new research and treatment center specifically to work on preventing and dealing with domestic violence. The Haggerty Center, if you catch my drift." She raised her glass and clinked with Sally, everyone following suit. "Great news for women and kids in this town. The bad news, of course, is that you let that particular fish get away. Come see me Monday morning, and I'll give you a new list of development prospects."

Sally's shoulders sagged a little; Hawk put his hand on her back, leaned over, and whispered in her ear, "Yeah, I know. What have you done for me lately, and blah blah blah. Let me convey my personal delight in the fact that you're not going to be kissing up to that scumbag Haggerty. Maybe I can even dig up a few rich guys for you. All of them will be seventy-five, fat, balding, and willing to give you money because they adore their granddaughters."

Sally grinned at Hawk. But she was hardly off the hook. Maude Stark was bearing down on them. Sally hadn't seen her since before they'd found Charlie. Maude probably wasn't too happy that Sally and Hawk had let her teenage niece maneuver them into taking her along on that nearly lethal escapade.

She looked around, wondering if there was any way she could escape. No hope. So she decided to go on the offense.

Maude was using her steeliest gaze, one of her best weapons, generally guaranteed to freeze adversaries in their tracks. But Sally countered by walking up to her with a huge smile and giving her a strong hug. Hawk, taking the cue, followed with a hug of his own. "Great to have something to celebrate for a change, huh, Maude?" Sally said.

"As luck would have it," Maude said, glaring right through and beyond the hug.

"I mean, Burt and John Boy's wedding. The happiness of the loving couple. That kind of stuff."

"And the fact that Bea Preston's sitting in jail, instead of picketing the reception," Hawk added. "Take a look outside."

They all looked. One forlorn picket stood on the sidewalk, holding a sign that said, "Queer Marriage Is No Marriage. Get Out of Laramie."

"Pathetic," Maude said. "Thank God."

Sally gave up. "Hey, look. I'm really sorry about the other night. I know we should have made Aggie go home, but we felt like we had to stick with Billy, and I was pretty sure Aggie wouldn't stay put. We really couldn't figure out what else to do."

Maude's eyes narrowed fractionally. And then she sighed. "I don't know what the hell else you could have done. One thing about us Starks. We're so stubborn that when we make up our minds about something, you couldn't shake us loose with a hydrogen bomb."

"Aggie," said Hawk, "appears to be a chip off the old block."

Maude laughed. "So they tell me. Although as a teenager, I was too much of a goody-goody to get into the kind of trouble that girl managed. If nothing else, this whole thing taught her a lesson she badly needed to learn. I doubt she'll be sneaking out to wild parties any time soon."

"Are her parents freaking out?" Sally asked.

"They're teachers, remember? They've seen it all. They were just surprised that Aggie had gotten around as much as she has. They're dealing with it," Maude said. "She's grounded until she's sixty-five."

"Are they sure that's long enough?" Hawk asked.

Just then, the sounds of guitar, bass, and fiddle tuning up wafted over the crowd. Burt and John Boy had taken tables out to clear a small dance floor in a corner, and they'd hired a trio to provide music. John Boy had been pushing for a disco DJ, but Burt had insisted that he was a down-home Wyoming boy, and he was going to dance to down-home music at his own wedding reception.

"I wonder what song they've picked for the first dance?" Sally murmured to Hawk.

She'd never have guessed, though the choice was perfect. Burt and John Boy walked out onto the dance floor, smiled into each other's eyes, took each other by the hand, and showed that they knew pretty much all there was to know about country swing dancing as the band struck up a lively rendition of the Carter Family's "Hello Stranger."

For the first time in her life, Sally really understood that song, about two people who could be strangers and rounders and friends and lovers, all at the same time.

Hawk smiled at Sally. She smiled back. They moved onto the dance floor. He pulled her close. She nuzzled his neck.

"Now let's see," said Hawk softly in her ear, as more couples began to dance. "About this calm, quiet, normal life we're going to lead."

"Maybe later," said Sally. " For now, I've got some other ideas."

"Nothing involving guns. No violence of any kind. No lawyers," said Hawk.

"Oh yeah. I agree. But how about this?" She pulled his head down, put her mouth close to his ear, and began to whisper. Then she drew her head back to watch his reaction.

She'd never seen him blush like that.